CHARMING HER MONSTERS

BEWITCHING MONSTERS BOOK TWO

YVE VALE

CHARMING HER MONSTERS

BEWITCHING MONSTERS
BOOK TWO

YVE VALE

Published by Entraverse Publishing

Sedona, AZ 86339, USA

YveVale.com

AUTHOR'S NOTE

This is book <u>two</u> in the Bewitching Monsters series, a dark yet humorous paranormal why choose romance. Book one must be read to enjoy this novel:

www.books2read.com/bewitchingmonsters1

The female main character will end up with more than one of the love interests. Group scenes are on the agenda.

This series also has quite a bit of M/M romance within the group that will occur with and without the female present. But there's no cheating.

So if this is <u>NOT</u> your jam, then put this book down now and walk away. You won't be happy with this series, because there's going to be sword fights.

Wink wink nudge nudge. You know what I mean.

If you believe love is love, you like to have some laughs too, and of course, some spicy times, then please charge forward!

This series also contains several dark themes that some readers may be sensitive to.

For more information, visit: yvevale.com

1

MISSING

ARRAN

*O*bsessive worry pulls my attention away from the chaotic scene I'm in, making me no use to the victims who are relying on me to rescue them.

Yet, I can't help it. I need to get back to *her*. My heart, my love… my future mate, Jade.

I don't know how long I've been moving debris and rescuing innocent supernaturals from the destruction of the community center, but it feels like days. However, perhaps that is only my dread. When I check the old grandfather clock that somehow escaped damage, I see it's been less than an hour since my pack has been here to help.

I hate that so many have been hurt, and the longer we take to find the rest of the victims, the less likely their chances are to survive. Fortunately, reinforcements have arrived, allowing me a moment to take a breath.

Another pang of dread hits me. This time it feels different

from the worry over the victims here. I scan the huge, demolished room and the frantic supes here to help.

Maxum has dropped his glamour and is in his huge demon form—red skin, horns, tail, and wings on display. Flint is in his stony, gargoyle body. Together, we are tossing huge beams and concrete aside as part of the rescue mission. But I don't see our phoenix.

"Where the fuck is Calder?" I call out.

Maxum looks around and then turns back at me with confusion behind his eyes. "I don't sense him nearby. I can't say I have for a while now."

That's not good. The unsettling feeling that's stabbing at my heart takes on a new urgency.

Is he okay?

Then my next thought is… *where is he?*

And … *would he hurt Jade?*

I sure as hell hope he wouldn't. But he's been on edge more than ever since Osen died. I don't think he will ever recover from that loss.

Ironically, it only pisses Calder off more that Osen's spirit has attached itself to Jade. You would think he'd be happy that his former lover wasn't completely out of his life.

My heart pinches with hurt again. As though I'm losing a mate.

"Something's wrong. *Jade.*" My skin ripples. My berserker beast is begging to be released. That's not good. He might attack anyone in sight with his fear. Despite his crazed persona, he likes Jade. Dare I say he loves her—if that cursed part of me could ever love someone.

Could it be that our death-omen-sensitive phoenix felt Jade was in danger and checked it out on his own? It's not out of the realm of possibility, but with his hatred of witches, I doubt he would care.

Unless my pack mate was worried about how Maxum and I

would feel if we lost her. Or he might only care about Osen's spirit trapped inside Jade.

I shift into my giant, dire wolf form and rush to the door.

"Wait!" Maxum calls, racing after me. "A portal will be faster."

I keep moving but stop far from the commotion of the community center.

Maxum and Flint follow me.

Behind a shielded corner of a building, so no one can see the location of our safe house, Maxum opens a portal a few houses down from ours.

As I reach our house, I shift back into my human form so I can open the door and charge through. In my hurry, I neglect to test if there's a magical booby trap waiting for us.

Maxum curses behind me. When he sees no spell has been activated, he runs inside and admonishes me, "You need to be more careful! If only for Jade's sake."

He's right that I can't die on her. She'd be pissed. Who knows what kind of power she has? She might catch my soul and punish me for decades for being a bad boyfriend.

"Jade!" I shout and run into my bedroom, where she's slept since she's been hiding out with us. "Calder!"

No answer, and she's not in my room. I shout for her and Calder over and over. I check Maxum's room, the bathroom, then Flint's bedroom, and finally head to Calder's.

"What's all this racket about?" a tiny voice grumbles at me. It's Jade's accidental and unofficial guinea pig familiar, Trouble.

He's giving me a glare for waking him and the rest of Jade's small rescue animals who now have taken up residence in Calder's room.

"Where's Jade? Or Calder?"

"I don't know where Calder is." Trouble yawns. "But I heard Jade talking to the grumpy ghost. She left... maybe two days ago."

"Two *days* ago?" I shake my head at his complete

miscalculation. Most animals don't have any concept of human time. I have the same battle with my wolf half.

"Did you overhear where she was going?" I ask.

"Death." He does the guinea pig version of a shrug. My stomach turns, and I almost vomit at the thought of Jade dying.

"Calder's car is gone," Flint reports.

I turn back to Trouble. "Did Calder take Jade somewhere?"

"No. I think she left by herself. She was arguing with the ghostman."

Since Maxum and Flint can't hear them like Calder and I can with our shifter abilities, I tell them what the magical creature said. "He says Jade left on her own to go to Death with Osen. What the fuck is going on?"

"Osen's death spot?" Maxum guesses. "He probably coerced her to go there to investigate."

"Open a portal," I demand.

Maxum glowers at me because he doesn't appreciate being bossed around. Yet, he wants to find Jade just as much as I do, if what I sense about his feelings for her are correct. He opens a portal, and we all step through.

I realize now that I'm naked and hope there are no police officers on the other side. Otherwise, Maxum will have to fuck with someone's brain so I can escape a public nudity charge.

It's late enough at night that no one is around. At least, no one we can see. Supernatural creatures might lurk in the shadows. It's what they do in this neighborhood.

We spot Calder's car parked on the side of the road, not but a dozen yards from the alleyway where Osen was murdered.

The heavy, metallic scent of blood fills the air. I glance over at Maxum, and see by his flared nostrils he smells it too.

"Danger," Flint announces. His sense of smell isn't like ours, but he can pick up danger or if someone needs protection.

Part of me doesn't want to look down the alleyway. I fear that the woman of my dreams is already dead.

She might still be alive and need my help. I have to push forward and see what's going on.

When I brave my fears, I see both Jade and Calder sprawled out lifelessly on the ground. There's so much blood pooling around them. I'm sure they are dead.

Then I notice a glowing bubble over them like a protective shield. A small flower faerie huffs with the effort to keep it going.

"Help!" she shouts at us. But her voice is faint, weak from the strain of casting magic outside of her own realm.

"Are you slowing down time for our friends?" Maxum asks as he runs up to her.

"Yes. My mate and I stumbled upon these poor things being attacked by a strange warlock. We projected images of giant trolls, and he took off."

"Smart," Maxum approves.

"My mate left to get someone to help them."

"A healer?" I ask.

She nods.

I continue, "How much longer can you hold this bubble?"

"Not much longer." She grunts with the effort. "I'm sorry."

"What's your name, warrior?" Flint asks.

"Tavi of Elorith," she says with a raised brow. "You are my first gargoyle. What do they call you?"

"Flint." He grimaces that his kind is so rare she doesn't know any. Besides, most gargoyles aren't likely to associate with the flower faeries. "Tavi, we appreciate you helping our friends, but I sense you are harming yourself to do this. If you need to release the time bubble, you should."

"Flint!" I shout. "Jade might die."

He turns to me and stares deeply into my eyes, which unnerves me. Only Jade dares to do that, since she doesn't understand what a challenge it is to my primal nature. "Arran, we don't know how badly she is hurt. She could recover. And Calder… he will be reborn if he's too far gone."

Maxum places his large hand on my shoulder and squeezes. "No matter how much we want to, we cannot ask the faerie to sacrifice herself for Jade. I recognize Tavi's name and description. She is a leader of her people and a friend to the Fae Queen."

Shit. I can't piss them off. Just as I'm about to give up my pressure on Tavi, a portal opens up.

All three of us react defensively. I shift back into my wolf and the others brace themselves for battle. We can't know yet if the newcomers will be friends or foe.

A woman steps through with a half-shifted phoenix. His wings are out and flaming and he looks ready to defend his partner against us.

I snarl. She is a witch by the smell of her magic.

I can smell the magic of a hellhound on her, too. I back down, confused. What in the world? Why is this witch working with supernaturals?

A male faerie flies through before the portal closes behind them and rushes to help his mate hold the bubble in place.

"Amira?" Maxum asks in disbelief.

"Maxum?" she questions in a similar tone of shock. "It's been ages."

I shift back into my human form and demand. "A witch?" I sneer.

I suppose my prejudice against witches runs deep, and only Jade is acceptable in my eyes. Besides, I was hoping for a mage to heal her. A supe's magic usually works faster.

The witch turns toward me with a glare, but her phoenix jumps in the way, blocking my nakedness.

He grumbles, "Do you mind not waving your dick and all that sexy in my mate's face?"

"Mate? What the fuck is going on?" I say, but they all ignore me.

Maxum takes charge of the situation and informs the newcomers. "Our pack mate, a phoenix, looks to have severe head trauma, maybe more. It's hard to tell. I don't want him to go through a rebirth, but at least he can. We are more worried about the woman. She also looks to be banged up and losing a lot of blood."

"You mean the *witch*?" Amira says with a curled lip of disgust.

Hmm. That's odd… a witch-hating witch?

"Jade's not like that. She didn't even know that she was one, or that magic was real until a few days ago," Maxum explains. "She also has a spirit attached to her."

"Well, that's… different." Amira nods to her mate. "Raithe, when Tavi drops the bubble, can you look after your brethren? I'll do what I can to stabilize the witch."

"Jade," Maxum corrects.

Amira frowns, stares at him for a second, and cocks a brow. "Oh, I'm sorry. I didn't realize you had a bond with her."

What does this witch see with her special sight? Did Maxum and Jade create a mate bond, and I just didn't sense it?

The witch's eyes shoot over to look at me. "Hmm. You, too." Then she smirks at her phoenix. "Things are getting interesting. Let's help this woman recover so she can return to her mates."

I want to argue that Jade hasn't accepted my bond. But my wolf argues it doesn't matter. She is ours, and we will do anything for her.

"Do you have somewhere we can take her so I'm not treating her in the street?" Amira asks.

I finally notice a large bag the woman is carrying.

"Yeah." Maxum walks closer to the bubble. "As soon as she's free, I'll open a portal, and we can go to our place."

My instinct is to not allow this witch into our safe house. But Maxum seems to trust her. Flint isn't protesting, so he must not be getting bad vibes off her either.

"Maxum, you can open the portal. Raithe, you grab the phoenix." Then she looks at me and my beast flashes over my body. Her eyes go wide and then she looks at Flint, "Can you carry her?"

"No." He staggers backward, looking downright panicked. "I can't."

Poor guy. He just can't get over his trauma.

"I should do it," I say. "I can keep my beast at bay for this."

Besides, I need my hands on Jade to feel her once more. I need to pour my love into her, so she knows I'm here. Maybe it will make the tiniest difference to her staying alive.

Goddess, I don't even know if she wants my love. Would it make a difference to her? Could she ever love someone as broken as I am?

Just because she had sex with me doesn't mean she wants forever or even tomorrow. Maybe when she joked about monster fucking being on her bucket list, that's all it was... a fuck.

My wolf howls inside my chest. He doesn't believe that. He tells me she cares about us.

"Okay. Here we go," Amira calls out.

The flower faerie—a creature with more strength and fortitude than I originally would have guessed—sucks in a breath as she releases the time bubble. I will have to track her down and her mate at some point and thank them for their assistance. No matter what the outcome is here tonight. They were brave for risking themselves when it was clear this was a dangerous place to be.

"Thank you," I say quickly, with a nod of gratitude.

I scoop up Jade into my arms.

Her body is cold. That's not a good sign. She doesn't grunt or react to being moved, and my concern for her grows. Her beautiful silver-gray hair is matted with blood. My heart twists in my chest.

"I got you, my love," I whisper in her ear. "Hold on for us, okay?"

Maxum has the portal open, and we are all running through.

He's portaled us right into our backyard. Which means he plans for us to abandon this safe house since it's possible someone with the unique ability coupled with enough power could track the magical trail.

I carry Jade inside, following Maxum and Amira as they race ahead.

"On the table," Amira orders me.

I hope Amira's healing skills will work fast enough, and that since witches and warlocks usually have compatible magic, it will be all Jade needs—if not, we are screwed. Unless Maxum has a mage healer he's kept secret from us.

I set Jade down, but don't let go of her completely. I grasp her hand and look her over myself as Amira assesses the damage.

"She's breathing, and there's a weak heartbeat. She has a concussion from what looks like hitting her head on the ground or wall. Maybe both, if the two bumps and gashes are any indication. She's lost a lot of blood." Amira sounds confused. "But there's something else…"

"Her brain waves are all wrong again," Maxum says as he gazes down at Jade with heartbreak in his eyes.

"What does that mean?" I demand.

"I'll patch her up and give her a magical boost for the concussion… but there's something off, but I can't pinpoint it." Amira works, cleaning up the blood, applying salves, and chanting a spell for healing.

I look at Maxum. "What are you saying? Is it Osen messing with her? Is his spirit not attached? What?"

"A supernatural's spirit?" Amira asks curiously. "Not a witch or warlock?"

Maxum admits, "An incubus."

"Well, that might explain what I sense that's so odd about her."

"I don't feel either of their spirits right now. She feels…" Maxum bites his lip, drawing blood. He really doesn't want to

11

tell me. "Arran, maybe we should go outside. And let Amira work."

My head spins. He wants to contain my beast. There's only one reason for that. He thinks Jade is beyond return.

"No!" I howl and my berserker breaks free from my hold.

My claws descend and pierce Jade's hand. What have I done? I've hurt her more.

My berserker releases her and falls back to the floor, scrambling away.

"Arran, come with me," Maxum says calmly. I don't know how he can be so calm with Jade in this condition. Does he not care?

But I can't leave her. I shake my head because I can't speak in my full beast-like form.

"Okay, just stay there and let Amira heal our woman." Maxum stands between me and Amira, protecting the healer.

However, it's unnecessary. Even my crazed beast wouldn't hurt that witch, since her healing ability is the only thing preventing me from losing my mind completely.

2

DISASTER

FLINT

*M*y phoenix friend, Calder, doesn't appear as though he will pull through, but I know he will make it, even if it's through his death. Either this body will heal itself, or he will die and be reborn. My money is on the former. I've seen him go through worse and recover.

The unfamiliar phoenix, Raithe, is working on stabilizing Calder and patching him up. I know he's in expert hands with someone who knows how to treat his own kind.

So instead of worrying about the phoenix, I direct all my concern to Arran, Maxum, and their sweet little witch.

Our wolf shifter is a wreck.

Maxum's putting up a brave face, but the demon was more than charmed by the unusual female. I believe he is falling in love with her.

I also find Jade a genuine delight. Her chaotic, creative mind amuses my overly logical one. It's her pure heart that draws me in, enticing me in a new way I don't fully understand yet.

Surprisingly, she actually appears to be interested in being my friend, even though I'm an odd one even among the supernaturals.

If Jade passes away, the realms will be dimmer without her presence.

With the somber mood permeating the house, it feels like her death has already come to be.

In his beast form, Arran is curled into a ball on the floor. I've never seen his berserker side like this.

Maxum paces next to him, watching his old acquaintance Amira work her magic on Jade.

Jade's magical creatures quietly sneak into the great room and watch on as their witch battles with death. They also shoot worried glances in Calder's direction, as they'd started to bond with the phoenix in the last few days.

I wish I could assure everyone that it will be alright. But I don't know it to be true... not for Jade, at least. If she dies, Arran might lose his mind as he loses his heart.

My soul aches for him. He had just found his center and his anchor in her presence. Now this tragedy threatens to take that all away.

I wonder what happened. Why was she in the alleyway? Did Osen force her to go to his death spot? From what the guinea pig said, it sounds like this is the case. But what would be the purpose?

If it weren't for the precarious situation here, I would go investigate the scene myself. But as it is, I need to stay here and help Maxum if Arran's berserker goes wild and tries to harm anyone.

I stand vigil for what feels like an eon. The waiting is torture.

Finally, Amira says, "I've done what I could for her body. The swelling on her brain has subsided. With the wounds healed, she *should* wake up any moment now, but I don't sense that she is."

"Is there anything you can do to bring her spirit back?" I ask. "Don't witches have some ability to call souls?"

"Personally, I don't. But my other mate, a hellhound, might be able to give us some advice." Amira taps her lips, thinking.

I'm shocked that this witch is bonded to not one, but at least two supernaturals. Maybe Jade being with Maxum and Arran won't be such an issue after all. The couple before me seem to have a deep and loving bond.

"Darius might suggest for them to call to her," Raithe says from his place sitting next to Calder on the floor. "Maxum, it sounds like you have mind speak abilities."

"More like mind fuckery." Maxum sighs, waving him off with defeat. "I can pull out memories, scramble brains, or implant false memories, but I don't work with the soul... just the mind."

Amira looks at me.

I shake my head. "I don't see how my limited abilities can help her."

"Perhaps, just try calling her—all of you. Visualize her spirit, her soul, and ask it to come back." Amira waves Raithe over. "Maybe you can use your rebirth magic to assist if we find her?" She looks at the berserker. "Can you shift back to your human form for Jade?"

Arran nods, stands, and forces a shift.

I toss him a blanket from the couch for him to tie around his waist, since Amira's mate doesn't appreciate Arran's naked display.

The amenable phoenix gives me a wink as he passes by. "Thanks. He's too sexy for his own good."

I shrug. I wouldn't really know. I wasn't created to judge or admire sexiness. I only see someone's soul. And no one has called me to have more than a passing interest in exploring more. Well, except two. The first one was four hundred years ago, and now again, with Jade.

I can't say I'm sexually attracted to her, but I want to know her. I'd like to know what she likes to eat. I wish to hear her thoughts on the magical world and discuss the differences in what she dreamed up compared to what is real. I'd like to talk with her about all the things she finds interesting. This makes no sense, because I don't enjoy talking in general.

Yet, with Jade, I want to teach her all about this world that she's just discovered. However, I fear it's too late for me to share my knowledge or to share any moments with her.

"Come around," Amira instructs. "Imagine her in your mind. Place your hand on her body and call her back."

Fear, dread, and longing all smash into my chest. I feel like I'm sinking to the bottom of the ocean.

Touch her? I can't. Can I?

Without hesitation, Arran and Maxum each grab a hand.

Standing by her feet, I stare at her shoes. Slowly and carefully, I reach out to place one finger on the top of her slip-on shoe. That's safe. I can do this.

As soon as I make contact, even with a shoe, my body turns to stone. But that's okay. I'm touching her, and my mind and spirit can still call to her soul.

Fortunately, everyone is so focused on their own meditation they haven't noticed that I've turned to stone. Hopefully, Jade will wake, and her foot will be pulled away from my hand. Then I can return to my normal state with no one taking notice.

I'm glad Jade is unable to see the coward I am right now.

When I froze up before, she pitied me. I can't bear to see the sympathy in her eyes for my pathetic and debilitating anxiety.

Will I ever get over it? Could Jade help me through it?

I believe she could talk me through my fears again. Maybe next time I could be stronger. Maybe one day, without incident, I could brush up against her, hold her hand, or carry her in my arms as I take her on a flight through the clouds.

But first, she needs to return to us. To me. To be my friend, of course.

The image of her sweet smile appears in my mind from

when I told her a few facts about being a gargoyle. She's so inquisitive. She's so vibrant that I wonder if she could bring color and joy back to my existence.

"*Jade,*" I call.

I feel the others calling her too. In their hearts, Arran and Maxum are shouting, screaming, and begging her to return.

"*Please come back to us,*" I say in my mind, projecting out into the realms. "*We won't be okay without you.*"

A presence drifts into my perception. There's a weight to it.

How heavy is a soul? And are some heavier than others?

Would Jade be light as a feather like the feeling of joy she spreads? Or would she have more substance and fill up the space the way her smile lights up the room?

I imagine I hear an intake of breath, and Jade mumble, "Dying sucks."

My eyes fly open. Is it real?

Jade is stirring and blinking her eyes as if she can't see properly.

Arran snatches her up, pulling her off the makeshift exam table and into his arms. He clutches her to his chest.

By removing Jade's contact, I'm able to return to my normal state, but I remain stuck still with worry. Watching the scene unfold, I sense danger lingers.

Racing around the table, Maxum presses against her backside, sandwiching her between their enormous bodies.

She doesn't fight it or react, her arms hanging loosely at her sides. That's strange.

"Jade, can you move your arms?" I ask, since I think the others are only focused on the fact that she isn't dead.

With a grunt of effort, she twitches her fingers.

Thank the Goddess.

"What about your feet?" I prompt.

Another exertion, but she's able to shift her legs. I had been worried she had injured her spine. Humans are fragile like that.

"Flint's right. I should look her over before you manhandle

her anymore." Amira points to the table for them to return Jade to.

"Who are you?" Jade asks, eyes wide. "*What* are you?"

"Amira. Another witch," she answers succinctly.

Jade looks at Maxum and Arran. "I thought witches were bad?"

"Not all witches. Amira turned her back on the witches harming supes years ago." Maxum strokes Jade's damp hair back and settles her back onto the table.

Thankfully, Maxum had washed most of the blood out of it earlier when Amira worked on healing.

Her blood shouldn't have bothered me as much as it did. I see blood all the time in battle, but I couldn't handle the sight of *Jade's* blood. It was too much like… before.

Raithe adds, "And she mated with me. I'm a supe."

Jade studies him for a second. "You feel a bit like Calder, but not as smoldery. Are you something like a phoenix?"

"Smoldery?" Raithe chuckles. "Yes, I *am* a phoenix. It's good to have you with us. Your three males were about to lose their minds."

"*My* males?" Jade's eyes widen. She glances at Arran, Maxum, and then at me. "Uh, I… it's not… we aren't…"

"No shame, Jade. Amira has more than one mate," Raithe adds.

Amira swats Raithe away. "She doesn't need your matchmaking just after she returns from death. Can you check on your brethren while I finish up?"

Jade's face blushes with the matchmaking line, and then she almost launches from the table when she sees Calder on the floor, still unconscious. "Oh, my fuck! Calder?"

"Settle." Amira says calmly and holds Jade's shoulders to the table. "You can't do anything for him at the moment. It's more important that I inspect you for any lingering damage."

"But—" Jade points to Calder on the ground, worry and pain clear in her face. "He's hurt."

"We know, but you are too," Arran says, his voice wavering with emotion. "Please, just let Amira look you over so we can feel better."

"Okay." Jade weakly lifts her hand up to touch Arran's cheek. Her arm can barely make the journey, so Arran helps her along by clasping her hand in his and kissing her palm.

"Jade, how does your head feel?" Amira gently touches places over her scalp, focusing on the back of her head.

"Uh, I feel a bit groggy."

"I'm going to check under your shirt and pants now to see if there is any other damage we missed. Okay?"

Jade's gaze catches on my widening eyes.

I quickly turn away to give her privacy, and Raithe follows my lead. We exchange a look and both distract ourselves by checking on Calder.

After assessing Calder's condition, Raithe says, "I think he's going to recover without needing a rebirth."

It's good news, because depending on the nature of the death, it can be a long process. Usually, Calder forgets things about his last life. Sometimes, he mostly remembers the bad. He gets some of his original self back, but not all. He's a bit different after each incarnation.

"Where did you get *this*?" Amira's tone holds fear and a touch of anger.

My spine goes rigid, my instincts wanting to fight. To protect.

I turn to see Amira pointing to the necklace around Jade's neck. Fortunately, Jade's breasts are still covered by her half unbuttoned shirt, so I don't make her uncomfortable.

Why does Amira seem so upset by a necklace?

3

HEIRLOOM

JADE

This witch, Amira, pokes and prods my head for residual damage.

I don't know how long I've been unconscious, but it appears the guys somehow found Calder and me in the alleyway not long after Rob attacked us.

How did Rob find me? And for that matter, how did Calder know I was in that alley? Why did he save me from Rob's clutches?

I thought all four guys had left me alone to help the community center, after it had been attacked with some sort of explosion. Was it all a lie?

Calder appeared to be protecting me... or protecting Osen inside me.

The last thing I remember is Osen's vision of his death. We saw someone who looked like me or perhaps my grandmother, although I thought she'd been dead for nearly thirty years. But the woman apparently killed Osen. Though the more I grasp at the image, the more wrong it feels. *Fake.*

I don't understand how it could be possible for my grandmother to be the one to kill Osen.

Perhaps someone used a glamour to disguise their true face?

I'm also freaked out that Rob grabbed me with shadows, much like Osen's incubus ability.

I believe Calder and I were both knocked unconscious, when Rob tossed us aside. Why did he give up so quickly? Was his magic fading?

When I dip into my mind, I don't feel Osen anymore. I'm worried, but he's slipped into the background before. Maybe that's what's happening now. I hope it's not because Rob snuffed out Osen's soul.

I have ugly and selfish thoughts: Will Arran's and Maxum's feelings for me change if I don't have Osen attached to me anymore? Will they still feel the same? Or subconsciously, was Osen my whole appeal? The incubus ghost probably radiates some strong sexual vibes. His influence would explain my sudden appeal to the local monster population.

Amira announces she wants to check out the rest of me. Arran and Maxum hurry to help. Sweetly, Flint looks embarrassed and turns to give me privacy.

The witch unbuttons a few buttons on my shirt. She sneers and points at my grandmother's pendant. "Where did you get *this*?"

"My grandmother?" I lean away from the witch. My hand instantly clasps the necklace protectively. "Why?"

"I thought they said you didn't know you were a witch? When I accidentally touched it, something pulled at my magic."

"I'm sorry." I put out my hand in a feeble attempt to protect myself.

Arran draws me back to his chest and snarls, picking up on my fear.

"Everyone, calm the fuck down," Maxum snaps.

"You did *not* just tell two witches to *calm down*." Amira glares at him.

Maxum wisely says, "Sorry about that, but we need to keep our heads right now. Arran is about to beast out to protect Jade, and you don't want to deal with his berserker. Let's figure out what secret this pendant holds, because from what I'm picking up from Jade's surface thoughts, she has no clue that it holds any actual power."

Amira's shoulders relax, yet she eyes me like I might start throwing spells.

I can't even *throw hands* right now. Or ever, if I'm being honest. What can I say? I'm a lover, not a fighter. Now, if I could subdue my opponent with ear scratches and belly rubs, then I'd win every fight.

Hmm, I suppose I worked that move with Arran. I just didn't know my new dog was actually the enemy at the time.

Maxum touches the pendant. "I don't feel a pull on my magic. Perhaps it only draws upon witch magic?"

Arran tries and has the same results.

Staring down at the jewelry in question, I explain, "My abuela gave me this pendant. She said it was a protection charm and not to take it off. I've had it for over thirty years. It can't be that bad."

"Don't assume that to be true." Amira studies my face and then the offending piece of metal. "So your abuela is the one with the witching lineage?"

"I guess so." I nod. "She told me when I was little. But my mom didn't let me talk about her much, and I was told she died when I was a child."

"Wait," Maxum stops me. "Why does it sound like you don't believe that anymore?"

I look at Amira and then back to Maxum, unsure what to share with this stranger about Osen's vision. "I'd rather talk to you and Arran in private about that. Let's just focus on the pendant for now?"

"Her being alive might be pertinent," Amira says. "If this thing attempted to drain my magic, it might be slowly siphoning yours."

"Take it off," Maxum says. It's a request more than a demand, but he will insist. I can hear that much in his tone.

The unease that idea creates in me is overwhelming, as if an irrational fear takes hold. My hands hold the chain, but I can't lift the damn thing over my head. And it isn't just because I'm feeling weak right now. "I… can't."

Amira sighs, but pivots her approach. "It looks like a locket. Can you open it? Have you done that before?"

I stare at my heirloom and wonder what secrets it holds. "I've tried before, when I was a kid, but it didn't open."

"You should take it off and see how you feel," Maxum encourages me with a hopeful look.

"But I've never taken it off." I clutch it in my hand and dread stabs my heart.

"That alone worries me." Amira softens her energy. "Someone could be influencing you."

My grandmother's face flashes in my mind. However, it's not from when I was a child, but from Osen's death vision. Are witches the bad guys here? Is it possible I am related to one of the worst? Or was it a glamour like the guys are able to use?

I want to scream in frustration. I don't know if I can talk to the guys about this revelation. If Osen returns, he will tell them I might be a traitor after all, because he thinks it was me or my grandmother who killed him.

Just before Rob's attack, it seemed like he questioned whether that woman was me. Yet, is it any better if it's my relative and my ex-boyfriend who attacked him?

Probably not.

As a show of good faith that I hope wins me some points in the future, I remove the pendant from around my neck. When Amira doesn't appear interested in touching it, I drop it to the table beside me.

We all stare at the damn thing like it might explode.

"How do you feel?" Arran asks, nuzzling into my neck.

"Same?" I shrug.

"You could be so thoroughly drained that you might not notice anything right away. I don't sense much magic radiating from your aura, even now," Amira says thoughtfully. "I would have used my psychometry to read its energy and purpose, but I don't want it to drain my magic, too."

"I can try to open it at least," Maxum offers. "Most curses don't harm me."

I grasp his arm as he reaches for the pendant. "No. I'll try. I don't want you to get hurt. It probably won't harm me."

"You don't know that." Maxum caresses my cheek. "I don't want anything else to happen to you."

Unholy demon cocks. Why does he have to be so sweet?

I snatch up the locket and wedge my fingernail into the crease. It doesn't budge.

"Use the spell, *patefio*," Amira suggests.

I almost object to the idea, but remember, I'm supposed to be a witch.

"*Patefio*," I whisper, still feeling a bit foolish.

The locket loosens. Encouraged, I repeat it and finally the blasted thing opens.

Inside, strange symbols and inscriptions are revealed. After a quick scan and not recognizing anything, I look up at Amira and Maxum for answers.

"Looks like a tracking spell," Amira mutters. "And a siphoning and containment spell on the other half."

"Shit. That must be how Rob found me in the alley!" I shout.

Maxum snarls. "This also means our safe house has been compromised. He could find you here."

"You aren't safe," I say. "Do you have somewhere you can go?"

Arran turns me in his arms, and searches for understanding

in my eyes. "Why does it sound like you don't intend to come with us?"

I avert my eyes under his scrutiny and stare back toward Amira. "We should probably have this conversation privately."

Amira takes the hint and wraps up her visit. "Jade and Calder will need to be monitored, especially with Jade's necklace removed. I don't know how her powers and body will react to being free for the first time."

Oh, damn. I didn't think about that complication. What if I explode?

"I'll be able to help her through that." Maxum rubs his hand down my back reassuringly.

"Call on my assistance again... only if you need it." Amira gives Maxum a hug. She whispers something in his ear.

Jealousy and frustration rise up in me. I don't like a beautiful woman touching him. And I don't like secrets, because I know she's keeping something from me. I will have to get him to tell me when we are alone.

Amira's mate, Raithe, nods goodbye as they portal right out of the damn living room.

My jaw almost drops to the floor.

One, I didn't know witches could create portals. And two, it's the first time I've actually witnessed it myself. I was knocked out when traveling through portals before.

Arran doesn't waste a second, turning me again to look at him. "What's going on?"

"And what have you been keeping from us?" Maxum adds. His tone is firm, but he's not angry.

"It's okay, Jade. You are not in danger," Flint says, and I meet his kind eyes. "I would sense it. You can tell us what's wrong and what happened tonight."

With his deep rumbly voice, his words put me at ease, oddly more so than if Arran or Maxum had said it. Perhaps because they both are personally invested in me. But that also means they might be more upset by what I have to say.

Maxum seems to sense how uncomfortable I am. "Let's go sit down on the couches, then we can be near Calder to keep an eye on him."

Arran picks me up, carries me over to a couch, and settles me on his lap. "We'll have to check the rest of you for more damage later. Okay?"

I nod, but I don't know if they will toss me out after everything I confess. "Shouldn't you be relocating right now since I inadvertently compromised your safe house?" I ask.

Maxum shakes his head. "I don't think anyone will attack in the next few minutes while we figure this out."

My mouth is dry, and I cough. Instantly, Flint is there with a glass of water in his hand as if he already knew I would need it.

"Thanks." I take a sip and use the few extra seconds to organize my thoughts. "I'll just start from the beginning."

"That's often a good place." Maxum grins.

"First of all, I didn't know about the pendant tracking me."

"We know," Arran says. "Go on." He nudges me as he strokes down my back.

"Osen insisted I go to his death spot, or he was going to take over my body and do it regardless. While we were there, he had a vision, but I don't know how much is real, or what it means. It's very confusing. Then Rob attacked me, trying to get Osen out of my head. Suddenly, Calder appeared out of nowhere, and I must have hit my head during their scuffle. I don't remember anything until I woke up here."

"Let's go back to what happened in this vision." Maxum puts his hand on my knee and I half worry he will probe my mind and scramble it like he says he can do.

"Well, if Osen's memory was accurate, then it seemed like Rob was there the night of his death." I study all three of their faces, but they don't seem surprised.

"The weird thing—the part that makes little sense—is that someone who looked a lot like me was also in Osen's memory.

Although she was put together and Rob seemed to defer to her. At first, Osen thought it was me. However, I thought it looked more like my abuela than it did me. We looked a lot alike. Heck, even my mother looks very much like me, just twenty years older. However, only my grandmother would have had a connection to the witch world since my mom hated the notion of magic."

"But your grandmother is supposed to be dead, right?" Arran asks.

"So you don't think it's me?" My eyes widen in surprise. I'm rarely trusted, even when I do nothing to warrant suspicion. I didn't expect them to accept what I'm saying at face value. They are supposed to be my enemy.

"We don't even know if Osen's memory hasn't been twisted," Arran explains. "When he first possessed you, he was extremely confused by times and dates. That confusion might not have passed entirely."

"We don't know if his soul is intact," Maxum adds. "We also don't know if he has pieced himself together and superimposed your image over his trauma. He *is* living in your imaginative head."

"Oh, yeah. I suppose you're right about that part." I frown when I think about my circumstances. Just like I might work out a troubling plot point, my mind catches on a problem. "I appreciate you not immediately hating me, but I might be connected to Osen's death through my ties to Rob. I'm pretty sure it was actually Rob who attacked me tonight. And that would suggest it was him in Osen's vision."

"Rob does appear guilty of being an accomplice to Osen's death," Maxum agrees.

"Okay. But now, I'm freaking out about the pendant. How is Rob able to use my grandmother's pendant to track me? Did my grandmother want to drain me of my magic? And why?"

"Take a breath." Maxum squeezes my knee reassuringly.

"Rob is a warlock, and he's had unfettered access to you, even while you were sleeping. At any point, he could have replicated and switched out your pendant. Or he could have altered your grandmother's pendant to do those things."

"But how did Osen's soul get attached to me?" I ask. "That might suggest I was there when he latched on. What if I am to blame?"

"Or it could mean Rob went to your house afterward, triggered the spell he has on you, and then somehow attached Osen to your mind, hoping to get information through you," Arran argues. "This wasn't the first time you had a spirit linked to you, right?"

"No. Well, I don't think so. But none of them have been as strong willed or aware as Osen is."

The problem is we don't have a clue what's been happening to me.

We might never know. Life isn't often wrapped up in simple answers, revealed to us at the perfect time. No. Sometimes we never know why or how something happens. That being said, I want answers, and I'm determined to get them.

I don't mention that I can't feel Osen anymore. He might still be there and is too weak to reach out after everything that's happened. I don't want to upset the guys if he's only gaining his strength back.

Deep down though, I know the real reason I'm omitting this is the insecure part of me that worries they will abandon me when I'm not useful anymore.

Maybe they are only attracted to me because an incubus is in my aura.

What if all these loving feelings they seem to feel for me are just transference?

"Hey?" Maxum calls me, and catches my chin gently in his huge hand. "Why do you feel so sad suddenly?"

I don't want to confess my insecurities. What if they confirm my fears about what's happening between us?

So I divert his attention. "Is Calder going to be okay?"

"Is he?" a tiny voice says.

Arran points to Maxum to get something off the floor. My demon reaches down and then places Trouble next to me on the couch. My rabbit and hamster join us shortly after.

"He should be fine, hopefully awake soon," Arran tells them.

"Have you been okay?" I ask the other two, "Can you both talk too?"

"Scared for you!" my bunny Sage says.

I pick up the sweet little lop-eared rabbit and snuggle with her. "I'm sorry I scared you, and that I didn't know that you could talk before."

"We know." She licks my fingers and pushes under my chin, her soft fur tickling me. "The metal stopped you."

I point to my neck where my pendant would normally be. "My locket?"

"Yes."

My guinea pig, Trouble, rolls his eyes. "She thinks she *knows* things."

I chuckle at the arrogant tone of the familiar I apparently have. Of all the things for me to think are crazy, my rabbit sensing stuff is not farfetched at all. In fact, that sounds down right normal anymore. I don't poke at Trouble's theory that my blocked 'witch-holes' have been cleared by Maxum's and Arran's dicks.

But honestly, I can't necessarily rule that out. Maybe we need more research in that area to see if their dicks can power up my magic somehow.

Cocks for science. I really should get shirts made for them.

"Sage is probably onto something," I say as I return to the conversation. "But you're right, it was likely also my ignorance about the supernatural world altogether."

Trouble grunts as though validated.

Just as I allow my shoulders to relax and feel the fatigue hit me, something stirs on the floor.

Huge wings blaze with fire, taking up my entire vision.

Calder.

4

FLAMES

CALDER

*M*y life force finally coalesces in my body, and I hear the soft voice of a woman speaking sweetly. For a moment, I'm almost lulled into a false sense of safety with the sound. Then I remember women can't be trusted—especially witches.

Opening my eyes, I see the witch snuggled in Arran's arms, playing fucking innocent and chatting with Trouble, the guinea pig.

My body roars to life, and my anger returns with my last memories. Apparently, I didn't die since I don't feel like I've lost another part of myself.

I lift from the ground and my wings spread out to their full span and catch fire, likely scorching the ceiling.

Flint and Maxum are now in front of me, blocking my path to the witch.

"Move," I snarl at them, not moving my stare from the now frightened witch.

Arran pulls her closer to his chest, readying to race away with her in his arms.

"She's behind Osen's death," I say, firmly. "I heard them fighting at his death spot."

Maxum steps into my line of sight. "Sorry. Old news, buddy. While you were taking your little nap, we got the entire story."

"No." I shake my head. "Osen said it was her that night."

"He remembers someone who *looked* like her," Flint explains. "But his memory could be faulty. Jade said someone there looked a lot like her, but not exactly."

"And you trust her explanation?" I demand. "What does Osen's spirit have to say about this?"

"He hasn't surfaced yet," Arran growls. "Stand down, or my beast is going to tear you apart for threatening Jade."

"You would kill me? Over *her*? A witch?" I shout.

The pain of rejection slices at my soul, along with the thought of the permanent loss of Osen.

"Put your flames out and listen for a moment," Maxum asks of me in his calm, reassuring voice that he laces with his mind-bending influence.

It isn't enough to make me forget my warpath, and it pisses me off that he's using his powers against me—for her sake.

"Stop it, Maxum," Flint says softly. Then he looks at me. "Calder, you have a right to be upset and confused. However, there are few things that have come to light since you were hurt. Jade appears to be innocent. I don't sense danger from her end. We need to keep our heads and leave soon. Someone was tracking Jade without her knowledge. I sense we are all in danger if we stay here much longer."

My fire fades, and I no longer see red. I don't know how Flint is able to calm me. Possibly because he's the most logical of us, and if he's certain, I should take heed.

"We need to go to my last resort safe house," Maxum says, taking a step back when he sees I'm settling.

I don't trust her, and I'm still pissed. I won't believe anything until I hear it from Osen.

But that's the rub, isn't it?

If she has access to Osen's thoughts and personality, then she can lie and mimic him.

How can we trust *anything* that comes out of her mouth?

Maxum palms my shoulder and grins. "I'm happy you have returned to us whole."

He means my rebirth process. I can't say I ever have returned whole, and I don't feel complete now. Without Osen, I feel hollow.

Yet, even when he was around, something was missing. Part of my soul was destroyed when that witch tortured me to death.

"Let's pack our things," Flint suggests, tilting his head toward the hall to our bedrooms.

I follow along, glaring at Jade the entire time.

On my way past her, she says, "I'm happy you are okay. Thank you for saving me." Her eyes are downcast, and she's so quiet and timid.

It's as if she's afraid I will attack. Maybe she *is* afraid of me. Could that mean she isn't as powerful as I assume?

Or maybe she is only grateful that I stopped Rob from attacking her.

But I don't see how she cares if I'm okay.

Besides, her life wasn't the only reason I stopped Rob from diving into Jade's mind. I didn't want Osen's soul harmed, and I wanted answers about what had happened the night of Osen's death.

I grunt as a response to her thanks and follow Flint.

As I leave the room, I hear Maxum and Arran coddling her. They will help her gather stuff from her house before we leave.

It seems like a foolish thing to trust her, yet I get the sense that they actually do.

Even after all that's happened in their past? With her?

She might have a spell over them, since this isn't like them at all.

Trouble and his magical creature mini-pack race after me into my room. I want to tell them to leave me alone, but they are too fucking cute.

"Are you okay?" Trouble asks, the unofficial spokes-*creature* of the bunch.

"I will be." I grab my oversized duffle and start tossing my stuff inside. "What happened when I was knocked out?"

"Jade almost died. The other witch healed her."

"Another witch?" I hiss, shredding the shirt I have in my hands with my rage.

"Yeah, and the other birdman was looking after you."

I sniff the air and scent another phoenix. What the hell?

I had been so focused on Jade that I hadn't been paying attention.

That woman is a distraction, if nothing else, which is just as dangerous as being a conniving witch.

"Then they found a metal thing on her neck so that the warlock can find her and maybe take her power," Trouble continues.

Well, shit. One would think that if Jade was a knowledgeable witch that she wouldn't have allowed a tracker or something to drain her. However, she might just have allowed her power to be drained temporarily so she could *pretend* she was weak—to get everyone to trust her.

"I know you don't like her, but she worried for you," Trouble adds.

I didn't realize that my disdain for Jade had been so evident to the creatures. However, just because she acts concerned doesn't mean she is.

"She tried to jump off the table to help you."

I scoff. "She has no healing ability. She isn't even a real witch, according to her claims."

"She might not know about her powers, and she might be weak," Trouble argues, his feisty spirit coming back into play. "But that doesn't mean she didn't want to help you."

"You want to believe the best about her, but—"

"I've lived with her for a long time," Trouble interrupts me. "Rob knew about her being a witch, but she didn't. I heard him talking to her under a spell, even after she told him never to come back."

"What did they talk about?"

"Rob would ask her questions, but it wasn't really Jade who answered. And she was hurting. Rob is bad and mean."

"I figured out that much," I grumble, throwing the last of my stuff in my bag.

"Don't be mad at Jade anymore. She is a good witch."

I don't promise the little guy anything. There's no use in arguing with him. He loves her. Perhaps he's right. Perhaps she is just a victim of all this, but I don't like any of it. Osen's death is connected to Rob. And Jade's connected to Rob. I really don't like this ex of hers. He almost killed me. I could have lost most of my memories of Osen with that. Would that be a good thing, though? Would it lessen the pain that I feel?

I have to remind myself it's only been a week or so since he died.

I wish I could trust Jade, and that Osen really is coming through her. But does it matter when he will probably fade away soon, and I will lose him all over again?

"Maybe you should help her," Trouble says.

I frown, not wanting to even entertain the idea. "How?"

"Do what the demon and the wolf did. Clear her witch holes."

I cough and then actually laugh at the absurdity of the idea. "I will *not* be touching her… holes."

"Too bad. It seems like it makes her happier," Trouble says with a touch of disappointment. "And the demon and wolf were happier, too."

I say nothing to that.

I don't know if I *want* to be happier. Perhaps I want to wallow in my grief.

5

SAFEHOUSES

JADE

I hate that Calder hates me. From his perspective, I'm the enemy outsider, connected to his beloved Osen. I've invaded his tribe.

The problem is, until things get resolved with Osen's spirit and his murder mystery, I don't think even Calder will let me out of his sight.

Beyond that? I'm not sure what will happen.

After I thank him for saving me, Calder could light my ass on fire with the glare he gives me.

Arran's muscular arms surround me, and he reassures me that everything will be okay.

I'm not so sure.

Being positive is all well and good, but... life. Well, it isn't always wine and lubed cocks. Or however that saying goes.

It's hard to think clearly with these two hotties pressing close with all their sexy.

Maxum's obsidian gaze locks onto me. "Is there anything else you need to tell us?" He doesn't sound mad, just concerned.

"I didn't realize about the necklace. I would never have put you all in danger." My eyes sting as I acknowledge I'm in trouble, and I don't know what I should do about it. I reach into my mind again to see if I sense Osen, but I feel nothing in response.

"Uh, guys. Hear me out... I should stay behind," I say, focusing on my hands instead of looking at Maxum or Arran.

They suck in a breath to argue, but I hold up my hand for them to stop.

Damn. This is harder to do than I thought. How could they get under my skin so fast?

"Before you argue, I need to confess that I haven't felt Osen since I've woken up. So I can't help you with finding justice for him." I gesture to the pendant left on the table. "And now that you've found the tracker, I can pack up the most important things, skip town, and vanish. I can write from almost anywhere, so I can get lost for a while. I should be safe."

"Safe?" Arran huffs. "Rob and his partner in crime will probably want to abuse your magic again. They will hunt you down. If they have a witch portal maker like Amira, they can follow you into other realms, let alone another part of the country."

"He's right. Until we deal with Rob and probably the entire ASO, you are a target," Maxum says.

"What about Osen? I'm afraid he's gone for good."

Here it comes—they will say don't worry, he'll be back. Then I'll know that's why they want to keep me around.

"Hold on. Do you think that's why I want to keep you safe? For Osen?" Arran asks, hurt rings clear in his voice.

"Uh, partly?" I shrug. A woman can only get rejected so much without expecting the other testicle to drop.

Arran catches my chin and forces me to look at him. "Jade, you are mine. Understand?"

"But I—" I protest, but he shuts me up with a consuming kiss that makes it impossible to think.

When Arran finishes exploding my brain cells with his passion, Maxum captures my attention, his hand cupping my jaw. "You aren't getting rid of me, little witch."

I gasp at the intensity with which these guys are claiming me.

Maxum leans in and licks over my parted lips, then dips in. He growls into my mouth and pulls back. "This will have to wait until I get you somewhere safe. Then I will make sure you understand."

That threat of pleasure rings my clit like a gong. I wish I had more energy to demand he make me understand right now. However, I am still recovering from yet another near-death experience. This is becoming an ugly habit.

Arran stands, lifts me bridal style, and carries me down the hall to his room. He gently places me on his bed and packs his things.

Maxum nods to me from the door. "I'm gathering my stuff. When we are done here, we'll pick up what you need at your place, so think of what you want to bring."

"Okay." My heart flips a few times, dismissing the possibility that they only want me around for access to Osen.

Could whatever is developing between us be real?

The thought is both scary and thrilling. I've always dreamed and obsessed over having someone truly love me. Hell, I write books about it, getting lost in that idea for months at a time. I become each one of my characters, imagining what it must feel like to be so desperately wanted that the men would move mountains or kill any enemy in their way for me.

Now that the potential for that sort of devotion is right in front of me, I'm a bit terrified of how I will fuck it up, and I probably will.

I'm set in my ways. I'm a loner. The relationships in my books are (mostly) in my control. I don't know how to manage an actual relationship with all its ups and downs. Working out healthy compromises and overcoming day-to-day challenges are not my forte. In other words, I can write them well, but suck at real relationships.

Besides, I'm hyper-focused on my career… *usually*. But not lately, since they have been an enormous distraction. Well, and Rob trying to kill me a few times has definitely disrupted my work-life balance.

"I thought I lost you forever," Arran says in a quiet voice as he places the last of his personal items in his luggage.

"I'm sorry to scare you. Osen insisted I go. If I didn't, he would have taken over my body—maybe for good. And I had no way of telling you what was happening."

Arran kneels down at my feet where I'm sitting on his bed. He clasps my hands in his. "I'm not blaming you. I know exactly how obsessive Osen could be. It's what got him killed, and now he's risking your life."

"I still feel like if I were stronger—a better witch—that I could have stopped him."

"I don't plan on letting you out of my sight. But if I have to leave you alone, I will have Maxum or Flint watch over you."

"To babysit me?" I huff.

"To protect you." Arran tucks a loose lock of silver hair behind my ear and tilts my chin to meet his eyes. "At least until you can learn to use your powers and protect yourself. Good news is Maxum can train you."

"Can he teach me *witch* magic?"

"Maxum knows how to do almost everything—it comes with being alive as long as he has been. He gets bored," Arran explains.

The mention of Maxum getting bored hits me harder than it should. How do you keep a relationship fresh when everything in the universe feels stale? I expect love for people who live forever can be complicated. Maybe long-lived supernaturals have to break up before they get too attached? Or do these relationships rarely last because one gets old and the other doesn't?

Or are they like most relationships? Love and lust fade, and life gets in the way of a happily ever after.

It's something to think about while moving forward with these guys—longevity in all senses of the word. When I asked about lifespans, Maxum told me witches can live longer than regular humans, usually around one hundred to hundred and fifty years. It all depends on the strength of their magic.

Arran leans in to pick me up again, but I put out my hands. "I can walk."

Yet, when I try to stand up, I have a hard time getting to my feet.

"Compromise?" He quirks his full, kissable lips and snakes his arm around my waist to help me walk.

I hook my arm over his shoulder so I can stay upright and slowly we make it to the hallway.

"Ready?" Maxum asks.

I look around and don't see Flint, Calder, or my fur babies.

"They went ahead with your familiars," Maxum says when he figures out what I'm looking for. "We'll meet up with them after we get your stuff."

My demon boyfriend chants and waves his hand to open a portal.

I curse with my surprise. "This time, I can feel magic buzzing. I don't think that will ever get old."

"You've never sensed magic like this before now, have you?" Arran asks.

When I shake my head, Maxum growls, "That pendant was holding you back your whole life. Whatever her reasons, your grandmother wanted to keep your power contained."

"Do you think she was the one who put the draining spell on it?"

"Likely." Maxum waves me forward to go through the portal. "We'll never know about the tracker part unless Rob confesses."

"I doubt we'll get him to do anything," I mutter.

Arran and I step closer to the portal, his arm wrapping around my waist. I hold my breath as we move through to the other side. It feels like stepping in and out quickly of a steamy room with a dramatic pressure change, but other than that, I might not think much of the shift from one place to another.

I exhale when I am securely on the other side, standing in the middle of my living room.

Arran chuckles. "Did you just hold your breath?"

"Don't judge. No one gave me any indication of what it might feel like. I'm flippin' brave for just walking through without a thorough explanation of the effects."

He kisses my cheek. "Very brave."

"Don't patronize me," I laugh.

Maxum follows us over and closes the portal. "Actually, your body handled going through a demon portal quite well for someone new to them. It usually takes a while to get used to this sort of travel." Maxum eyes me like I've done something bizarre.

That ability seems odd to me. I get carsick, but I can jump through demon portals with no problem?

I glance around my house, wondering what I'll need.

"Are we going somewhere that has internet access? Or electricity?" I ask, because for all I know, they are taking me to the woods in faerie land.

"Electricity, yes. You should be able to use your cell phone. Just keep it away from me, or I will probably drain it or make it implode."

"Should I take my phone?" I ask. "Rob could have loaded it with a tracker, too."

"Didn't think of that." Maxum frowns.

"But I will need to access the internet. Oh! I have a traveling router. I doubt Rob knew about it."

In my bedroom, Maxum helps me pick out my clothes and neatly places them in my luggage.

When I chuckle about it, he looks at me quizzically.

"It's a bit strange to have a badass demon be so careful with my things," I confess, hoping he doesn't take offense.

"It's a misnomer that we are misbehaving terrors. That's only during sex and in battle. Well, okay, it's true, we are a menace. But I would *never* damage a woman's clothing that wasn't on her body. Then your delicate panties are fair game as I tear them from your luscious body."

A shiver goes up my spine as his obsidian gaze devours me. He must actually like me if he still thinks I look good after the harrowing night I had.

Since Arran is able to go near technology in short, controlled ways, he packs up my laptop and tablet, and places them in a special lead-lined case they brought along for that purpose.

Then he rummages through my kitchen, probably looking for snacks. He better be grabbing snacks.

"Snacks?" Maxum asks as he zips up my suitcase. Then he shouts to the open bedroom door. "Arran, pack up Jade's junk food!" He winks at me. "Got to take care of you."

I catch his hand in mine, use it to stand up, and look him in the eye. "Are you sure you should take me?" I whisper. "I already got Calder hurt."

"Calder got himself hurt." Maxum wraps his arms around me and pulls me against his firm chest. "He ran off without telling us where he was going or why. And Osen forced you to leave the house. This is on them."

"But I—"

"Nope." Maxum places his huge finger over my lips. "Even the stuff Rob did isn't your fault. Or your grandmother. You were innocent, and they took advantage of that." He leans down, kisses, and nips my bottom lip. "But you won't be innocent in *any* way, shape, or form after I get some time alone with you."

My heart beats wildly with his suggestive talk. "Yeah?"

Arran clears his throat as he walks into my bedroom. "Did you get all the toiletries?"

"I can take care of our woman," Maxum says, his eyes never leaving mine. "Let's get you safe, sweetness."

6

HOME

MAXUM

I open the portal to the fae realm, Elfhame, so that we can shake any tails we might have acquired at Jade's house. I don't want supernatural trackers following us to my home and endangering my people.

My woman.

Correction... *Our woman.*

Arran has a stronger claim on her than I do.

But I don't plan to let Jade slip away, no matter what comes of Amira's warning that there is something odd about Jade's magic.

We'll unravel what's going on, solving the mystery of Osen's murder and Rob's involvement. After that, we'll tackle the mystery of Jade's unknown past and her powers. Then we will live out the rest of her days making love and sharing myself in ways I've never contemplated before.

If I've learned anything in my many years of experience it's that nothing is what it appears at first. Also, I can handle whatever comes at me.

I'm sure the same is true for Jade. She's already proven she can handle what life throws her way—maybe even more than the rest of my pack.

Case in point, Flint and Calder still haven't gotten over their respective traumas. Even Osen was a mental mess before he died.

I'm sure his death has fucked him up even more. Damn, that even sounds weird to me.

My mind drifts to thoughts of Osen. I loved the motherfucker, but he was a pain in the ass too, not always in a good way. Now that he's dead, he's still causing a bloody mess. Leave it to that bastard to piss me off from the afterlife.

Jade gasps, and my attention is brought back to my mate.

Fated mate? Yes, she is mine.

"Is this really...?" Her mouth hangs open in awe. "Faerieland?"

Through her eyes, I see the beauty of the fae realm again. "Elfhame," I correct. "Yes, you are in another realm. However, this isn't your first visit, is it? You've likely astrally traveled to other dimensions in your sleep before, been here in your special dreams."

"Yes, but it's so much more vibrant than in Osen's memories." She smiles brilliantly at both Arran and me. "I suppose it was usually nighttime during his memories, though."

A flower faerie flutters over to us. Their arrival is a response to the call of amnesty that I requested from the fae royalty so we could travel through the fae realm with a witch. Fortunately, during Jade's time of need, I have people in high places who owe me favors.

"Tavi!" I greet her. "Good to see you have recovered."

She smiles shyly and looks over at Jade. "And I am happy your witch is recovering. The Fae Queen and her consorts grant you permission to travel freely. Oh, and Hollis says hello and to stay out of trouble… if that's possible."

I grin at the mention of my former student. He has outdone himself from the scrappy teenager I tutored.

"Please send the Queen and Hollis our regards and our thanks."

"The Queen would also like to extend an invitation to the witch to visit anytime she wishes."

Hmm. That's interesting and a bit odd. But perhaps this is a play to get more witches on the supernatural's side and put an end to the violence. "Much appreciated. However, until we are able to secure my witch friend's safety, we won't be making any rounds of visits."

Arran clears his throat. "Tavi, I want to thank you and your mate for saving Jade. I plan to bring you a gratitude offering in the near future."

"I appreciate the gratitude, but it is unnecessary. May the Goddess light your way." Tavi does a little bow midair and then flies off. However, I doubt she has left. She'll be watching us until we leave her realm. No doubt Hollis' instruction was to make sure that we find our way out peacefully.

I pick up Jade and carry her cradled in my arms.

She squeaks and bats at my chest. "I can walk."

"Barely," I argue. "Besides, I need to do this. You frightened me with your alleyway stunt. And you are much slower than we are," I say with a laugh at her pout.

"Am I too slow?" She rolls her eyes. "It's not my fault that my legs are so much shorter than yours. You are both giants."

"No," Arran says. "But we could introduce you to some actual giants."

"Really?" Jade practically bounces in my arms with excitement. "Wait… are they cool or assholes?"

"Depends on the giant." Arran shrugs. "We'll have to wait to go on an Elfhame tour until things have settled down."

"In the meantime, we can teach you about different species

and proper etiquette." I move faster since I want to get to our next portal point. That one is a permanent fixture, so there won't be a trail of my portal magic to follow to my house.

We jump through another portal and to another. Then finally, we trek away from the last one, and I open up one to my house.

The traveling has exhausted Jade, but when she sees the lakeside cabin, her eyes light up. "Please tell me this is where we are staying."

"Because you are done with the portal hopping?" I joke, feeling vulnerable with her seeing the place I call home.

"Well, a little. But no, this place looks exactly like one of my dreamscapes." She's studying her surroundings and appears fascinated by my home.

"Dreamscapes?" I ask as I carry her closer.

"Yeah. It's what I call the places that feel real to me. Like I can go back to them over and over and they don't change or morph into something else like regular dreams do."

"Maybe they weren't dreams at all?" I suggest. "You could have dream magic. It makes sense. You could have traveled here astrally."

"But why would I come here all these years? You think it was like a premonition of sorts?"

Should I tell Jade it is because her soul was seeking mine all these years? That my heart tells me she is my fated mate? My match? That we are destined to be together... No, she isn't ready for that. She doesn't believe it when Arran tells her, and she has a deeper connection with him than me.

No, she's not ready yet. Jade's beliefs and sensibilities are still mired in the human world. Even if she plays with the idea in her books, she doesn't truly believe there are people out there meant for us—who are fated.

Jade wiggles to get me to release her, but I hold on tightly. I'm going to carry her over the threshold into my home, just like the bridal tradition the humans have stolen from supes.

"Oh, Wolfboy? Don't shit in my yard," I poke at Arran.

Jade hides her snicker in my arms.

"Fuck, dude! You aren't ever going to let me live that down, are you?" Arran metaphorically tucks his tail between his legs.

"You took a dump in our mate's back yard. How am I supposed to forget that?" I egg him on.

"I cleaned it up!" Arran whines.

"Throwing it at my head doesn't count," I deadpan.

"He did what?" Jade laughs a bit too hard.

I glower at her, though there isn't much heat behind it.

Then I focus back on our destination. I whisper words of power as we approach, and the wards allow us entry to the property.

When I near the front porch, I use my will to open the door.

Jade squeals with delight, like a child seeing her first magic trick. She makes everything feel new and exciting. I can't wait to delight her for all the years we may have together. She even lets out a playful giggle when I carry her inside.

When I set her down on her unsteady feet and wrap my arms around her waist, she gazes up at me adoringly. My whole body vibrates with happiness. I don't think I've ever experienced this giddy feeling.

She lifts onto her toes, and I lean down to give her a kiss.

Then, like a curious puppy, she bolts away to explore, even though I can see it's taking the last bit of energy she has to even move.

Flint and Calder are already here, as they used a quicker set of portals to travel and had the spell to unlock our place.

I'm about to call out to them when Flint steps into the hallway.

In her excitement, Jade is practically flying at him. She screams, not out of fear of him, but that she will crash into his stone body and upset the lug. Her momentum is such that she will collide, so instead, she purposely falls.

Sliding on the slippery hallway wood flooring, she barely misses Flint's legs.

Her head thuds against the wall and then the floor.

"Jade!" Flint cries out and then almost tries to pick her up. He stops himself at the last second when he realizes what he's about to do.

Arran is there in the next moment, aggressively shoving Flint out of the way, and dropping down to check on Jade.

"I'm fine. Just banged myself up a little." She waves him away, but her eyes are glassy, and she doesn't move to get up.

"You can't afford anymore head trauma," Arran says with the bite of reprimand. "You are quickly killing me, *woman*."

"So dramatic." She laughs it all off. "Flint, I'm sorry for coming at you like a damned baseball player sliding into home. I should have been more careful with my surroundings."

Ugh. I hate that she has been conditioned by jerky ex boyfriends and an unloving mother to take responsibility for everything, even when it isn't her fault.

"Please, don't apologize to me," Flint says with so much sorrow that I feel it pierce my heart. He despises this part of himself, and Jade is only rubbing the old wound lately. "It's my issue. Please, don't hurt yourself to avoid me." He runs outside and takes off, flying over the lake.

"Well, I keep making a mess of things. He won't ever get used to me, will he?" Jade frowns as Arran helps her to her feet.

"He will, but it might take more than a couple of days," I assure her.

But will Flint heal? Could she be the one to help him finally come out of his self-inflicted and literal shell?

"Sweetness, you should get some rest," Arran says. "Today was a lot."

Jade pouts as she glances down the hall. She wants to explore, but that isn't a good idea right now. My cabin is no tiny hovel, it has eight bedrooms and six baths.

I bought it twenty years ago, hoping we all could settle here and give up fighting in the wars. Or at the very least, take a break from the life of revenge. Collectively, we've taken two breaks in total. However, I make use of this retreat and come here alone whenever I need to get away from the noise of city life—which is more often than not.

"Come with me." I take Jade by the waist and help her down the hallway to my enormous room on the first floor.

Jade looks up toward the stairs. "Five bedrooms up there?" she asks. "And three down here?"

I nod at her accurate guess. She *has* been here before in her dreams, further confirming she is mine... *ours?*

"One room is set up as an office of sorts. You can use that as a space for your writing," I offer, hoping she will understand the implications of allocating a piece of this house to claim as her own. "It also has a daybed if you need your... space from our energy. Though I would rather you sleep with me. You and Arran are more than welcome to share my bedroom with me while we are here. The bed could easily fit all of us. Since it's on the first floor, it will be easier for you to move around while you recover. And I have an ensuite bathroom so you won't taunt Flint or Calder with all your delicious naked flesh."

"*Taunt* is a strong and wholly inaccurate word for what I do to them." She brushes me off with a chuckle. "At least when paired with my nakedness. I'm not even trying to be an annoyance! Apparently, I'm just that good at being frustrating."

I push open the door to my huge bedroom. "You frustrate me, but in a good way."

"How so?" She smirks.

"Because you wear way too many clothes and I want to have my dick buried deep inside you at all times."

She shakes her head. "It seems as though we may experience a lot of sunburns and chafing if we played it your way."

I smile at her joke, but my statement wasn't one. I'd love to live inside her. Maybe I can get some sort of harness and I can fill her up while tending to other tasks that I can't avoid.

Hell, my mind now wanders to sexy scenarios just as much as the witch's dirty mind does. We are perfect for each other.

She moves across the room with an awe-filled face. Her hand reaches out to stroke the floor to ceiling tapestries hanging on the walls, then over a jewel-tone damask fabric duvet and pillows that cover the mattress of my four-poster bed. She grins as her fingers trace the gauzy fabric drapes that hang down and over the dark wood of the bed frame.

Overall, the decor creates a sensual space. And it feels as though I've built it all with her in mind. Pride wells up inside me when I see admiration clear in her beautiful eyes.

I rarely allow anyone inside my personal sanctuary. I think this might be the first time Arran has even seen my room.

Jade smiles from ear to ear. "Maxum, it's like you're an omega princess with a pretty nest," she jokes.

"I'll show you who's an omega when I rut you through a heat." I swat her full, plump ass, and she yelps.

"Holy shit!" She pants, worked up. "How do you know about omegaverse?"

"Where do you think humans got the idea?" I waggle my eyebrows.

"Fucking knot me," Jade sputters. Then she hugs me sweetly, clinging to my side. "But seriously, it's so fuckin' gorgeous. I'm not sure what I was expecting, but it's prettier than any place I've seen. It's like a fantasy come true."

"You don't remember my room from your dreamscape?" I ask, sad that she didn't recognize it.

"No. I was never allowed inside the bedrooms, just in the common areas."

Interesting, but it makes sense. Our rooms are sacred to us and each of us has our own form of warding to protect them from outsiders. Even my mate's spirit would need some sort of permission to enter. I feel myself relaxing with the thought.

Jade yawns, but tries to hide her sleepiness as Arran and I set all the luggage down.

Striding over, I give her a kiss on the lips, and then the top of her head. "Get some rest. I'll make sure all is well on the property before I return."

She hums her acknowledgement, then grimaces at her dirty clothes. "I don't want to mess up your beautiful bed."

"Never worry about that, my sweet witch." I wink. "I'm sure we can make you more comfortable." I slowly unbutton her blouse.

Arran comes up from behind. Reaching around, he unfastens and unzips her pants. She kicks off her shoes. The wolf-shifter slides her pants down slowly, skimming her silky skin with his fingertips as he goes.

When I pull the shirt from her shoulders, I'm both aroused and concerned. Aroused by her silky flesh and ample breasts on display. Concerned because she's covered in bruises from her brush with death.

Jade stands before me in only her skimpy underwear, and I admire her strength and resilience, especially for being a witch. They are not built like supes.

Gently, I touch her damaged flesh. "I will heal these with my magic after you rest."

She bites her lower lip, and her voice comes out husky. "Sex magic?"

"Would you like that?" I ask.

"Is it illegal to own six dildos in Texas?" she quips as an answer.

She doesn't know how much I love weird facts, and I chuckle.

"Yes. Yes, it is." I boop her nose like a silly demon and leave her be so I can ensure the safety of my pack and my mate.

7

INTIMACY

ARRAN

*J*ade falls asleep immediately in Maxum's amazing bed. I feel like I need to spruce up my bedroom before she visits it, to make her feel as comfortable and lavished in expensive fabrics as she is in Maxum's space.

I'm lacking as a provider. To be fair, Maxum is far more wealthy than any of us combined—not that he usually flaunts it. He doesn't think much about his wealth at all, from what I can tell.

On top of his ability to lavish her with whatever she dreams up, he can heal her and protect her better than I can.

Besides Maxum being a better provider, I'm also lacking in a whole other way that I don't know how to fix: I might still be a danger to her. Sure, my berserker kept his violence under wraps during sex with her. But Maxum and I kept him reined in the entire time, making sure he didn't get rough. The threat of Maxum ripping him to shreds probably helped to keep him passive, but I can't even make love to her in my human form. I want to be intimate with Jade without my beast. Otherwise, every damned time, I will probably have to invite Maxum to make sure my beast doesn't hurt her.

Will I ever have that? Will I ever be able to lose myself completely in passion with her and in my own body? Or will I always have to hold back?

After a few hours, Jade stirs and stretches. Her mesmerizing hazel eyes instantly find me watching her. "Hey, creeper," she teases, but admires my naked chest and pulls on my shoulder for me to kiss her. "Are you okay?"

"Yeah, why?" Damn, she can see right through me.

"You don't have to lie to me about stuff anymore. Tell me the truth."

Well, that stings more than I expected. She's right, though. The time for lies is done.

"I was just overthinking everything," I confess, then place gentle kisses over her face until she's laughing and pushing me away to catch her breath.

"I should freshen up." She grabs a lock of her matted hair and wrinkles her nose. "This is a fully formed rat's nest. Do you have a hacksaw?"

"That's a little drastic." I guide her to the bathroom and offer, "I'll help with untangling your hair."

I leave her to pee and come back when I hear she is washing her hands. "Sit." I point to a vanity stool, because, of course, bougie Maxum has one. Oh well, I can't fault him for wanting the finer things in life when I know the life he was born into.

Jade smirks, "I didn't know Maxum was such a fancy boy."

I pick up a comb and some oils to untangle Jade's hair and say off-handedly, "I'm sure, with his age, he's been just about everything. Except for being in love, until now."

Jade inspects a lock of her hair, starting at the ends. "Do you mean with me? That's an awfully big assumption."

"Not really, but I suppose it isn't my place to say how anyone else feels."

My witch stares at the mirror and watches my muscles flex as I brush out her hair. I pretend not to notice, but I preen under her attention. I've never cared much about my looks, only that I was strong and honorable.

Now I'm pleased that my woman finds me attractive. Jade even called my wolf handsome. She claims she has no problem with my berserker's looks, but I know she was only trying to make me feel better.

My wolf inside me bounces around, wishing to get some attention, too. He misses Jade from their long days in her home. He demands ear scratches.

I make him wait until I'm done with her hair.

"You are a miracle worker!" Jade swings her long, silver threaded strands.

I grin and then kneel to look her in the eyes. "Beast... my *wolf* misses you. He would like to visit."

Jade strokes my face. "Are you okay with that?"

"Yeah, he's been patient."

"May I ask how this shifter thing works? It sounds like the wolf and the berserker are separate from each other and from you."

I take in a deep breath. This isn't easy to explain, and it sounds baffling to most humans. But I remind myself that Jade writes stuff that isn't far from the truth.

"I suppose it's much like a split personality. Except I'm aware of him, and he is aware of me. His emotions are usually in line with mine. But similar to when you might feel conflicted about something, we can be at odds at times. Usually, that happens because he operates from his instincts and heart. I operate from my mind, humanlike feelings, and sometimes, if I'm lucky, with logic. Then there is the berserker."

"So instead of a dichotomy, you now are a trichotomy," she jokes, trying to ease my tension.

I nod. "Suppose so. We all are impulsive, and that can get us in trouble."

"Like chasing me down from the bar?" Jade smirks.

Thank Goddess she thinks that's funny now.

"Yeah. That's one example. The other is how I got cursed."

Jade covers her mouth. "Sorry. I didn't mean to bring up a sore subject."

"It's okay. I don't want anything hidden between us. And now, this is part of who I am—unfortunately."

"You mentioned it was a witch who did this. Is that why you don't like witches?"

"Partly. Jade, I will understand if you no longer like me once I tell you how I was cursed."

"Well, shit. That's not a great setup to a story." Jade places her hands on mine, calming me instantly. "Just tell me what happened and let me decide what I can handle."

Choking down the emotions bubbling up in me, I begin, "Many years ago, Osen was attacked by a witch named Tanil."

"I remember that name, vaguely." Jade gazes into the distance, lost in the memory she plucked from Osen's soul.

"You might also remember that she had gutted Osen and threw iron in his wound. For a fae-born supernatural being, iron poisoning can be a death sentence. Somehow, he managed to escape. I think she wanted him to be found in the wild, and we couldn't pin his death on her. Using Flint's sense of danger and protection, and Calder's ability to sense death, we were able to locate him and get him the help he needed. We were supposed to wait until Osen recovered, then attack Tanil together."

"But you didn't go along with that plan," she guesses.

"No. I was filled with so much rage for my friend and occasional lover that I raced off when no one was paying attention and attacked her. I tore Tanil apart. I could barely tell she was human by the time I was done."

Jade waits for me to go on, but the tension in her body grows. She probably wants to drop my hands and run away.

"But Tanil wasn't alone. Her coven mates attacked, cursing me with dark magic sealed with Tanil's blood. From then on, whenever I feel potent emotions, my berserker is awakened and takes over."

"Oh."

"Oh?" I squeeze her hands in mine, unsure what to make of her response.

"I mean, I'm so sorry they cursed you like that. But it sounds like there was an ugly cycle of revenge going on. I probably would have gone after Tanil too, if she had hurt one of my people."

"So, you don't think I'm a monster?"

"Technically? Yeah. You are. But *what-the-fuck-ever*. Humans are monsters for much less and for no reason at all." Jade shrugs. "Why did Tanil attack Osen?"

"He believed it was because he broke off their fling."

"Well, trying to kill Osen for a break up seems like a bit much," Jade says flippantly.

I bark out a laugh. "Yeah. A bit much. She knew he was a fickle incubus from the start."

"Anyway, I get why you killed her. She tried to hurt your pack because she was mad she was ghosted." Jade kisses my lips.

"But I murdered someone—a witch," I argue.

"Do you regret it?"

"I wish I had done things differently. Maybe we could have avoided all the violence." I rub my face in frustration. "But we've now come to believe that she was a spy from ASO, and she always intended to kill him. We may never know the truth of it all."

"Then you can't keep beating yourself up about it. Okay?" When I nod, she bounces in her chair. "Can I watch you change into your wolf? Is his name really Beast? Or is that just a joke Maxum made?"

I'm surprised how she drops the subject of my violence so easily.

"My wolf didn't have a name, but he likes it when you call him Beast. He thinks it makes him sound formidable."

Jade palms her face, embarrassed. "Geeze. How dumb was I that I didn't realize a wolf wasn't a dog?"

"To be fair, most wolves don't just trot inside human's homes when invited." I smile with the memory. "And there are some breeds that look a lot like wolves."

"Can I say hi to him now?" Jade asks.

I stand and drop my boxers. My cock being at eye level has Jade licking her lips.

"Next, I want an appointment with your snake." She waggles her eyebrows.

I shake my head but chuckle. Then I sober up with my next thought. "I should tell you, I will only be able to have sex in my berserker form. I won't be able to be with you like that in my human form."

A tear forms in her eyes. The reality of our relationship has set in.

"That upsets you," Jade says, like that fact doesn't affect her.

"Doesn't it upset *you*?" I ask, my brow wrinkles with confusion.

"Only if you don't like it." She frowns, thinking, then asks, "Do you feel all of it? I mean, the werewolf is part of you, right? Do you enjoy the sensations? *You* feel my touch?"

"Well, yeah. But I won't be *me*—in this body. And I can't guarantee your safety with him. I kept him mostly calm before, but he dug his claws into you during sex. We were fortunate that Maxum was able to heal the cuts so easily."

"We'll figure this out." Jade places her cheek in my palm and kisses my wrist. "But now, I need puppy time."

Beast instantly shifts without my permission. One moment, Jade is holding my hand and staring up at me, the next, she has a massive wolf standing in front of her.

He licks her face, chin to forehead in one swipe, and she shouts her shock.

"Beast! Settle down." But she's laughing and rubbing his ears. Hugging him around the neck, she buries her face deep in his fur. "I missed you, sweetie."

He whimpers, conveying he feels the same.

"I'll make sure to spend time with you more often, okay?" she promises.

Beast barks his joy and runs around the room.

"Come here. I don't have the energy yet to chase you." She picks up the brush she had just been using on herself and moves it over my wolf's head and neck.

Without even knowing it's about to happen, my berserker bursts into being, pushing the wolf back into my body.

Jade doesn't even miss a beat as a giant werewolf kneels before her.

"Be good," she warns and continues brushing, but now she's treating my berserker werewolf like a naughty pup.

And… he fucking loves it.

I don't step in and stop it. Not yet. I'm curious what he will do and how he will react, because he doesn't seem crazed with emotion, aggressively possessive, or ready to hurt someone.

He just wants attention.

Love.

So do I.

Since he *is* part of me, I suppose Jade needs to accept him, too. But I feel so exposed while she studies my true werewolf face. She didn't get a good look at me before when we had sex. But now, we are calm, and she strokes my furry body with her brush.

The berserker closes our eyes in bliss as she brushes down over our chest. Methodically, she works the brush over our sides, moving to our waist, but no further.

"I'm going to stand up and brush your back now, okay?" she informs us. Smart—she doesn't want to startle him.

Berserker grunts his approval, and she moves behind him.

Her position makes him vulnerable since he cannot see what she might do to him. I'm shocked he allows it.

Then the feeling of trust wells up in our heart. He really trusts her. Loves her. As I do.

However, that doesn't mean he might not accidentally harm her. He is a brute, after all. Am I any better, since I'm an impulsive asshole?

"Your coat is gorgeous. It looks so nice brushed out," Jade says, running her palm over our back, following each stroke of the brush. "Softer than I expected too." When she gets to my lower back, she surprises us and encourages, "Stand up."

Behaving like a tamed beast, Berserker gets to his feet.

Jade kneels and brushes over our ass and down our powerful thighs and calves. She even fusses over our tail. This is the most intimate thing I've ever experienced. My ugliest parts are on full display, and every inch of me is being loved and caressed.

I'm reeling as I feel the love pouring off her. Her acceptance. I've never accepted this part of me. Maybe I've never fully accepted and loved myself in any way—ever. But Jade makes it seem so easy to accept my monster and to love me completely.

Berserker wags his tail. *Wags! His tail!*

I don't even recognize this creature right now.

Jade gasps quietly, likely just as shocked as I am.

I thump her face with our flailing tail. Oh my goddess, how embarrassing.

"Turn around," she asks with a smile in her voice.

We do, gazing down into Jade's adoring hazel-green eyes.

She's on her knees at our clawed feet, looking up at us like we are a god. Her sweet pink mouth is only inches from our hardening cock.

I've never felt so naked or so cherished.

I'm surprised once again when my berserker doesn't grab her face and fuck into her lush mouth. The loving way she looks at us right now, she might let us do that.

But even Berserker knows this moment isn't about fucking.

Jade touches our huge hands and slowly traces the line of my giant razor-sharp claws. "These aren't innately bad, you know. You can use them to protect the ones you love. Just be careful when you get excited with me, and I will be okay."

Maybe there is potential worth in my alternate self. I can protect her.

What would happen if I accepted this part of me? Would it heal this perpetual wound I have?

My berserker nods his understanding of her words. He sees himself as her protector already. Lightly and experimentally, he skims his sharp claw over the back of her hand. He doesn't even leave a mark.

She smiles up at us and continues brushing our thighs and shins. Then she moves up over our crotch, brushing around our cock and balls.

During this sacred moment, she has, only with her actions, told us how much we mean to her.

She moves to stand and Berserker reaches down and helpfully lifts Jade to her feet. He then licks up the side of her face very much like my wolf did minutes ago.

Jade laughs and hugs us, holding *him*.

After a moment of enjoying the affection, Berserker relinquishes control over my body. It's the first time since my curse that he's willingly allowed me to come back. Every other time I have to fight him to win back control and return to my human form.

"Oh!" Jade scare-jumps from my shifting into a human, of all things.

She's so weird. It's my normal appearance that gets her spooked, but I sort of love it.

I'm six inches shorter and less bulky in my human form. And I dare say less furry.

She snuggles her cheek into my bare chest and hums happily.

"Thank you," I whisper. "For accepting them… me."

Jade leans back in my arms to look into my eyes. "Of course. You have accepted me even though I'm your enemy."

"You were never my enemy. My love, you are my savior." I press my lips to hers, luxuriating in her softness.

"Well, that might be taking it a bit far." Jade blushes and tucks her head under my chin.

"It's not. No one has made me feel at peace like I feel right now. You accepting my berserker makes me accept him, too. He doesn't even feel feral at the moment."

"I'm happy I could help a little bit."

"A lot." I squeeze her to me, wishing I could make her part of me too. I suppose when… *if*… I claim her, she will be part of me. "Maybe witches, in general, should have never been my enemy."

"People, no matter what kind, can be amazing or they can be jerks. I don't think it's wise to lump whole groups together and assume we know everything by the behavior of a few."

"If you're finished fixing the world's problems in my bathroom, would you like to come eat the meal we whipped up for you?" Maxum asks with a smirk in the doorway.

"A chef too?" Jade hurries to him, pulling me along by my hand. "A demon of many talents!"

8

MEALS

JADE

*T*ears had formed in Arran's eyes when he was a berserker. I don't think the monster within him is all beast.

Volatile? Impulsive? Dangerous?

Yes, he is all these things, but also... more. It wants to be accepted. Loved.

It isn't just an *it*.

I hope that my affection for the berserker might persuade it to allow Arran to be with me in his human form. Not because I need to have Arran in his non-monster form, but because *Arran* wants to be with me in that way.

Holding both the demon's and werewolf's hand as we enter the kitchen and open dining room, I feel weirdly giddy and happy. Considering everything that's going on, I shouldn't feel this happy. I almost died—again. I'm on the run. My career is likely in jeopardy of taking a nosedive if I can't finish my next book on time.

Yet, it's reassuring to have these two brave males by my side, willing to help me figure out the next completely overwhelming and new phase of my life. It's also more than I expected or hoped for.

I still can't believe what my life has become. First off, I'm a witch. With that, there are realms of existence beyond the one I've always known. There really are magical beings and creatures. I've had sex with three kinds of supernaturals... no, make that four magical people if we include a stupid warlock named Rob.

Might as well add him to the list, as it makes my low 'body count' sound more impressive.

The kitchen and dining area are open to the living room, which has a magnificent stone fireplace. My eye catches a huge framed image I hadn't noticed when I arrived. It looks like a blurry photograph of a werewolf.

"What is... *that*?" I rush over to it. My eyes pop out of my head when I catch sight that all around the larger photograph are framed newspaper clippings.

Each clipping features a blurry, furry *monster*—named to be bigfoot, the Jersey devil, chupacabra, unknown species, etc. Now that I know how the camera distorts a supernatural's image and how Arran looks in his beast form, I recognize the famous and *previously believed to-be-a-hoax* images. "Is this you?" I ask my werewolf lover.

He grimaces and tucks his head down.

Maxum chuckles. "Every time he's been caught by a camera, I like to remind him of his reckless behavior and frame it up for him."

"Maxum!" I admonish, but find myself chuckling too.

"We all have clippings around the house, but Arran is the most famous," he informs me.

Shaking my head in amusement, I turn back toward the kitchen.

Looking shy once again, Flint is back and helping to dish up dinner.

The dining table is set with medieval-style forks with only two pointed prongs and sharp knives.

The plates are thick ceramic and appear extremely retro—like centuries old retro. However, the gas stove is cutting edge and looks like it belongs in a fancy restaurant.

At the head of the table, Maxum pulls a chair out for me next to his, and Arran sits on my other side. Calder storms in and plops down at the far end, clearly stating his objection to my presence with a hard glower.

Flint serves us our plates, being extra cautious around me.

I want to joke that my arms aren't going to flail around and accidentally touch him, but I don't want to draw attention to his discomfort. Besides, I'm slightly klutzy and I might actually bump into him.

My plate has a thick slice of meat that takes up almost the entire surface. It looks mostly like beef, but doesn't quite smell like it. Also on my overly full plate are a variety of unknown vegetables, a chunk of fancy cheese, and a fresh dinner roll. On the table in a big serving bowl is a pile of my snack chips, all mixed together.

My eyes go wide with that last offering and Maxum addresses the weird *dish*. "Flint thought you might want some as an appetizer."

Shaking my head in disbelief, I say, "This is a fuck-ton of food."

"Is that a metric ton?" Maxum asks with a smirk.

I grin at his joke, then slowly look back at my plate. "I appreciate how generous you are with the servings, but I can't eat all this."

"But you have lost weight." Flint leans forward in his seat, with an earnest expression. "You need your strength."

I don't use scales. Not that I've had time to locate and use one lately. But now that he's mentioned it, my pants have been a bit looser. "I've lost weight?"

"Yeah," all four of the males say in unison—with a frown. Even Calder joined in, which blows my mind. Why would he care or comment?

"I need you healthy for what I have planned for you later." Maxum grins wickedly at me. "So, eat what you can."

Healthy? He means curvy. But I can't say I mind them enjoying my curves.

I love my curves more and more the way they adore every inch of me.

Glancing around the table, I see they are all waiting to start —Calder, too.

"What's happening?" I ask. "Do we need to say grace to the Goddess or some supernatural being?"

"You are our guest, so we are waiting for you to take the first bite," Arran explains.

"Oh." Eyeing the meat and veggies again, I ask, half-joking, "Is this unicorn meat? Because it's not beef."

"Unicorn meat is much too gamey," Maxum says. "This is pegasus meat. They are far more common than you would think and quite a nuisance."

"What?" I push the plate away from me. "I don't think eating magical creatures is a good idea. Supes are already pissed off that I was even born."

"I'm just messing with you." Maxum laughs. "It's buffalo. And it was ethically sourced. The buffalo lives out its normal lifespan, with magic to keep its body healthy. And then it passes peacefully in its sleep."

"Are you still screwing with me?" I ask, because who knows with this jokester.

"That's the truth."

I take his word for it, because honestly, that sounds like the most ethical thing you can do if you are going to eat meat. I cut and spear a small piece on my jabby fork and try it.

"It's pretty good," I say, and they all dig into their food. It still has a different taste than the buffalo I've had before, but maybe that's the magic flavoring.

I taste the veggies on the tip of my tongue one at a time and find they taste okay. The seasoning is a bit different from what I'm used to, but I'm adventurous enough.

"So, where are we? Earth?" I ask, since it doesn't have that colorful hyperrealism look that the fae realm has.

"Yes, but I don't want to tell you exactly where, because if someone infiltrates your mind in your dreams, they will know where we are."

"I suppose a lake house is generic enough," I note.

"No landmark features around here for a reason except for a lake. But there are 125,000 lakes in the Continental U.S. alone... if we are even in the States." Maxum winks. "Since you are untrained in blocking, you would be the most likely to reveal our location accidentally."

I don't mention that when I have access to Wi-Fi with my travel router, I'll be able to pinpoint exactly where we are. I don't plan on doing that for exactly the reason Maxum outlined. And thankfully, I've already turned off my GPS location on my devices.

"I don't want to be the weak link," I say.

"Too late," Calder grouches.

"I wouldn't point fingers if I were you," Arran growls. "You botched the whole alleyway incident from beginning to end."

"Stop it," Maxum raises his voice.

I quietly shovel food in my mouth because I still feel guilty for not stopping Osen from demanding I go to that alley. I remind myself I didn't have the tools or magic to stop the incubus.

"Will you really be able to help me block out people like Rob?" I ask Maxum.

He studies me for a second. "Yeah. Your magic is coming in. Soon we will see what kind of power you actually have."

"I'm nervous," I admit openly. "I don't know if I can handle suddenly being powerful at forty."

"You already are powerful," Arran says and strokes my arm. "You're an amazing medium, even when the talisman was draining you, and you have dream magic."

"And you are a fucking grown-ass, professional business woman who has carved her way through a male dominated world," Maxum adds.

"Okay. You're right. I just need to brace myself for whatever happens."

"We'll be here for you," Arran promises.

"Can we lay off the sugary positive affirmations for a few minutes so I can choke down this food?" Calder asks with a sneer on his face.

Having enough of his attitude, I say in a calm but firm voice, "Can you lay off being a dick to me for five minutes? I get you hate witches, and I get you don't trust me because of Rob. But it upset me when you got hurt. One, because the asshole Osen loves you, and two, because I don't hate you."

Calder doesn't respond, which I'm taking as a good sign. Then finally he asks, "You haven't felt Osen again since the alleyway?"

"No. I'm getting worried."

"Why?" he asks firmly, with more than a hint of disbelief. "He's just some cosmic parasite now, if it's really even him at all."

"I've seen a bit of what he's been through—what all of you have been through. Believe it or not, I've grown to care about him. It doesn't matter what you think about me, because I hope he's okay." I offer an olive branch. "If he returns, I'll make sure you get to talk to him."

Calder grunts and focuses back on his plate. I'll take it as a win.

9

ANOTHER ROUND

JADE

*T*he guys encouraged me to eat way more than I had planned. I'm stuffed, and they probably could roll me away from the table.

Fortunately, they don't erase the small amount of dignity I have left by going for that option.

Flint gathers up our empty plates and cleans up with Calder's help.

Maxum takes my hand and walks me back to his bedroom with Arran in tow.

"I know you suggested a night of sexy times, but I'm too full and exhausted for that," I inform him as we step into the beautiful bedroom. "I'm frustrated now."

"I know, little witch," Maxum purrs. "I thought we'd give you a bath and then let you sleep. The sex will have to wait until you can handle what I plan to do to you."

My clit tingles with his sexy threat.

Down, girl.

"Arran, get these pesky clothes off her, and I'll get the bath going," Maxum says and darts into the ensuite bathroom.

My wolf shifter shrugs innocently as he steps closer. "Boss's orders. Nothing I can do, miss."

"Well, if Mr. McBossy said so…" I help Arran along and lift my arms so he can pull my top over my head.

Instead of helping me all the way, he leaves the shirt stuck over my face and arms trapped, and he sucks my exposed nipple into his mouth.

"Arran!" I laugh, hurrying to pull the shirt all the way off. I run toward the bathroom and crash into Maxum's arms.

Arran collides with my backside and presses me between them.

"Mr. Maxum McBossy needs his witch naked by the count of three." Maxum stares at me sternly. "One… Two…"

Behind me, Arran drops to his knees and pants me as he goes. His sharper than normal teeth bite into my ass, and I shout my surprise.

Maxum lifts me, and Arran removes my pants from around my ankles.

The water spout is rapidly filling a gigantic tub that could hold all three of us comfortably.

Maxum's hands stroke up and down my sides, from hips to breasts. "Beautiful."

My eyes drift to the hot water blasting out of the faucet. Wow, he has amazing water pressure here. That's going to feel amazing in the shower.

Focus. I don't want to be sidetracked by future pleasures when I have a current experience happening now.

Fragrant steam wafts off the hot bath water and fills my nose. The floral smell is like nothing I've experienced before. I suspect he added other worldly oils to my bath.

Other *realmly*?

Realmly isn't a word, is it? I'll have to look that up. Probably not. It's likely another one of my new words. But I'm exactly like Shakespeare, making up words to fit my wild stories.

I pull on Maxum's tight long sleeve shirt, and he obliges, removing it over his head. No way I was reaching over his six foot five height. These guys are all so tall it makes me feel like a tiny thing.

My fingertips trace Maxum's tattoo-like crimson markings. He's in his human glamour, so it's striking against his lighter skin tone.

"Why don't your markings disappear with your glamour?" I ask.

"Not sure why, but we can't make our life marks disappear. I suppose it could be considered poetic—my life history is always with me."

"I like that answer."

There's a rustle of clothing, and then I feel Arran's naked body and his hard cock pressing up against my back. He moves the mass of my thick hair away from my neck and shoulder and presses sweet, tickling kisses on my skin there.

"I thought you said no sex?" I'm not sure which answer I want.

"*I* didn't say no sex," Arran purrs and his hand reaches around to cup my breast.

Maxum chuckles, tests the water, then lifts me up and into the deep tub. "Arran, she needs to recover... unfortunately." He sits and sets me down between his powerful legs. His right hand strokes up my inner thigh. "But that doesn't mean we can't tease her."

"Naughty demon!" I smack his hand.

He doesn't stop his exploration, and with his left hand on my left knee, and his tail wrapped around my right leg, he opens me up.

Arran joins us in the water. His hungry gaze locked on my exposed sex.

Arran scoots closer, lathers up his hands, and washes me from my toes, moving up to my hips.

Maxum washes my hair, massaging my scalp with his deft fingers. Oh, wow, I could get used to this sensual spa treatment.

After he rinses the shampoo out, I lean back against Maxum's broad chest and luxuriate in his ministrations as he slides his fingers over my pussy and stimulates me, slowly working me up.

It feels so good that I drift off into a strange half-asleep arousal.

Or I think it's half-asleep.

"Is she snoring?" Maxum asks, with mirth in his voice.

"Dude, she full-on just zonked out during our sexy times," Arran says with a laugh.

I try to wake up, but the jaws of sleep are clamping down on me. I murmur, "Good little monsters are very relaxing."

"Everything you said in that sentence is wrong," Maxum sighs. "We are not little monsters. Morally gray at best. And we shouldn't be relaxing. We should be making you come right now."

"I'm coming, just tomorrow." I mumble.

I'm lifted out of the warm water and the most sensual, huge towel is wrapped around me and I'm in love with it.

"That's a wrap!" I call out like a drunken movie director.

I can feel a deep rumble from Maxum's chest when he lifts me up and carries me out of the bathroom.

I'm tucked into the massive bed. It's so big that I could get lost here for days.

"I'd like to get lost in bed with you for days, too," Maxum says.

"You read my mind?" I ask, snuggling into his chest and feeling Arran tucking in behind me as my big spoon.

"You're saying everything out loud," he informs me. "And I'm a bit jealous of the towel."

"Rain check on the magical dicking?" I ask.

I feel a kiss on the top of my head and drift off, happy to know my two monsters are safely in my bed.

Darkness surrounds me, but I know I'm not awake or in bed next to my guys.

No. I'm lost in a forest.

When I allow my consciousness to reach out to the dark, like Osen inadvertently showed me how to do when he took over my body, I sense I'm in Elfhame.

Not that I'm all that familiar with the fae realm, but I had a good dose of the energetic feel of the place during our cross-realm trek to Maxum's home.

Why am I here?

Of course, my first instinct is to wonder if I'm reliving another one of Osen's memories. I don't have the same sensations as I did when we were connected, though.

I fear, once again, that our incubus is lost. *Ours.* When did I claim him as mine?

Even though he's inhabited my body and brought me immense sexual pleasure, I don't know if I have the right to claim him that way. Or in any way.

"Osen?" I whisper. It's my voice, not his, that cuts through this dark quiet.

So if I'm not in his memory, or anyone's memory, where am I? And why? Maybe I have dream magic as Maxum suggested.

This feels too tangible to be a normal dream.

Eerily, I can hear a woman hum a song—like a lullaby. It echoes around me, from everywhere and nowhere. This song feels familiar.

It sounds a bit like... my abuela?

Now, I'm very confused. If my grandmother was a witch, why is she in the fae realm?

"You shouldn't be here, mija."

"Abuela?" I ask. "Where are we? Are you alive?"

"You are here, because your pendant is gone," she says.

Is this real? Is this now?

"How do you know about the pendant?" I ask, "Why did you suppress my power?"

"I meant to come back and teach you about your power. I didn't get the chance."

"Are you working with Rob? Did you kill Osen?"

"No. Never." I can almost hear her shaking her head. "Your pendant was meant to protect you... hide you... from those who would harm you or use your power."

"What powers?" I wonder if there's more than my mediumship and dream magic. "Why would someone want to harm me? Or use me? Why me?"

"There are always those who crave more power," she answers cryptically. "Those who are filled with hate and bigotry."

"What power?"

"You already know you are unique."

"What? Because I can channel the soul of a supernatural being?"

"Yes, that sort of gift hasn't happened before." She sounds so sad.

"Why can I do it then?" I ask.

"You..." she hesitates, as if she doesn't want to tell me. "You are made differently."

"Are you in the spirit realm watching over me or something? How do you know what I can do?"

She ignores my questions and says, "Now that your full magic has been freed, you need to learn to use it. Quickly, mija. You are in more danger now that they can no longer control you. They won't suffer a witch such as you."

"Why didn't you warn me before? With Rob?" I demand.

"He turned your pendant against me, blocking me," she explains. "Before he corrupted my gift, I had visited."

Conflicting emotions collide inside my chest. "That was really you in my dreams."

"Yes, after I was killed." She warns, "You feel safe with these males, but you aren't meant to be with them."

She was murdered?

Why would she tell me they aren't for me? Her words conflict with the knowledge I have in my soul that they *are* meant to be in my life. It hits me like a lie. Anger rises up in my heart. I wonder now if this is actually the spirit of my grandmother. And if it is, does she care about me? Or is she just mean like my mother?

"Go now. Don't return."

An unknown force shoves me backward and I shout as I fly back into my body. I wake up in bed with hot, heavy limbs weighing me down, pinning me to the bed.

I scramble to break free, not realizing at first it's just my guys snuggling me.

"Jade? What's wrong?" Arran asks. "Is Osen attacking you?"

"What? No." I shake my head. In the darkness, I barely can make out the shapes of them next to me. Why did he instantly think Osen was hurting me? "I just had a weird dream about my grandmother."

Arran's eyes now glow gold, as if gleaming with worry. Maxum's flame with red, and I can actually see their faces with their light.

"Are you sure it was *just* a dream?" Maxum asks, his voice wary, and he appears ready to attack anything that moves.

"It might have been her spirit." I frown, but relax into their hold. "I need to learn how to have more control with this dream magic."

"As soon as you have recovered, I will teach you what I can." Maxum strokes my cheek and gazes into my eyes.

"I wish I could do more to protect you," Arran says.

"It isn't your jobs to do that," I argue. "I need to do it myself."

Both males growl. They don't like that idea, but don't debate my statement either. They know the wisdom in it, even if they're acting out the trope of 'touch her and die vibes.'

Can't say I mind having someone fighting on my team for a change. It helps that they are actual monsters that would have no problem tearing someone apart that was about to hurt me.

My naughty bits tingle with excitement.

"Jade?" Arran sniffs the air. "What are you thinking about, you minx?"

"Just how sexy it is to feel as though you might do almost anything for me," I admit.

"Might? Almost anything?" Maxum cups my chin, his intense gaze dangerous and feral. "You have to know we *would do anything for you.*"

I gulp with his intensity. "Not to be a Debbie Downer, but I'm not used to that. My mom essentially disowned me as soon as I was eighteen. And as you know, my ex-boyfriends are the human equivalent of black mold—and that's being generous."

Again, they curl their lips with disgust at the mention of my ex.

"We won't let you forget it," Arran promises. "Even if you no longer wish to be with me intimately, I will always show up for you. I will always protect you."

Well, fuck.

I'm not crying, it's just all the emotion floating in the room that gets in my eyes.

I snuggle back down between the two living heaters and get some more sleep.

10

MUFFINS

JADE

I wake up to the delicious smell of breakfast. Only Arran is with me now, and I give him a soft peck on the lips.

His golden eyes open, and he grins at me like I'm his favorite thing.

"I'm fairly certain Maxum opened up a portal to the land of milk and honey in the kitchen," I joke. "We should get in there before the bounty is all gone." I jump out of bed… Okay, that's a lie. I roll out of bed, then I head to the bathroom for a quick pee and mirror check.

"You're perfect." Arran catches me frowning at the mirror and races forward, throws me over his shoulder like I weigh nothing at all, and takes me to the kitchen. I don't think I'll ever get used to how strong these guys are.

I'm finally allowed on my feet when we get to the dining table. It's overfilled with several serving plates: muffins, scrambled eggs, fruit, home fries, bacon, some things I'm unfamiliar with, and, of course, sausages. Not just the guy kind…

"Whoa." My eyes almost pop from my skull. "You guys eat a lot!"

"Actually, we don't need to eat very much," Maxum says, shaking his head with a smirk.

"Then… why the big spread?" I gesture at the table and sit down.

Standing in the kitchen, Flint, the quiet, nervous looking gargoyle, rubs the back of his neck. His face tints a peach color—his version of a blush, apparently. "When I heard humans need food several times a day, I realized we haven't fed you enough." With a coffee mug in hand, he races over, then slows down as he nears me. "They informed me you like morning bean tea."

"Coffee?" I smell the tale-tell aroma of dark roast. "Yes, thank you."

"Cream and sugar are right there." His thick finger points in front of me.

My heart almost bursts from his adorable attempt to take care of me properly. I truly never expected this level of concern from anyone, but his urge to provide for me is giving me all the warm fuzzies.

The urge to hug-attack the gargoyle is strong, but I keep myself rooted in my seat.

"You should pick up the book, *The Proper Care and Feeding of Your Human*," I say with a straight face.

Flint asks with eyes wide with interest, "Where can I purchase this book?"

"Don't worry, I'll get you a copy." Maxum grins at me, mischievously.

"I appreciate all the thought and effort, but remember, I can only eat small portions at a time." I point to Maxum's plate with a reasonable portion of food. "I usually eat about that much.

And honestly, I'm not great about eating three times a day. So please, don't go out of your way just for me."

Calder shuffles into the room, and his eyes widen at the sight of the spread. "Are we not allowed to eat for the rest of the month?" he jokes. He takes a seat, gathering up a huge portion of food. It probably took a lot out of him when he almost died.

I place a bit of everything onto my plate to show Flint that I appreciate his hard work. I take a large bite of a muffin.

The baffling burst of jalapeño causes me to choke.

"Are you okay?" Arran asks and rubs my back as I sip some water.

I feel my face turning red. "I just wasn't expecting a muffin to be… spicy."

"I thought you liked it spicy." Flint glances innocently at Maxum and Arran. "Is this untrue?"

"Oh." I clear my throat and take a sip of water. "I write what they call spicy books, but it has nothing to do with food. I'm sorry about the confusion."

Maxum gives me an evil grin which makes me think he was in on the misunderstanding or wanted to see how it played out. He's such a trickster.

"You don't like it then?" Flint asks, looking completely deflated.

Ah, fuck. "I… they are good. It just was a surprise, since muffins are usually sweet."

"I'll eat your spicy muffin any day." Maxum gives me a wink.

I remember he added a fair amount of hot sauce to his eggs when we went on our brunch date. He places two muffins on his plate and appears victorious.

Rolling my eyes at my sneaky demon, I turn my attention back to Flint. "You are amazing. I appreciate all of this work."

He gives me a shy grin. "If you need anything, I'll make sure you get it. All you have to do is ask."

Calder grumbles under his breath, which sounds a lot like *kiss ass*, but I ignore him as does everyone else in the room.

"Thank you." I turn to look at everyone else. "Are there any plans for the day that I should know about?"

"I'd like to train you to block out psychic invasions soon," Maxum says and takes another bite of his muffin. "But only after you are healed."

I tuck in to my food and then say, "I need to see if I can use the Wi-Fi here, and I need to get some writing done. I'm so far behind on my schedule, but I suppose near-death experiences will put a hamper on timelines."

"I put all your writing stuff in the office," Arran reminds me.

"We are in the human realm," Maxum confirms. "Will you still be able to access the internet with your travel device?"

"Depends if there are any cell towers in the area, but humans have them pretty much everywhere now." I glance out the huge windows at the beautiful lake. "You have a gorgeous place here. Thank you for sharing it with me."

Maxum subtly preens and inclines his head to acknowledge my thanks. "I've been wanting these jerks to spend some time here for a while now, so I suppose our situation has been a good excuse. And now, I get the delightful bonus of having you here."

"Are there other residents living around the lake?" I ask. "I don't see any houses or docks. Do we have to be careful about your true forms here? Or if I shoot off a *premature e-magication*?"

Maxum snorts, then shrugs. "Uh, yeah, no one else lives around this lake."

"How lucky is that!" I take another bite of the spicy muffin and find the taste growing on me.

"Well, I own the entire lake."

I choke again. "What?" I sip some more water.

Then I realize he's been alive for centuries and probably made some smart investments along the way.

"Oh, did you buy this area up when the country was still being formed?"

"Uh, no. It was a couple of decades ago." Maxum turns a brighter shade of red.

"You're… rich?" I brush it off because I don't want him to get the wrong idea. "Or you were rich, *before* you bought this entire area?"

"So now you're a *gold-digging* witch?" Calder sneers.

I level a look at him. "FYI, I thought you were all hot before I knew a single thing about you. Even though you all look like some punk-ass thirst trap models, I would have taken you home for a snack." I snap. "Besides, I don't really care all that much for money, except that *I* make enough to live comfortably so I can keep writing. I'll gladly pay my way while you all help me out." I look at Maxum. "Do you think it will be safe to e-wire transfer you some funds? You have a regular bank account, yeah?"

"Jade, you are not giving me any money. I know you aren't here for a free ride." Maxum looks pissed. He stands up, then glares at Calder. "You need to back the fuck up, or I'll adjust your attitude for you."

"I just—" Calder protests.

"No." Maxum crosses his arms. "Apologize and then drop this bullshit. Jade is innocent, and you know it. She isn't the witch who killed you. She is a victim of other witches, and who knows what else."

What else? I don't like the sound of that.

"I'm sorry that you were upset by my joke," Calder grits out.

It wasn't a joke, but whatever. Also, his apology is blaming me for being upset.

"That's such a weak-ass apology." Arran shakes his head. "Might as well say 'I'm sorry you have feelings.'"

I stifle a chuckle at Arran's comment.

Calder frowns at his half empty plate of food and huffs. "I'm sorry. I'm still not recovered from the attack the other night—

both physically and emotionally." He pauses and asks, "Has Osen come back yet?"

"I'm sorry… not yet." To give him some hope, I add, "But he could be still recovering from the attack too."

He hums and doesn't look at me for our entire exchange. It's progress, nonetheless.

After breakfast, I wander into Maxum's office and unpack my gear. I really hope my computers don't melt with all their magic swirling around.

What if I eventually have enough magic to cause problems all on my own? Will I be able to write on my laptop? Or will I have to write longhand and send my work off to someone to type it for me?

Once I have my stuff on the desk, I figure out my travel router, which actually works. No matter how much my curiosity pesters me, I don't check to see where in the world we are. I'm guessing North America, probably the States, since my router works without issue. Beyond that, I don't know, and apparently, it might be dangerous for me to know if someone invades my mind.

I also don't like or comment on any of my public social media posts. If Rob really is watching for signs of me, then I don't want to let him know I survived his attack.

I notice one of my author friends has sent me several direct messages in the last couple of days. I find it odd because she rarely notices when I've locked myself in my writing cave for too long. Somehow, she must sense I'm in trouble. Perhaps she has a bit of psychic intuition. As much as I want to respond, I don't.

Sales are doing okay since my assistant is still promoting, and my ads are running fine. I remind myself it's only been a few days, but part of me is disappointed. I had hoped more people would notice I was missing.

Why am I irked that the world didn't fall apart when I wasn't constantly there? Does that mean I could have taken a day off once in a while before now? Nah, I don't want to believe that.

Opening up my manuscript file, I sigh happily. I finally have climbed over my writer's *wall*, but I've had barely any time to write. Now, I might get the writer's retreat of my dreams, with sexy monster lovers to test out all the sex positions I can think of.

My personal supernatural research and development team is on call.

With that, I'm wondering what kinds of fantasies Maxum wants to make come true for me. I need to write out a lengthy and thorough list of things to try. I had no one I trusted before to do kinky stuff with. Will he chase me through the woods for a primal fuck? Tie me up and edge me to oblivion? Fly me into the sky and fuck me midair?

I open up a notes file and jot down some of these ideas. Never hurts to be prepared.

I'm lost to my imaginings when I feel Arran's presence. I don't even have to turn around to know it's him. Is this a witch's power? Or because we are bonding? I've never had a connection to someone the way I do with him.

"Hey, Arran," I say before I turn.

When I look, he's standing in the doorway. His gaze is locked onto my computer screen as if he eagerly wishes to sneak a peek. The fragrant scent of my favorite herbal tea is wafting from my favorite tea cup.

I squeak with happiness and rush at him. Then blessedly, I remember the scalding hot water, so I stop, place the cup gently down on the desk, and *then* jump him.

He catches me, holding me up by the ass, and my legs wrap around his waist.

"Thank you." I pepper kisses over his gorgeous face. "That was so thoughtful. I was out of my mind and didn't even think to grab it."

"Of course, my sweetness. I know how it's part of your writing ritual."

I think about how he used to watch me as his wolf, unbeknownst to me. "That reminds me—no more peeking! I thought you were a dog that couldn't read. I don't like when people read my stuff before it's done."

Maxum enters the room, his brow cocked and eyeing how I'm plastered to Arran like a baby monkey. "If you are healthy enough to jump on werewolves, then I think I should heal you up and give you your first magic lesson."

"Oh, yes, a magic sexual healing will commence forthwith!"

11

HEALING MAGIC

MAXUM

I hate to break up Arran and Jade's little snugglefest.

Actually, I don't mind one fucking bit.

I want her ass in *my* hands, her legs wrapped around my waist, and her wet center taking my length.

My dick wakes the fuck up with that and wants to say hello to the curvy, unwitting seductress. She has no clue how hot she is.

Thankfully, I'll be balls deep in her pussy in a few minutes, convincing her of her sexiness.

I also have to convince her that my need for her is more than a meaningless fucking. I need alone time with her. Jade is my fated match. I have to know all about her. Because with her modern *human* sensibilities, spending quality time with her will be the only way to make her believe I crave her like no other.

If she were a supernatural being, or raised in any magical community, then she'd already know without question that I'd die for her, even though I don't yet know her like I intend to.

I will discover every ticklish spot on her body, figure out how her wacky mind works, read all her books, learn how to cook her favorite foods, explore her favorite positions and fantasies, understand what makes her laugh, and what brings her comfort.

However, right now, I plan to take care of her body and heal the ugly bruises and cuts that Rob inflicted on her the other night.

Fucking Rob.

I will hunt him down and bring Jade his severed head on a pike.

Is that too much for a mating gift? Not enough?

I'll have to brush up on my courting etiquette.

Ultimately, I blame myself for leaving Jade alone.

I should have expected that *stupid prick of an incubus ghost* Osen would coerce her into sneaking off. What was he thinking, taking an inexperienced witch to a dark alley in a supernatural beings-infested neighborhood where he had died?

What really pisses me off is that he didn't trust one of us enough to escort them there. I would have done it *after* I checked out the entire area and had everyone in our pack there as backup. But like always, Osen does everything in his own reckless way. Damn the consequences.

Look where that got him. He's dead, and now his soul is probably obliterated.

Fuck, and he almost took *my* mate—Arran's mate—away from us.

Jade studies my face as she climbs off Arran's body. "You okay, big guy?"

"Yeah, just remembering how we almost lost you. I'd kill Osen if he weren't already dead."

Sadness and regret flash over her face as she saunters over to me. "I think your wish might have come true."

"Let's see if he's able to return after we have sex. Osen might just need to power up." I smirk evilly. "*Then* I'll rip his soul to shreds."

Jade playfully bats my bicep and winces. "Ow! What is that thing made of? Flippin' steel?"

I flex my naked chest and watch as her face lights up with excitement. "You didn't know that demons were made of carbon steel from the depths of the Earth's core?" I deadpan.

Her mouth drops open briefly and then her eyes narrow. "Don't fuck with me. It's not nice."

"Oh, I plan on fuckin' with you, and I can be as nice or as wicked as you like." I lift her up over my shoulder, and she squeaks. I look at Arran, wondering about how his beast will handle my taking her away like this. "You good?"

"Yeah. I actually am. But I'm going for a run around the lake, so I don't have to hear it… just in case I'm not."

"Aw," Jade whines. "I want to explore the lake, too."

"Another time." I swat her rump, turn, and rush to my bedroom. As we enter, I rip the seam of her leggings, and I slide my fingers over her wet center. "I also have something wet I'd like to explore."

"Maxum!" She wiggles as I keep her trapped to my shoulder. "You ruined my pants!"

"Now, I'm going to ruin your pretty pussy."

"Fuck," she hisses to herself as I circle her clit.

"And these leggings are old and worn out. I'll buy you new clothes so I can tear them all off you." I toss her in the middle of my bed and grab her ankles. "You ready for me, my delicious witch?"

"Uh, getting close," she says with wide eyes as I pull her by the ankles, so her ass lands at the edge of the bed.

With her leggings still on, I descend a claw and use it to slice the hole of her pants a bit more and cut her underwear at the crotch, allowing me free access to her pussy.

I lean down and give her obscenely exposed center a lick. I pull off my pants to reveal my hard cock throbbing with desire.

Jade's eyes widen even more as she takes in the sight of my huge and naturally studded dick. She bites her luscious lip, likely wondering how I taste. Soon, I'll have her suck me and drink me down. But not until I've healed her.

I drop my glamour, revealing my horns, red skin, tail, and enormous wings.

She sucks in a breath. I scent her arousal increase. I love that she loves the real me.

How there is no fear in her eyes is beyond my understanding. She should run away screaming, not into my arms.

But her legs fall open even more while she studies me. "You're gorgeous."

"I'm just a demon. You are gorgeous."

She blushes at my compliment and laughs as if I'm being silly.

"You have no idea what you do to me, do you?" I ask. There is a dangerous edge to my question, and she rightfully shivers.

"Me?" She looks up and down my naked body, seeing the tension I'm holding.

I have to hold back most of my desire so I don't accidentally hurt her. But I want to pound into her for days, consume every drop of her honey, and wring cries of passion from her until she is exhausted and ruined for anyone else.

"Are you going to work your magic on me?" she asks.

"I don't like seeing bruises and cuts on your beautiful body." I tell her. "It reminds me how badly I messed up by leaving you alone with Osen."

"Well, if sexy times with you are what I get out of it, I'm good with that."

"How about I'll give you *more* sex if you stay out of harm's way?" I ask. "Then I can make all your fantasies come true without having to worry."

She grins. "I started a list."

"Do you have any special requests for me?" I ask with a

wink. "Any kinks you would like to explore right now?" I snap my sharp teeth and growl.

"*Ohmymightyclit*, Maxum. I think you just made me come. Why do you have to be so fucking amazing? I can't think straight when you look at me like that." She squirms to get the friction between her legs that she craves. "How about dealer's choice? I can show you my list later when I'm not gazing at my fantasy guy come to life."

My chest puffs up a bit with her praise. I can't help it. No one has ever made me feel desired the way she does.

"Shit. Did it sound as if I'm objectifying you for demon sex?" She reaches out to me in apology. "I totally value your brain and great personality, too. You know that, right?"

I chuckle because of the role reversal happening here. "I know, sweet witch. Would it bother you if I told you I only wanted you for your curvy body?"

"Not at all." She smiles shyly. "I like that you like my body. Also, I don't think that's entirely true. You like my weird personality a bit, too."

"You're right. I *love* your weird personality."

Jade gulps at my use of the word love. She's not ready yet for my full affection. That's okay. I knew it would take time for her to accept it.

"Enough talk." I hold open her legs and lean forward, flicking my forked tongue over her center.

She moans as she watches me, her breathing and heart rate increasing.

My large hands massage up her thighs and then slide up to her tits. My claws scrape over the swell of her breasts. As I suck her clit into my mouth, I rip the front of her shirt in half, exposing her flesh.

Jade shouts in surprise, then places her hands over mine as I knead her mounds. She strokes up my huge arms and takes hold of my horns.

Steering me where she wants me, I lave up her sweet honey

as she comes undone. I could easily join her, just by witnessing her pleasure. Pleasure that I give her.

She glances down at me, and we make eye contact.

"Come," I command, my growly voice vibrating her sensitive flesh.

"Maxum!" my witch cries as she undulates and surrenders herself to me.

I tear away the rest of her leggings and notch my dick at her opening. My arms wrap around her body, cradling her.

"You ready for me?" I ask.

"Yes, please." She tilts her hips, sliding me into her heat.

Pressing further into her, I groan when I feel how tight her pussy grips me. "Do you know how perfect you are?"

She glances away, trying to play it off.

My hand grasps her throat, just below her jaw, forcing her to look at me. I seat myself completely and grind my hips into hers, causing my soft spikes at my base to stimulate her clit and labia.

As I shallowly grind into her, I tell her, "You might not understand how I can feel so much for you, but you aren't part of the human world anymore. Supes usually listen to their instincts. We know when we have found our mate match. Plus, with my magic, I can feel you and read you on another level. When we were together last time, I tasted your soul."

"You did?" Her eyes are beginning to glow a haunting green. I didn't think witches could do that. "What did I taste like?"

"You taste like a winter's dawn, a summer's night, an inviting hearth, and a whimsical feast for a starving spirit—all rolled up in one. Your soul tastes like magic itself. You taste like coming home."

Jade opens her mouth to reply, but she can't respond. A tear rolls down her cheek. Then her lips crash against mine. She kisses me with the passion of someone finally accepting the love being offered after years of rejection.

I kiss her back with the same intensity and sentiment.

We both have been lonely for so long.

Slowly, I pump my entire length in and out of her slick channel. She moans with the sensual motion, and I swallow down her sweet sounds.

My tail wraps around and fondles her puckered hole.

"Do it," she whispers.

After picking up a bit of her wetness, it slides into her ass. Feeling her next climax coming along, I begin my healing chant.

"Maxum," she whines, the energy gathering around us and weighing us down. She didn't sense it as much before since she was half dead at the time.

I press my forehead to hers to anchor Jade in her body. It works, and her orgasm crashes over her. I unleash my own and follow her over the cliff.

Opening my eyes, I see the strange glowing pattern of light over her body that happened the last time I used the sex magic on her.

I search for identifiable glyphs or symbols, but there's nothing I recognize. However, it doesn't appear to be random lines. There *is* a pattern.

I release my accumulated magic, and her bruises and cuts vanish. I let out a puff of air in relief.

I worried both times I'd used my unique magic, thinking it wouldn't work on a witch. This time I worried since she is no longer being blocked by her pendant that her own magic might reject mine. But it seems her magic welcomes me. It validates my belief we are meant to be.

Jade's eyes are closed, and she appears to have passed out. Her mind is quiet, which is unusual for her. But when I scratch the surface of her being, I sense she is at peace, which is also uncommon for her.

Idly, I wonder what her mind feels like when she's writing.

I don't want to break this contented bliss she has found, though. I would keep my dick hard and deep inside her and my arms braced to keep my full weight off her forever if it meant she was happy.

My witch inhales deeply and grins. Slowly, she opens her eyes and gazes up into my face. With a lazy voice, she says, "Today's pleasure is brought to you by the words: demon dick."

I burst out with a laugh, my cock bucking inside her. With a soft peck on the lips, I roll off, and then I move us to rest properly on the bed. I jump up and get a warm wet cloth and wipe her clean so she can relax comfortably.

"I like this," she says. "Being taken care of. It's weird to experience, but nice."

I snuggle up next to her, pulling my wings back into my form.

"That is so cool." Jade strokes my cheek and then traces her finger around the base of my horns, and I shiver.

"You have something interesting as well. You probably haven't noticed, but when you orgasmed while I was working my sex magic, you glowed. It was a complicated pattern. I couldn't make sense of it."

For whatever reason, she grabs her boobs and looks down at her body in shock. "I did? Why?"

"I don't know why," I say calmly, to ease her concern.

"You've never heard of this?" she rushes to ask. "When you used healing magic on other people, didn't it happen to them?"

I answer truthfully. "I've never used my healing magic on someone before."

"What?" She sits up, her mouth dropping open. "In all your centuries, you've *never* done that? Why did you use it with me?"

"I've never wanted to save someone the way I needed to save you."

"Me? The weirdo romance writer?" She shakes her head. "You need to get out more," she scoffs.

"Don't do that," I urge her, with my voice dropping low, likely scaring her a bit. "Don't belittle yourself."

Nodding, she doesn't argue with me about this. "Do you think my light show could be a bad thing?"

"While I didn't sense evil or ill-intent, it's a mystery I'd like for us to explore. Likely, it's connected to your witch magic. I don't know as much as a witch like Amira could teach you about the various magics you could possess, but I can give you some basic lessons on channeling and controlling your magic. When your power presents, we will know more about what to research."

"I would think you would have plenty more important things to do besides teach me basic witch skills." She quickly adds, "I'm not being down on myself, just the facts. You have the war brewing and supes being killed."

"You realize you are part of my effort to stop all that, right?"

"Oh. If we can unlock what I can do, you might discover who killed Osen, and what Rob was using me for."

I pull her body on top of mine and stare into her questioning eyes. "Don't for one second think that's the main reason I want to train you. My first concern is to keep you safe. The rest, if it materializes, will just be a bonus. Understand?"

"Yeah." She rests her head on my chest and yawns. "I'm exhausted."

"Sorry. Rapid healing can do that." I kiss the top of her head. "Rest now."

12

TAKING FLIGHT

JADE

J'm shocked when I wake up and find Maxum is still snuggled up with me at midday. His outrageously muscular arm is holding me to his side. My head is resting on the rock he calls a pec. Aw, and yes, I do indeed have a bit of drool leaking out on his fine crimson tattooed chest. Apparently, this is my informal claiming procedure.

I've drooled on him, now he's mine.

Hey, we all got to have our signature move. Casually, I lift my head, and rub my hand to remove the evidence.

He does not need to know about this.

Despite my best efforts, Maxum thwarts my crafty plans when he captures my wrist and says in a deep, raspy voice, "I *know* what you've done."

"Uh?" I play innocent. "What do you mean?"

"I have to bite you to claim you. Drooling or licking doesn't work in a cosmic bonding ceremony."

"What? How did you…?" I stir and prop myself up to gaze

down at him. Damn, he's a sight. His obsidian eyes remind me of unfathomable depths—the surrender to the oblivion of an orgasm. "An abyss of bliss…" I mumble to myself.

"Is that my new nickname? Seems a tad long," he jokes and wipes the drool from the corner of my mouth with his thumb. How can he make that sexy? Must be a magic demon thing. "But I can make it part of my formal title." He gives me a sweet kiss, and my heart melts.

Arran flings open the door and rushes to greet me. "I was trying so hard, but I couldn't stay away for another minute." He snatches me from Maxum's grasp, and my wolfman clutches me to his chest, inhaling deeply, taking in my scent.

I didn't know it was possible for my heart to further turn to goo, but yeah, it happens.

Flint appears in the open doorway, his back turned to me so he gives me and my nakedness privacy. "I have more food for you." His stone skin around his neck turns a lovely peachy color from his embarrassment. "Don't fret. It is not as much as our last meal."

"You are too sweet," I say. "I'll be right there."

After Flint disappears, and we can hear he's in the kitchen, readying things for our arrival, Maxum whispers in my ear, "It appears our gargoyle might have caught feelings after four hundred years of immunity."

"He's just being nice." I wave Maxum off. "Maybe you don't realize people can be nice without needing to mate."

Maxum shrugs. "True, but he doesn't make *me* meals of his own volition."

My head spins with what he's implying. Is the anti-touch, anti-social, and stoic gargoyle developing feelings for me?

Arran thumbs the crease between my brows. Apparently, I've been frowning. He attempts to reassure me, "It probably doesn't matter much since he won't want to actually act upon them."

Disappointment and sadness rise within me. I kick myself. I

should be happy that I have two amazing guys in my bed right now. And if Osen isn't gone, maybe I'd have him, too. I don't need to *catch them all* like this is one of my why choose books or pokémon.

I doubt Flint would be up for sharing my affection even if he could get over the mountain of issues we would have to overcome.

I will just have to be friends with him and ignore my growing attraction—no matter how many spicy muffins he bakes for me.

Fortunately, there is less food this time, and the meal is uneventful, since Calder doesn't show to haze me.

The sun is setting on the lake. It's stunning, and I gasp at the sight of cotton ball clouds of rich peaches and pinks.

Standing from the table, I drift over to the huge picture window and gaze at the beauty. Always being cooped up in my writing cave and getting so caught up in working every single day, I've been missing out on life.

Maxum walks up behind me and wraps his arms around my waist and rests his chin on the top of my head, both of us taking a moment to absorb the beauty.

I suppose it has taken near-death experiences and these caring souls, who the human world considers monsters, to slow me down enough to question the pace of my life.

"How many spectacular sunsets have I missed?" I ask no one in particular.

"I don't know, but maybe the question should be: what are the beautiful moments we have left to share?" Maxum squeezes me. "I know that for the first time in forever, I look forward to finding that out—because of you."

Arran walks over and kisses my cheek. "Me too."

"Would you like to take a flight over the lake?" Maxum asks.

When I sputter instead of answering, he checks in with me. "Are you afraid of heights?"

"Not particularly. But I just didn't think you'd offer."

"I told you… *all* your fantasies."

"Okay, but no sex—*this time*. I'll need to see how scary it is first."

"Oh." Maxum chuckles darkly, leans down, and nibbles on my ear. "What makes you think I would be so damned reckless as to fuck your sweet body amongst the clouds?" He growls for good measure.

My core tingles, and my knees threaten to give out. I grip his brawny forearms and tremble. "Unholy hell, you're gonna make me pass out."

Picking me up like a doll, Maxum rushes through the doors and launches into the air. I can't help it. I scream with excitement and cling to him like a baby ape.

I leave my stomach behind on the veranda, and it takes a moment for me to acclimate to the bobbing up and down from his wing beats. I just try to imagine the pumping motion is sex. That calms me a bit.

The cool evening air whips my hair around my face, and I can barely see. If he had given me any warning, I would have grabbed a hair tie.

"Whoops," he says as he notices my predicament. "I got you." He chants low and in a strange, likely demon, language.

My hair swishes back and twists in a ponytail. "Can you teach me how to do that?" I ask in awe.

He grins and gives me a quick kiss. "Depends if you have an affinity for air."

"I guess we need to figure out what the hell I am soon."

"I wouldn't have guessed you were a hell species, but maybe you are since you light a demon's heart on fire," he jokes. "And yes, we will investigate your magic soon. I feel it building inside you."

"You can feel my magic?"

"Yes. And you will become familiar with sensing magic—your own and others."

As he says this, the glorious sunset catches my attention once again. This is a kind of magic—the beauty of nature and the beauty of experiencing life with Maxum.

He was right that there aren't any landmarks to indicate where we are in the world. There are only trees as far as I can see and rolling, nondescript hills in the distance. This lake could be anywhere, and no one could pluck the location from my mind.

I dare to release one of my death grips on his shirt and stroke his cheek. He makes a strange purring sound, and my center wets with need.

"You sure about not fucking this time around?" he says with a wink.

Goodness! He can sense my arousal even while flying?

"It's tempting."

With my words, Maxum's lips crash onto my mouth, and quickly his tongue tangles with mine. My head spins that I'm in the air with a demon who is consuming any fears I had about flying. When he breaks for a breath, I'm now dizzy from the heights and his wicked kiss.

Maxum turns me so my back is to his chest. He beats his wings fiercely again and we climb higher until we really are in the mist of the clouds. My head is spinning. "Shouldn't we be careful about someone seeing us?"

"No one will see us," he assures me.

His hand slips down and inside my pants and underwear. His thick fingers find my pussy wet and needy. "I think my sweet witch wants to come, doesn't she?"

"Yes," I say, breathy and desperate.

Damn, this demon knows how to work my body like a master. He strums my clit with the perfect pressure. Which, kudos to him, for being able to do that while he's keeping us hovering in the sky.

"Maxum," I moan, praying for release.

His two thick fingers sink into my channel and the heel of his hand grinds against my clit in a rhythm attuned to my body and pleasure. If he were to break up with me, I would mourn the loss of someone who seemed to understand me on every level—physically, sexually, and mentally.

"Come for me, Jade," Maxum commands, and my body that aches for release complies.

I scream out to the surrounding heavens and twist with pleasure as my pussy clamps onto his hand.

"Such a good little witch," he coos, as I pant, attempting to regain my sanity. Then he licks my juices off his fingers and hums with delight.

"Do you know you're too sexy for your own good?" I ask.

"No. But I might be too sexy for your own good." He chuckles, kisses me, then scans the horizon.

I follow his eyeline. With a sweeping gaze, I take in all the area around the lake and realize we are entirely isolated. Which is disconcerting, since that makes me entirely dependent on them to get me out of here. I don't even see a car around his house. Maxum's portals or his wings are my only way to leave.

"Is there a town nearby?" I ask with a tinge of anxiety in my voice. "Anything?"

"Yes." Maxum points to the south. "Ten miles down that road. If, for some reason, you can't rely on one of us to get you out of here, head that way. Mostly humans live there."

I sigh with relief that I have a way to save myself if need be. But it's also unnerving to have someone who can literally read my thoughts and emotions.

We hover, his massive wings beating and keeping us high above the world. Maxum senses my mood shift yet again. "Hey, I won't ever push into your mind and hurt you."

"I don't believe you would, unless you felt it was truly necessary to save someone you care about."

"I care about you," he assures me. "Is there something else bothering you?"

"Are we really safe here? What if the glowing markings are another level of magic that could be used to hunt me down? What if you all get hurt? And we are stuck out here with no one to help you?"

"Take a breath. It sounds like you are trying to work out every possible plot twist for one of your novels."

"Well, I'm not crazy. It could happen."

He shifts his wings slightly, and we glide back toward the house. "Yes, you're right. So many things can go wrong. Or they could go right. But let me worry about the possibilities... for now. You need to recover from all that's happened—all that you've learned about the world. Gather your magic. Write. This is the moment for you to take a break and find some clarity."

His words make sense, but I'm not used to taking a break. "I don't know if I know how to relax. I feel like I'm being lazy if I'm not constantly striving and working toward something."

"That is a problem. Humans are conditioned to be in constant survival mode. Living in a continuous loop of anxiety and stress. It doesn't always need to be do or die. Sometimes, you can take a break from the never-ending spinning wheel."

"Is that something you've learned over your many years?"

"It's something that I've *forgotten* since my early days. I used to know when to remove myself from stressful situations, now I charge into the middle of them. But after meeting you, I've realized I should slow down and enjoy your company."

Warm fuzzies fill my chest. I don't know how I got so lucky.

As a person unaccustomed to good luck, it makes me nervous.

Will all this be taken away from me?

13

DREAMING

JADE

*M*axum and Arran insist I get some rest once I'm back at the house. I insist on writing a bit. I grin wickedly when I think of a prank to pull on Arran. It only takes me a few minutes to set it up.

Finally, when I'm done, I head to our bedroom. Maxum is brushing his teeth when I come in. But Arran is nowhere to be seen.

"Where's Arran?" I ask. "I thought he'd be waiting eagerly for his snuggle time."

"Up to no good. That's all I can tell you." Maxum shrugs.

I smile, since I'm pretty sure I know exactly what he's doing.

Arran bursts through the bedroom door, looking downright frantic. "Cheaper by the Dozen? You need twelve guys?"

"What's this now?" Maxum's interest is piqued and stands at attention.

Oh, boy. This prank may have worked a little too well.

"Jade... she... wrote—" He stops, realizing he's been caught crossing my boundary, but he keeps going, unable to deal with what he's read. "Her female character... she bi-locates to two separate groups of guys and then fucks them all at once! Twelve supernatural guys total in different dimensions! She has to do that because it's the only way she can ever be fully satisfied." Arran falls to his knees. "Jade? Do you really need so many? I don't think my berserker can share you with anyone outside of our pack."

"Wow." Maxum strides up to me, challenging me with a look. "You think you can handle that twelve guys *and* a career?"

Defiantly, I cross my arms. "I have many skills."

"Juggling cocks doesn't seem like one of them." Maxum shrugs. "But what do I know?"

And now I'm wondering if my readers will enjoy a juggling cocks sticker.

"Jade?" Arran holds my hands. "Are we really not enough?"

"You are more than enough." I caress his face and let him off the hook, because I hope he's learned his lesson. "Sweet wolfie, I only wrote that whole thing to prank you. I thought you would see it for the joke it was meant to be. I warned you not to snoop in my manuscripts before I'm done with them. I left it open on my computer to be a brat."

He wraps his arms around my hips and kisses my belly in relief. Next I know, Arran has lifted me up and tossed me in bed. "I need extra snuggles now."

"Not sure if you deserve them. You've been a naughty boy," I tease.

"I promise I won't do *that* again."

They both snuggle with me in bed as I pet Arran to soothe his ruffled hackles. Even though my mind is spinning, once I stop petting him, I instantly fall asleep.

Becoming lucid in a dream, I find myself standing in a hazy and gloomy forest. It's oddly illuminated, much like what Osen called his shadowscape. Apparently, this is another plane of existence where incubi and succubi can interact with their sexual meals. With that thought, I'm reminded that was much of what I was to him, a way to feed his power, even in his death. He'd hinted he might feel more for me. Was it a lie, or was Osen only getting caught up in a heated moment?

I don't know enough about cubi, their personalities, or their abilities. Maybe this is a question for Maxum and Arran. If I have some unusual magical gift with dreams and channeling spirits, then I should know more about this shadowscape realm as I sense they are connected to my power somehow—however loosely.

Thinking he might be here in the shadowscape with me, I reach out with my senses to locate Osen, but I don't feel his energy. I had become familiar with his presence. I felt his passion and protectiveness, which often blurred into anger and resentment.

His energy has a taste and smell to it—tart cherries and wildfires. He was volatile. A fairly classic romanticized psycho, who would burn down the world for the person he loved, and while it's all well and good in a book, I sort of surprised myself that I was into it in my real life.

I don't know if he's still with me, hidden and weakened by the fight with Rob.

If Osen suspects I betrayed him, and he comes back, will he try to kill me?

"Osen?" I call to the dark corners of the room. "Are you there?"

A breeze tickles over my cheek. Is that the incubus? Or just my mind playing tricks on me?

How far could our relationship really go beyond sexcapades in my dreams? I believed things were taking a positive turn for us until we visited his death spot.

I doubt he could return to the living without a body to inhabit. He doesn't have a body left lying around somewhere anymore. Or if he does, it's not viable anymore. I doubt someone would volunteer for him to take over, and I don't want him taking over my body permanently. I'm not a fan of him taking control, even briefly. It's scary, and he makes poor choices.

If it were possible, would he need another incubus body to inhabit? Does he need a body that will align with his powers? Here I go again, imagining all the possible threads. We don't even know if he's still haunting me. First things first.

He might not trust me anymore, which will be bad for me if he returns. Maybe he wouldn't even like me if he hadn't been stuck in my brain.

"Osen?" I call for him again.

Another breeze answers.

Could it be?

My thoughts rush to Calder. Not as I see him when he looks at me, with anger in his eyes, but through Osen's eyes, showing me how he looked at the incubus when he was alive.

Calder's image materializes and moves to stand face to face, hunger in his eyes. I realize I'm taller. Could this be Osen's memory? Is it a leftover from merging with Osen? Or is this memory being pulled from Osen right now?

During our first days together, when his ghost was completely drained, this was how things unfolded. My hopes rise that I will return my guys' friend to them.

The nagging doubt also returns that some, if not all, of their attraction to me is only because of Osen's seductive presence.

No point dwelling on the negative. Enjoy the ride and all that. Nothing is guaranteed. They might talk a big game and perhaps even have the best intentions, but life isn't filled with happily ever afters.

I might have to take the '*happy for now*' for as long as I can.

In this memory, Calder doesn't have the haunted look I have

come to know. Perhaps this is from before his last death caused by the witch. My senses tell me I'm correct.

His hand reaches up and strokes the side of my face—*Osen's face*. "Please, hold off your shadows so I can have this moment."

Ah, yes, the incubus shadows will immobilize Calder when he is ready to feed. Does this mean that Calder can never actively participate when they are intimate?

My heart aches from the longing in his eyes... to return a loving touch.

"I'll try," Osen says. "But you know how much I need you."

"More than the others?" Calder is so vulnerable—emotions raw.

It feels wrong to be here, but I can't leave. I've tried.

"You know you are special to me, do you really need me to say it?" Osen asks.

I want to slap the damn fool. Of course, Calder needs it. I can see it written all over his pretty, desperate face.

Osen sighs wearily. "You are the only one who satisfies me." Then his patience is gone, and he slams his mouth against Calder's, claiming him.

The phoenix goes stone still from the paralytic shadows wrapping around him. I'm relieved when I hear Calder's moan of approval.

Osen's hand clenches Calder's jaw. "You are on your knees today." His shadows shove Calder to the ground. "Do you like that? Do you want to suck my cock?"

"Yes, sir, please," he begs.

Well, damn. I feel a rush of power as Osen's shadows feed on Calder's lust.

"Then be a good pet and open your mouth for me."

From my encounters with Osen, I know a cubi's feeding partner can only move their eyes and mouth.

But seeing Calder's hungry eyes stare up at Osen and open his mouth for him, I'm more than turned on by this power dynamic in action. Osen loves being the dom, and Calder is an eager submissive.

I idly wonder if he's only a sub for his incubus. Or is this what turns him on in general? I'm guessing it's the latter and that's why they are a good match.

Osen plunges his cock into Calder's mouth… and holy hell, I can feel all of it. I can never tell the phoenix that I know how it feels to have him suck my cock.

He pumps into Calder's mouth, and his shadows stroke and explore Calder's body.

I swear I think I'm going to orgasm in my sleep. Will Maxum and Arran know how naughty I've been watching this pay-per-view sexy incubus feeding?

When he comes, I think my soul might hiccup right out of my own body.

Osen drops down to kneel in front of his love. He kisses him, tasting his cum on Calder's tongue. "Goddess, I missed you."

The incubus wraps his arms and his shadows around the phoenix, and I feel the love he has for Calder. And weirdly, I sense the love Calder has for him. Then I remember an incubus can feel and feed off powerful emotions too.

Their love overwhelms me. It's all consuming.

Will I ever have love like that? If some part of Osen is still inside me, then my fears might be real. The guys are only attracted to me because of his power.

I wake and stare at the ceiling. I don't like this feeling that I will soon be rejected.

The two living heaters next to me snore softly, but it's too loud for me to go back to sleep. Maxum is pressed too close to my one side and Arran's beast form is practically on top of me. Aw, the berserker really does like me. Weighted blankets have nothing on these guys.

I sort of hate the attention and love it at the same time. I love that they are so affectionate with me, because yeah, who wouldn't love two amazing, hot guys loving on them. They are so attractive, that even the straightest of straight guys would question moving away from their sexy bodies.

But alas, I must pee, and I need to clear my head after the mind fuck I just had.

When I try to extricate myself from the supernatural puzzle pieces, they mutter and groan. I assure them I will be back...

But maybe not this morning... We'll see how it goes.

I open the door to the bedroom and feel a strange sense that someone's watching me. My eyes instantly lock onto the space in front of me.

I am not alone.

14

NEW SENSATIONS

FLINT

I'm startled when I sense the enchanting witch has awoken.

She cracks open the bedroom door and peeks out. Her eyes instantly land on my location, even though it should be impossible for her to see me.

I wonder—not for the first time—what the nature of her power is.

"Hello?" she calls quietly. "Who's there?"

I make myself visible, and she gasps. Her pretty hazel eyes widening in surprise.

"How did you just appear like that?" She frowns, having realized I'm stalking her. "And *what* are you doing out here?"

"I'm making sure no one comes to hurt you." I rub my neck nervously. "Even if it's only to ensure that if Osen is inside you, he doesn't make you do things against your will again."

"Oh, Flint."

With my keen eyesight, I can see her sweet, pale coloring turning a shade of pink.

"You don't have to do that... you need to rest too, don't you?" she asks the last part with confusion, wondering if I do.

"Yes. I need to rest, but not as much as a human. I only came out here to keep an eye out for trouble when I sensed Maxum and Arran drifted off."

She closes the door behind her and joins me in the hall, but keeps her distance. Distance she creates because she knows *I* need it.

I curse myself for my problems. I never wanted to make her uncomfortable or make her hurt herself like she did when she arrived at the house.

"Are you worried that I'm going to bring more trouble?" she asks.

"Not you... not on purpose. I'm worried *for* you," I explain, so she doesn't get the wrong impression. Just because I'm not in her bed doesn't mean that I'm in Calder's camp.

"You didn't know that Trouble is my middle name?" Jade sighs and frowns.

I have failed her. "I didn't. Is this why you named your familiar Trouble? Please, forgive my ignorance. I will learn what I can to better protect you."

She folds over with mirth and almost reaches out for my arm to stabilize herself before quickly pulling back. Once again, I regret my condition.

"Oh, sweetie. I don't expect you to know anything about me. And I'm sorry. I was just messing around. I thought you would have heard that joke before."

I've been far too serious for too long. Maxum tries to jest with me. So I take a page from his book. "Well... I thought your parents may have had a premonition and knew your nature."

"You have been around for centuries, right?" She smiles and somehow I don't feel like she is mocking my ignorance. "Wait a minute! You are messing around with me! You knew my parents didn't name me Trouble from a premonition!" She is wheezing with laughter.

It makes my heart thump wildly that I've made her joyful.

When she settles a bit, I answer, "Yes, I have been around for four hundred and twenty three years. However, I'm not usually attuned to the current lingo or… jokes." I hang my head in frustration. The knowledge that I have missed things because I haven't been more adaptable in my long years or engaged in banter with the pack more often weighs heavily in my mind.

"Hey, I didn't mean to make fun of you. I only tease the people I like." Jade bites her lip and then asks, "Were you really that worried about me?"

"I am worried. Osen shouldn't have forced you into the alley, and I'm frustrated with myself that I didn't sense the danger you were in. You almost died."

"Do you always sense danger?"

She knows so little of our world. Maxum and Arran need to correct that. I suppose she is asking me now, so I should impart whatever wisdom and knowledge that I can.

"I do. It isn't a foolproof detection system—obviously. However, I can usually sense when an innocent is about to be harmed."

Her lip protrudes in what I assume is a pout. "Maybe I'm not all that innocent. What if I did something wrong, and I just don't remember?"

I step closer and then realize that might intimidate her because of our size differences, especially in close quarters, so I take a half step back. "Do you believe that?"

"I don't remember what happened when Rob hypnotized me with a spell. So, what else could I have done?"

"If he used you, then you would still be innocent." A silence settles between us, and I nod toward the kitchen. "Were you on your way to seek sustenance?"

"Yeah. A *snack*," she says with emphasis, subtly reminding me of the current vernacular. "I've been diagnosed with a medical condition."

My whole body goes on alert so I can help her with whatever ails her.

With a heavy sigh, she grabs a bag of chips out of the huge walk-in pantry. "I have insom-*nom-nom*-nia," she says as she munches on the crispy processed potatoes. Her eyes twinkle. It's not a metaphor, they truly light up like she is more than just a witch.

I grin at her jesting with me and because I'm delighted by her unusual magic. "I recognize that *is* a joke."

"I can't seem to help it." Jade worries her lip, thinking. Then she slides onto a stool at the kitchen bar, taking another bite of chips.

"You need something more nourishing than that." I nod to the bag and am tempted to pull the garbage food from her hands. But that's something Maxum or Calder might do, and I'm not that rude. "Your magic needs whole, clean ingredients to thrive. And you especially need good food since you are building your magic inside you to its full potential, possibly for the first time."

She drops the handful of chips back into the bag and sets it down. "I suppose you're right. I've been meaning to eat healthier for a long time now. It's just…"

Something inside me suddenly realizes *why* she's been holding back in taking proper care of herself. It's a feeling I'm all too familiar with.

I lean forward, daring to get closer. Even though there's an entire kitchen island between us, it feels like I'm pressed up against her body. Another feeling stirs within me… lower. I swallow nervously since I haven't felt *that way* in four hundred years.

Once I'm clearheaded enough to speak again, I say, "You are worthy of everything good."

Jade shivers ever so slightly.

"Are you cold?"

She must be. The tiny scraps of clothing she has on for sleeping can't keep her warm enough. Human witches are sensitive to heat and cold.

I rush over to the couch in the adjoining living room and grab a small blanket.

Turning around, I regain my composure as I cautiously approach her. Her eyes are wide, studying me. She's trying to hide a smile. Is she happy that I've thought of her? But my heart grows heavy—why does she feel like she has to hide any response?

"I have made you uncomfortable," I say, setting the blanket down over the barstool next to hers.

She shakes her head. "What makes you say that?"

"You were hiding a smile. You don't feel you can express your emotions around me."

"I was worried I might make *you* uncomfortable." She places the blanket over her lap and seems to be lost in thought. "Okay. I think I should try something."

I am intrigued. "What is that?"

"I'm going to be completely honest with you."

Alarm sets in. "What? You haven't been honest before now?"

Her eyes widen. "Oh, shoot. No. That didn't sound right. Okay. I mean… I will say exactly what is going on in my mind, but you have to try and be okay with whatever I say."

"Yes, we can try this." I'm nervous. I haven't been truly nervous in so very long.

"Just now. When you thought I was cold, I was really shivering because of your voice."

"The sound of my voice repulses you?" My already heavy heart feels like it has stopped beating. "I don't know how to change it."

"No." She smiles reassuringly. "I like your voice… a lot.

Maybe too much. When your voice dropped lower and with such intensity, it gave me good shivers. But I know you don't really like females, so I didn't want to smile when you were trying to be so nice and take care of me with the blanket. I didn't want you to think that I was expecting *something* from you."

"Oh." I think about what she has said. "I see, but I don't dislike females. I enjoy your company."

"So, is it just touching females that bothers you then?" she asks, her hands fiddle nervously with her blanket.

I want to tell her the story. For the first time in my life, I wish to share with someone who might understand. However, she might fear me afterward.

"Yes. I..." I'm at a loss for what to say. "I will tell you my story one day." I turn and begin to pull out ingredients from the pantry. "But for now, I wish to feed you. I want to see your magic grow. Then you won't be as vulnerable to attacks."

"Can I help?" she asks.

When I glance over, she looks ready to spring from her seat.

"No." Seeing her deflate a bit, I offer a compromise. "Maybe you can wash these fruits?"

"I can chop them up too." She hops off the stool, bounces around the island, and grins at me expectantly.

"I'm not giving you a knife," I inform her.

Jade blows out air in protest. "Uh, I'm not a child." She braces her fists on her hips. "I can wield a *blade*!" she announces dramatically, and grabs a knife out of the block.

Giving in to her demands, I warn, "I won't forgive you if you cut your pretty typing fingers."

"Awwww! You think my fingers are pretty?" Excitedly, she grabs her chest where her heart is and almost stabs herself with the action.

This woman!

"Give me the knife." I hold out my hand. "You almost killed yourself already."

"Nope!" She challenges me. "You can't take it from me."

I chuckle darkly at her assumption. Jade thinks that I won't because I can't touch her. She is a menace just as Maxum teases.

I reach out, my hand turning to stone as I wrap it around the sharp blade and tighten my grip.

Staring into her startled green eyes the entire time, I slowly pull the knife from her grasp, leaving her unharmed.

After an alarming moment when she moves closer, then she staggers backward. "Holy shirtballs, that was flippin' hot!" Then she sucks in a breath and bites her lips, like they are what made her say such a forward compliment.

I'm pleased by her praise. I never thought I'd feel that way. What is this witch doing to me?

Jade appears anxious, waiting for my response to her suggestive comment.

"You are enjoying the discovery of the supernatural world, aren't you?" I ask and turn to hide my smirk.

I've observed that she is easily amused by what she thought of as fantasy just days ago.

Jade exhales, realizing I'm not upset. "I suppose. Do you think I'm foolish or simpleminded because I'm excited?" she asks and turns on the faucet to wash the fruit.

I spin to capture her attention. "Never. I find it... entertaining. I learned most of what I know so long ago that now it feels like the world was never new."

"What's it like to live as long as you have?" she asks.

"Hmm." I contemplate my answer. No one has asked me this before. Honestly, no one has really cared to ask me deep questions about my thoughts about life.

Am I not a deep person? Or do they assume that my mind is filled with rocks? I suppose I don't dissuade them from that assumption.

After a moment, I explain, "Longevity isn't as exciting as it seems from someone as young as you are."

She snickers at that. "I'm not that young."

"I guess not in human terms." I continue, "At a certain point, you learn to navigate the world and how to live day to day as an independent person from your family. The assumptions I had about the world have shifted over time. Well, more accurately, how I exist in relation to the world has changed. Beyond that, I just have to keep up with the human world. After my first few decades, my personality did not change much. Is it pathetic that I have had little growth in all that time?"

"I'm sure you have had growth in all your years. But maybe it was so subtle that you didn't notice it happening." She glances up from the sink and shrugs. "There are two types of growth: gradual and catastrophic."

"I've had catastrophic events," I say with sadness and regret.

"Does it have to do with the touch thing?" she asks.

"Yes."

Her eyes lock with mine, and I want to confess everything. I crave to replace the horrific image of my worst experience with the pleasure of seeing Jade's face.

Craving. Such an interesting and new sensation.

I crave more of Jade.

What would it be like if I could allow myself to touch her?

Could I really change after all this time? I feel unchangeable, like an actual stone right now. But I remind myself that stone can be reshaped… usually by humans.

What if…?

A shout from upstairs grabs our attention, and we race toward the stairs. I move faster, even with my heft and size. Although Jade is faster than I thought she'd be for a human witch.

The shout is Calder's. I hear continued cursing and things being tossed about in his room.

What is happening? Is he being attacked? I don't like Jade running into a possibly dangerous situation with me, but I don't know how to stop her other than yelling at her to stay put. I can't bring myself to be a bossy alpha like the other males can be.

I hear the door downstairs to Maxum's room being thrown open. Good, we'll have backup. Maxum can hold Jade back from whatever is happening with Calder.

I fling his door open, even though it's sealed with magic, and I'm tossed backward by his magical ward. Fortunately, I don't collide with Jade, who is right behind me.

Calder charges through the door and into the hallway. His eyes are wild with anguish. He's so out of his mind that I don't think he even sees Jade. He's about to plow into her and knock her down the stairs.

I react without thinking and grab her arm, pushing her against the wall with my body, protecting her from Calder if he should attack or just knock her down.

He launches off the landing, releasing his fiery wings and then darts out the back door and takes flight toward the lake.

My body reacts to Jade's body pressed to mine, but not in the way I expect.

I'm hard... mostly below the waist. My hands are locked into place over her upper arms. Though I am only partially frozen, I feel incapable of moving away. I'm not sure I want to.

"Oh no, Flint?" Jade asks, worry and affection fill her hazel eyes. "Are you okay?"

"I... I don't know," I answer truthfully.

Maxum calls me. I glance downstairs.

When Maxum sees Jade is unharmed, he says to Arran, "I'll go see what's going on with him. You got this?"

Maxum launches after Calder when Arran shouts for him to go.

Arran comes up the stairs and sees me unmoving and pinning Jade to the wall. "Shit. Not again."

"Uh, no, it's different." Jade looks back up at me. "How are you able to move your head or talk? I thought..."

"I suppose you must have changed something inside of me," I whisper.

She shivers once again.

This time, I know it's because she enjoys the sound of my voice.

15

CRACKING STONE

JADE

"*I* suppose you must have changed something inside of me."

Flint's gravelly voice vibrates right down to my clit. Not fair. I'm trying to be a good girl and not the horny horn dogger who grinds against his boulder.

His massive, hard body presses me to the wall, and I can't say I mind all that much, especially when he doesn't look bothered by the touch. The concern over what is upsetting Calder fades into the background as I stare into the gargoyle's light gray eyes.

Flint's giant bat-like wings deployed when he was protecting me from Calder's outburst. I take a moment to admire them in their solid state before locking gazes with him again.

The shy guy seems just as surprised as me about his half frozen state. At least he can speak to me. And if the protrusion poking my stomach is any indication, his body is very interested in what's going on. Or maybe that's just his normal resting state.

Good Goddess.

My vision fades while I imagine what he might be packing and if he might wish to unleash it on me one day.

If any of them pull on my romantic heartstrings, it's this guy. I want to wine and dine him. Show him affection. Yet, I worry that his heart would literally crack if he suffered another heartbreak. I couldn't do that to him. Not that I'd ever hurt him intentionally. But what-ifs float and clog my logic-monster brain.

The most significant what-if circles around what secrets we will uncover about me and my past. Sure, Arran and Maxum would be upset if I turned out to be the true monster, but I didn't pursue them. They pursued me. And I can't chase Flint when I don't know what will happen in the future.

At the moment, I need to free myself from his hold before I lose my resolve and make a fool of myself.

When I wiggle, his hands feel solid and like stone.

"Are you *half... stone*?" Arran asks in shock, peeking under Flint's wing. Then he looks at Flint's grip on my arm. "Are you okay?" he asks me.

"Yeah." I look toward the room and wonder about my fur babies. "Can you check on my little guys?"

Arran's eyes widen even more. "Of course!" My wolfie rushes toward the room and I hear him curse. "The hamster is missing."

"Maybe that's what upset Calder?" I suggest. "He seemed to be really into the little ones."

I hear Arran inhale. Then he's stripping off his sweatpants as he says to me, "I'll sniff them out." He shifts into his wolf and races down the hallway of bedrooms, shakes his head and then rushes downstairs.

"It will be okay," Flint assures me. "They'll find them."

With all my worry, I briefly forgot I'm stuck with my half

concrete gargoyle. "I should have had them with me," I say, tears in my eyes.

"It's only been a day or so. They would have disrupted your healing, and you need to gain your strength and get some rest." Flint frowns. "From what I heard from Calder's room, he was constantly talking to them."

"I suppose they were probably pent up, unable to talk to me all these years."

Flint picks up on my guilt and frustration. "Don't blame yourself. You didn't know about the supe world. Everyone else before had failed you. Your mother, grandmother, warlock boyfriend. Maybe others you don't even realize."

My head spins with that realization. How many other people are 'in the know' and let me skip along through life with my ignorance?

I dare to look into Flint's stunning eyes again. They have been so full of sorrow and sadness, but now when I look, I see something else.

"I guess you are getting used to me?" I cock an eyebrow, wondering what's going on with my usually taciturn acquaintance.

"Yes, I... I'd like to get over my fear of touching. I don't want to be like this anymore."

I swallow down my own nerves, secretly wishing it's because he wants to do more than just touch me. "Why not?"

"I don't want to make you uncomfortable. This is the second time I've trapped you. It's dangerous. What if I need to act and I'm frozen?"

"I suspect if you really had to protect me, that something would make you act."

"Well, possibly. However, I wouldn't mind giving you a hug... you know.... for friendship. I sensed a few times you were open to doing that with me."

I don't say how I'd like to do more than just hug. Horizontal, naked hugging maybe. I'd hug the hell out of him and make him see stars if he'd let me. But I, too, would love a plain ole hug.

"I wish my arms weren't pinned down, or I'd give you a friendship hug now for making sure I didn't take a deadly tumble down the stairs."

"I panicked. I doubt Calder would have let you get hurt."

"We don't know that." I turn my head up to get his attention and make him see my truth. "I don't mind being here with you, even like this. I don't know what has caused this condition, but I want you to know that I trust you."

"Maybe you shouldn't."

"Did you hurt someone on purpose? A woman?" I ask, my voice soft. The question is out of my mouth before I have a chance to think it through. This is a problem for someone like me who isn't used to working with a filter. I usually try to allow all my wild thoughts their due so I don't censor what comes out. That's what the editing process is for. But in life, there's no delete button.

I hope I didn't strike a nerve with my invasive question.

He tenses, but then shakes his head. "Not on purpose. It was an accident."

"Maybe it will help to talk about it."

"You may be correct. Trying to avoid it all these centuries hasn't seemed to help."

"Ignoring trauma usually delays healing. I would know."

"I suppose you have had your fair share of trauma… in just the last few days." Flint regards me thoughtfully. "You find it helps to speak of your pain?"

"I do. I don't think it helps to dwell and go over it constantly because then it can become your only story. We all can fall victim to being a victim. I have done it too. Reliving the trauma repetitively can solidify it as our main narrative. But talking about it, and hopefully understanding why it happened or how the experience changed us, I think that can be therapeutic. It allows the space to heal."

"I thought not talking about it would make it go away. But it did the opposite. I've relived the tragedy over and over, allowing it to shape everything in my life."

His thumb moves, stroking my biceps ever so slowly and softly. I don't draw his attention to it. I want him to get his words out. Give him space to lance the wound that has festered for hundreds of years. I don't expect it will be easy for him.

"She was the first person I killed." Flint glances away, unable to look me in the eye anymore. Likely thinking I'll judge him.

"She was also the first human I saw. I was young, only eighteen years old. Marie was so pretty and sweet. She'd sing while I'd watch her gather wild fruits and berries, never knowing I was there since I used my gargoyle camouflage. One day, I decided to be bold and speak to her. For the first time, I used my glamour and appeared to her as a human. She was taken aback by my size, but otherwise was friendly to me. I told her a lie, that I was traveling through her area and would only be around for a short while."

He takes a deep breath and gains more courage when I nod for him to continue. "Marie invited me back to eat with her family behind the castle walls. I accepted because I was curious to see how the humans lived. I expected it to differ greatly from living in Elfhame and the rocky cliffs where my people are from."

I'm itching to know more about his people, but I file away the million questions I have for a more appropriate time.

"I met her mother and father. They were kind and friendly to me. However, no one knew what I was. Marie invited me up to the top of her liege's castle. It wasn't as fine as the ones in Elfhame, but the tower she took me to was high enough. As we climbed the stairs, I sensed magic, but it didn't feel like fae, so I ignored it."

I bite my lip. I fear what he's about to tell me next. And my guilt swells again.

"There was a witch in the tower, and she immediately sensed I was not human. She cast a revealing spell to force my glamour to drop. I was young and untested so I didn't react quickly enough to stop her. When Marie caught sight of my gargoyle form, she stepped backward. I reached out for her, but she was scared of my appearance, and she slapped my hands away. I failed to grab her. She fell..."

Flint's voice chokes up, and he doesn't continue.

"In her surprise, she fell down the stairs and died?"

He nods, his body shakes with his held back tears.

"My sweet gargoyle, that wasn't your fault." I place my hands on his forearms, the only thing I can reach with his tight hold on my biceps.

At my words, and touch, his floodgates are released. His body softens and almost his entire weight pushes me against the wall. His hands let my arms go, and he slides them around my waist in a hug, lifting my feet off the floor.

I return his embrace, feeling as if I'm holding him together, even if my arms don't reach all the way around him.

I'm not even sure if he knows he's doing it when he presses his forehead to mine. Not wanting to break the spell of the moment, I don't tell him he is almost crushing me, and take in shallow breaths instead.

His eyes pop open, and they seem brighter—glowing. He also appears a bit shocked by what's happening, being able to touch me without freezing up.

He pulls back enough for me to breathe again, but my feet are still dangling off the floor.

"I..." He loosens his tight grip around my waist. "Did I hurt you?"

Thankfully, he doesn't drop me out of instinct. "I'm okay. How are you?"

"I'm touching you," he says with awe, and looks down to see our hips are pressed together. "Oh, I'm sorry."

He moves to pull away.

I don't easily let him go. "This is all okay. Unless you'd rather not be touching me." He stops moving.

"But our lower halves are…," he whispers.

"Does that make you feel bad?" I ask. "Or good?"

"Good, but…" His skin flushes that beautiful peach color, and I can't help but wonder how far down it goes.

"What is it? You can tell me." I realize he might not know he can ask for what he needs. "If embracing me makes you feel weird, we can stop hugging whenever you want."

"It's not that… not exactly. It's just… you don't know the real me yet. My true appearance. How ugly I really am."

"I feel like I know you in many ways already. As far as your looks are concerned, I doubt I will find your appearance unappealing. Do you want to show me? Would that make you feel better about being near me? If I know the real you?"

"Uh, I think it would, but maybe not…"

"Hey, I get it. This is already a lot," I say gently as I stroke his sides affectionately. I want to lean forward and kiss him or stroke his cheek, but it feels like too much for his first experience. "Sweetheart, I never want to make you feel bad."

"You… you called me sweetheart."

"Is that okay?"

His smile lights up my entire being. "Yes. May I call you a name of endearment too?"

I giggle. I almost roll my eyes at myself for the silly sound I make, but he's so flipping sweet. "Of course you can. You can even try out different names until you find something you like."

"Thank you for being you, beautiful soul." He sets me down on my feet and takes a hesitant step back.

I'm flustered because I miss his solid body against mine. Even in its supposed soft form, it's almost as hard as stone. And if I'm not mistaken, he was getting harder below the belt.

"May I hold your hand?" he asks shyly.

"Anytime you'd like." I slide my tiny hand within his

massive one, and I shiver with the thought of his hands holding me in other places.

"Are you done with the mating dance yet?" my obnoxious guinea pig familiar says with his tiny hands on his hips. His beady little eyes glare at me.

"We weren't mating," I gruff.

Flint turns a brighter shade of peach.

"Did you have something to say? Or are you just acting out your name?" I ask my little furry brat. I recall how, even though I never knew he was a magical creature, I occasionally sensed his snarkiness.

He scurries from the room and tells me, "Shut the door and come with me."

"He wants me to follow him and close this door," I translate for my gargoyle.

"Sounds like a bossy little thing," Flint mutters and does as the furry boss says.

"Wait until he demands treats," I joke.

"Treats! Where?" After his outburst of excitement, Trouble huffs when he realizes I'm treatless. "Damn you, witch. That was mean. Unless you are hiding something…"

"You'll get some treats if you just get on with whatever you want to tell us and stop being sassy."

Trouble sniffs indignantly and continues, "I think… I think Floofer is a spy."

"Floofs? The hamster is a spy?" An icky feeling of betrayal washes over my body.

"Goddess dammit," Flint growls.

I try to remember but can't recall everything from the other day. "Does Floofer talk?"

"A little. I didn't think he could understand much," Trouble explains. "He seems… to have simple thoughts, like Sage. But now, I'm not so sure."

"Is that why Calder ran out of here in a panic?" I ask.

"Tonight, Floofer opened the ward on the bedroom door

with his mind. I saw a shimmer around him. He felt odd. By the time the birdman listened to me, Floofer was gone. I don't know if he also suspects Floofer of being a spy. I didn't have time to say anything."

"If he isn't a magical creature, what could Floof be?" I ask.

"*Where* could he be?" Flint scans the hallway and growls low, rumbling my body with the vibration.

Holy clitatory.

Flint doesn't even know how sexy he is. So protective, and I wonder what four hundred years of repression would be like unleashed in the bedroom. My body heats and thrums with anticipation.

Why is it *more* sexy when he has no clue what he does to me?

16

FLOOFING

CALDER

*S*taying in this house with the witch here is pure torture. I might as well be in prison. I'd probably be happier if I was locked up.

To hear her sucking Maxum's and Arran's souls out of their cocks is maddening. My entire existence is at war. My dick loves the sounds, but my mind revolts.

Even if she is innocent of Osen's death or all the other stuff that we've uncovered, she is still a witch.

To add to my suspicions, Osen hasn't shown up after the alleyway. Is she suppressing his spirit, so she isn't found out?

Ugh. The more I watch her, the more I realize it's likely she's just an ignorant witch. However, even an ignorant witch can cause a lot of problems.

I've been taking care of her magical creatures. Their warden of sorts, although they don't realize it. Sure, they all say Jade didn't know what she was, but there's something off. I just can't place my finger on what is wrong.

I can't shut Trouble up—incessantly talking, that one. And the rabbit, Sage, doesn't seem to be a schemer. Simple yet wise, much like her namesake. But that's animals for you. They carry their own kind of wisdom. Maybe superior in some ways.

And Floofer… *for all that is sacred.*

Could Jade have picked a more ridiculous name? I don't think he would have chosen that moniker, had he been given a choice. But what do I know? He barely speaks. I've only pulled out one-word answers from the hamster. Maybe he is a bit touched. Not all magical creatures are blessed with intelligence.

Hell, not all supernaturals or humans have been blessed with smarts, either.

That's what nags at me, I suppose. Jade is smart—smarter than she acts sometimes. She spaces out and often looks lost when I've been around, but then she can allegedly write books, making up entire worlds and magical systems all on her own. Yet she also appears to be perceptive and insightful. So I think the ditsy spacey shtick isn't real.

I suppose both could be true. She can lack focus *and* be extremely hyper focused other times.

I just… have never met someone like her.

To be fair, I don't get to know many people. At least, not since I died at the hands of that cruel witch. I'm not friendly or social anymore. Why should I be? The world is just out to rob me of any joy I have.

Losing Osen is just one example of that. In my last incarnation, I couldn't even enjoy his touch anymore. Now that he's dead, I will never have an opportunity to get over my pain, or help him get over his.

I've been tossing and turning in bed, trying to not eavesdrop on Jade and Flint in the kitchen. Except her voice is like a siren's call, and Flint's voice rumbles like an earthquake's incoming wave, ready to decimate the landscape.

Drawn to their conversation, because of course, I must know

everything that damned witch does. I get up and crack the door to better hear them.

Sounds like Flint is falling under her spell, too. He's yearning to bond with her in any way his broken spirit can. Why is it so easy for my pack to reveal their hearts and souls to this blasted woman? What am I not seeing?

Could I be jealous that she doesn't appear to want to catch me in her devious net? Or will I be her last conquest since I'm holding out and being a proper asshole to her?

Frustrated, I throw myself on the bed again and cover my head with my pillow. Not that it helps to block out the world. I chant a spell Maxum taught me to soothe my turbulent, broken soul.

"Birdman!" Trouble shouts, breaking my attention on my chant and the ugly train of thought I'm still riding.

"What is it?" I snap and spin to glare at him. He knows I hate it when he calls me that.

"Floofer is gone! He just ran out."

"What the fuck?" I feared something like this would happen. I hated to keep them cooped up in their cages. This is what I get for trusting them to stay in my room.

Another fear rises… one that I kept pushing down. What if the creatures aren't what they appeared to be?

I need to find him and discover what he is up to. I don't have the amazing sense of smell that Arran does. But my eyesight will do, even at night or before dawn, as it is now.

I glance down the hall and see all the doors are closed. So Floof must have gone down the stairs. Am I that obsessed with the witch that I allowed something to slip past me like this?

I am. I did.

Fuck!

I race toward the stairs and almost collide with Jade. Fortunately, Flint is quick with his reflexes and snatches her out of the way.

I'd stop and explain, but I fear I've fucked up. I can't look her in the eye and confess I lost her pet. Or worse, that I may have allowed a spy amongst us.

Either way, I'm pissed at myself.

Off the living room, I see the patio door slightly ajar. I'm out that door before it registers that Flint touched Jade.

I hear Arran and Maxum rushing out of their bedroom and figure they can handle whatever mess I made with the gargoyle and the witch.

My eyes frantically search the shadows. I'm completely screwed. A hamster could literally be under a leaf and I wouldn't see it.

Maxum joins me outside, flapping his huge wings as we both hover over the yard behind the house. "What the fuck is going on?" He rubs the sleep from his eyes and glances around.

I land, but continue to scan my surroundings. "Floofer is gone."

He touches down next to me. "What the hell is a floofer?" he asks, completely baffled.

"The hamster." I growl. I hate that he never took the time to get to know the creatures. "You should have investigated them!"

"You told me they were just magical creatures," Maxum says with confusion.

"I thought they were. Maybe instead of sticking your dick in the witch, you should have been probing their minds."

Maxum tenses, realizing this is more than a missing pet. "Explain yourself. What do you think is going on?" His eyes dart about, trying to catch sight of our potential infiltrator.

"Something felt off. It's possible he was a spy."

"Then you should have *asked* me to investigate."

I sigh. He's not wrong. "I should have. And this is just a guess. However, disappearing like this isn't a good sign."

Maxum glowers at the dark forest that surrounds the lake, and we walk toward it. "He's going to have a hard time getting outside of my wards."

"Unless he's a shifter and a mage. If he's powerful and skilled, he could break through."

"But why would a mage be spying on us?" he asks, confusion filling his face.

"On *Jade*," I correct him.

Maxum lets loose a string of inventive curses. After a moment, he gazes again into the darkness. But this time, I feel the swell of magic gather around him.

I try to shut down, quieting my wild and crazed thoughts so he can focus without me broadcasting all my messy ideas and worries.

The demon shakes his head and frowns. "Whoever… whatever Floofer is, I can't sense their thoughts. So either they are truly a dimwitted hamster or they are powerful enough to block me completely."

Dammit. I was hoping he could sense the hamster.

"If they are that powerful, why are they wasting their time masquerading as a hamster for a witch who isn't even at her full power?" he asks.

So many accusatory answers pop up in my mind, instead I focus on what we know for sure. "If she is ignorant of her power, then maybe someone wants to keep it that way. If she didn't know about the pendant's intentions, its presence would suggest someone wanted her magic weak. Or the hamster could be someone, other than Rob, who hoped to use her ability."

"None of the possibilities are good." He turns his attention fully on me and studies my face. "You really don't believe she's innocent?"

I must tread carefully here. He's bonding with her and I will be the enemy if I continue my stance that all witches are guilty simply by their existence.

"I don't know what to believe anymore." I shrug and as I say it, I know it's my truth. "Nothing about her has a clean cut explanation."

"Nothing in *life* has a clean cut explanation," Maxum retorts.

"Fair enough." I grimace and push on. "She represents everything that has ruined me. And then, on top of it, she's tangled up in Osen's death, whether or not she's innocent of any crime."

"You don't believe that she hurt him, do you?"

"No, not on purpose. But she might be a weapon that someone controls. Then she…" I can't even finish my sentence.

"She captured Osen's soul. I know that must be very upsetting… for you, especially." Maxum pats me on the shoulder.

I allow the touch because he means well.

"You aren't freaked out by that?" I ask with more than a bit of irritation.

"Yeah. But only because something like her has never existed before. At least that we know about."

"Don't you wonder how a witch can capture a supernatural soul?"

"That's why I plan to train her to reveal her magic. There's something different about her, and we all need to know what that is. Jade needs to know, too."

"She really has no clue?" I rub my hair and pace. I don't want to hear his answer.

"I haven't probed her mind deep enough to crack her marbles, but yeah, from what I've picked up, she doesn't have a clue. I can also tell she isn't trying to block me. She doesn't even know how to put up mental walls."

"Well, if she is as innocent as you believe she is, then you should train her. I have a bad feeling all of this is going to get worse before it's over."

"Let's just hope we are on the winning end of it when it's all done." Maxum sighs and gazes back at the house.

Even as dense as I am, I feel his longing for her as tangible as an ache in his bones. He wants to claim her, but he knows he can't—not yet. Maybe not even after we deal with Jade's situation.

With my keen eyesight, I turn back toward the house and see Jade and Flint staring out after us and holding hands.

Holding hands!

This woman has more natural magic than all of us combined.

17

INTERROGATION

MAXUM

*B*y the time I've circled my land and its boundaries several times over, in a fruitless attempt to locate the runaway hamster, the morning sun has quickly become noon.

When I enter the house, Arran is in his wolf form, curled up in the hallway outside Jade's makeshift office. The door is shut, and he looks about ready to whine.

If I weren't feeling the same distance created by the simple act, I might tease him. As it is, I want to grumble as well. She's likely making up for her lost writing days and the quote "never ending amount of promo stuff" she told us she had to do to keep her books selling.

Even if she doesn't accept my bond, I'd make sure she'd never have to worry about making money with her books. I've been around long enough to know writing is her passion so if I were to help her with the money aspect, it would be to hire people to help her with the advertisement so she could focus on writing and engaging with readers in a more pleasurable way.

Maybe she would take my money if I offered it in that context, as an investment? Then, if she is freed up from her constant striving, I might be rewarded with more quality time with her.

"Shift and tell me what's been going on here," I demand of Arran.

The wolf lets out a huff of air and drops his head back down on his huge paws. His golden eyes glance at the door, worry and vigilance in equal measure pour out of him.

"Fine. Keep your eye on the room, but we should move down a bit and keep our voices low so she isn't disturbed," I suggest.

Arran stands and shifts, walking down the hallway without letting his eyes leave the door. "I gave up the search, since I needed to be here, protecting Jade. But when I returned, she said she needed her space to work. She doesn't want me spying and reading her stuff anymore."

I grunt, indifferent to his need to read her books before she's ready to share. I have a whole set of books I grabbed from the stack at her house so I could read what turns this woman on. I'll share my stash with him when the time is right.

"Anything else going on?" I prompt, nodding toward the rest of the house.

"Calder has been searching through the house just in case Floofer doubled back."

"Smart."

"Oh," Arran lowers his voice and gets excited. "Flint touched Jade. He spontaneously grabbed her so she wouldn't fall down the stairs. After that, he was able to somewhat un-stone himself—for the most part. When I circled back to the house to make sure we didn't leave Jade open to attack in our frantic state, they were actually holding hands without him freezing up."

"He freed himself from his hangup?"

I didn't believe that the gargoyle would ever even *attempt* to break his self-inflicted curse. Jade really is something else. I grin, realizing she is becoming more entrenched in our pack. If only Calder would let his walls fall down, we could be a proper pack with a loving heart in the center.

Osen liked to believe he was the nexus of the group, holding us all together, but he was just as much of a divider as any sort of unifier. He was too obsessed with revenge, war, and sex to be a true center. If he's no longer inside Jade, I'd be okay with that. I worry he would only corrupt her and coerce her to risk her life for answers again.

I want answers too, but we need to be smart. His sneaking around almost cost my mate her life. If he's still with her, I'm going to demand he make a promise on his soul to include us in any plans. Or I will find a way to drive him out of Jade for good.

I hope the male I love is still whole enough to remember how amazing we once were when we acted as a team. Could being around Jade's energy balance him? I fucking hope so. He isn't so bad when he isn't obsessed.

We all need Jade. Osen would see it too, if he just took a moment. I dare say she is someone he would fall madly in love with as well. Too bad he's dead. Yet, it doesn't sound like that stopped him from enjoying her sexually in the shadowscape.

Once Calder lets go of his righteous anger, then he will be able to heal… likely with her love.

"I'm going to investigate the creatures and see what they have to say about all this," I tell Arran as I squeeze his shoulder. "Keep up your protection detail. We don't know if we are safe here now."

He places his warm hand over mine and smiles. Although his grin has melancholy behind it. Without needing to probe his mind, I sense he is a tornado of emotion—his love for Jade, his worry about her safety, their future, and how we will share the love of our woman.

He's also worried that we have drifted too far from each

other since his curse. What he doesn't realize is that it feels too good to have my companion back, and I won't let him slip from my grasp so easily next time. Besides, even his beast seems to have been tamed by Jade.

I head upstairs to deal with our possible spy situation. I growl, first at myself, then at Calder for not suspecting something could be off with the "fur babies" before now.

In my defense, they didn't radiate anything but magical creature vibes and brain waves. But if I'm to keep my mate safe, I need to do better.

I knock on the phoenix's door. "It's me."

"Come in," Calder bites out. He isn't happy. Well, join the damned fucking club.

I slip in and shut the door behind me.

The magical creatures sit huddled together on Calder's bed. Wide eyed watching their interrogator pace the room, they look adorable and nervous.

"How long ago did Floofers join your group?" he asks.

Trouble answers, sounding irritated.

Calder interprets for me, "He said maybe fifty years ago? You know how animals are with time, but it's probably been a while." The phoenix rolls his eyes and sighs, falling onto a wooden desk chair with exhaustion.

"May I?" I wave my hand toward the little tufts of fur.

"You won't explode their brains?" he asks.

The guinea pig squeaks and runs under Calder's pillow.

"I won't," I assure him, then add, "… probably."

"Be careful. If they are innocent, I won't forgive myself." Calder rubs his eyes and then decides he can't watch and covers his face with both hands and tilts his head down, using his elbows to prop himself up.

He likes to pretend he's such a hardass, but he's softer than all of us. That's exactly his problem. He knows he will melt into goo when Jade finally wins him over.

I wave to the guinea pig since he seems to be the most

human-minded. "Come here. I won't hurt you. It might feel uncomfortable, like someone petting you too hard. The more you fight me, the more it will hurt. I know you are brave, and I know you want to help Jade, so allow me to get some answers, and I will give you all the treats you can handle."

Trouble rushes toward me with the mention of Jade, and even faster with the mention of treats.

"Ready?"

Trouble squeaks, and Calder confirms it. "He's ready. He says he won't fight it. He has nothing to hide except that…" Calder chuckles softly. "Except that he peed on the carpet when Jade warned him not to."

"Don't worry. I won't share that with Jade," I promise.

The shivering mass of fur settles and closes his eyes, awaiting my mental probe.

Despite their small size, a magical creature's energy is sometimes bigger than the average human. I wonder if it's because their magic is just naturally bigger or because humans don't really connect with the world around them. I think it may be the latter. Human's natural magic has become diluted in the last several decades as technology has replaced thinking or being with nature. However, I've noticed that engaging their minds is beneficial for them.

Nevertheless, all the magic in a creature as small as this one has been concentrated. His brain is tiny. So I must be gentle, or I will accidentally squash it.

I decide instead of diving in, rooting around, and potentially causing damage, I should ask questions to bring the right thoughts to the surface. Then I will only need to skim his thoughts like I do with most people, without consequence.

"Remember back to when Floofer first joined you," I instruct.

The image of Rob pops up, and I also sense irritation toward him. The guinea pig isn't a fan of the warlock.

This is a good start.

"Did Rob bring Floofers to Jade?" I ask.

I get the impression that Rob first showed up in Jade's life and then Jade found Floofer immediately afterward, outside of her home. Rob acted as if he didn't like the magical creatures, but he almost completely ignored Floofer compared to the other animals.

"Did Rob ever take Floofer away from the rest of you?"

I don't see an instance of that in Trouble's memories, but that's inconclusive. If Rob could put a spell on Jade, he could have done something to the creatures as well.

"Did you ever witness Rob asking Jade questions when she was possessed by a ghost?"

In Trouble's mind, I hear the muffled sounds of Rob asking about names and locations of people. Jade's voice sounds odd, just like it did when Osen spoke through her.

I need to know if Jade was there *during* the murders. Maybe that's why Osen thought he saw her there at his death in the alleyway. Either he saw her in the weeks when he was investigating, or she was actually there against her will during his murder.

"Did Rob ever take Jade out of the house just *before* a spirit possessed her?"

Trouble doesn't think she was. He shows me a memory of her snuggling up to Sage and then a spirit rushed toward her, through the pendant, and into her body.

Shit. The pendant had been used as a focal point, just as I suspected.

It's also interesting that the guinea pig can see ghosts. Though I had heard that even regular animals, especially cats, often can perceive spirits.

"Is the last ghost still with her? The grumpy one?" I ask about Osen, and Calder comes to attention, waiting for any response.

I get the impression that something lingers around her, but Trouble has sensed nothing definitive since the alleyway.

"Well?" Calder asks Trouble directly.

The guinea pig chirps out a response, and Calder deflates.

"He might just need a power up," I try to console him. "Despite your claims, we haven't been relentlessly fucking Jade, so if Osen's still in her, he hasn't had many meals yet."

"I just can't get over all of it," Calder half-ass apologizes.

"You *can*, but you aren't allowing yourself to let go." I sigh, because I don't enjoy lecturing him, but he's not snapping out of his poor attitude. It's been years since he last died and came back. He's more twisted up than ever before. "Jade isn't anything like the witch who killed you."

"I know. But…"

"No. No buts. I'm not saying you have to be lovers or even best friends. I'm just saying give her a damn break. You are so focused on your anger, we might never get our answers if you aren't helping us find them. The pain of losing Osen made you miss out on a great opportunity to talk to him again. Hopefully, if we get him back, you don't let that opportunity slip through your fingers again. And you might be missing something else important if you keep this up."

"I…" he starts to defend himself and then stops. After a moment, he concedes, "You're right. I'm kicking myself that I didn't talk to Osen more when he was alive. And that I didn't pursue closure when he was in Jade."

"Promise me you won't make that mistake again?"

He nods, but doesn't seal the promise with his words. I just hope he doesn't fuck up his chances anymore than he has.

18

BOUNDARIES

JADE

*A*fter all the early morning strangeness with Floofer and the intense breakthrough with Flint, I attempt to write. Keyword: Attempt.

I get a few words on the page, but mostly it's just notes, ideas, and snippets of dialogue that I will have to expand and enhance for it to make any sense.

I can't focus with all that's happened recently, my mind is a chaotic mess. It was bad enough when I was just dealing with a jerky boyfriend and our breakup.

But everything going on in my life is so far beyond simple problems that I might as well be in another realm... which now, I suppose, I have been to.

What is my life?

It is no small thing to discover that your entire world is a lie. Or more accurately, completely misrepresented. What was up is now down. Monsters and supernaturals are real. My abuela really was a witch, not just loco, like my mother would have me believe. I have two (possibly more) lovers who are supernatural beings. Oh, and one of my fur babies might have been spying on me for the past few years.

I shudder, thinking how I petted him and held him to my breast when he might have been some mage in disguise. Ugh.

I hope the jerk hated every second of it. Otherwise, I want to be sick.

Ultimately, I'm just pissed off about how ignorant I was to literally everything happening in my life.

Every once in a while, I hear Arran whine softly outside the office door. His wolf, and-or beast, and-or the human part can't handle this closed door.

I can't say I'm a fan of it either, but I need to maintain healthy boundaries. As an introvert, I'm so used to being alone that this constant touching and attention feels scary and overwhelming. I'm collapsing in on myself with all the energy it takes for me to be around all these new people. I need time to gather myself.

After a slew of author administrative duties, I give up trying to force the words and curl up on the daybed. Weirdly, I can actually feel Arran outside in the hallway and Maxum upstairs. My magic must be coming to me. If I strain, I can even feel Flint in his room... pacing?

I suppose he's had his world rocked as much as I have. I hope our upheavals turn out to be good things in the long run.

I don't feel Calder though, and I wonder if that has to do with the fact I have no emotional bonds with him. I search inside myself and a shadow seems to brush up against me. Is it Osen? I hope he comes back in full form and is happy to be with me.

There's a soft knock on the door, and I sit up. "Come in."

Maxum opens the door, glances at the computer, and then thinks better of coming all the way inside. He stops, but Arran brushes past him to sit next to me on the futon. Apparently, shifters like Arran with little bonus magic rarely mess up computers.

"I couldn't find Floofer," Maxum tells me. "However, I successfully read Trouble's mind without hurting him. I believe Floofer was a spy, and was likely working with Rob."

"You're sure Trouble wasn't hurt?" I ask.

"Yeah. He's demanding extra treats for eternity for his bravery, from what Calder translated for me."

"Sounds like he's fine," I say, then move onto the other news. "What do we do about Floof? Do you think he is still hiding around the house?"

"I didn't pick up that he has crossed my wards or dismantled them, but if he's a highly proficient mage or witch, there's a slim chance that I might not know." Maxum pauses and then says what was likely on his mind this whole time. "I was thinking I should check in with my various contacts and see what they found out about Rob or his associates since I last asked."

"You are leaving?" My heart doesn't like the sound of that.

"Just for the day. I will be back before nightfall."

I jump up and run to hug him. "Promise?"

"Worried about me?" he says with amusement.

"Uh, yeah, of course. Should you be going alone?" I ask.

"I'm going too." Arran hugs me from behind, and I hear in my mind what sounds like a whimper.

I'm not worried about being left alone with Flint. It helps that he doesn't freeze up completely anymore, but I don't know about the phoenix. "You think Calder won't just let me be dragged off if it comes down to it?"

"He didn't last time." Maxum sighs and brushes the wild silver hair from my face. "He's promised to protect you, and I think he's beginning to regret his pissy attitude. Besides, Flint will be here too."

"Okay." I go up on my tiptoes and Maxum leans down to

give me a kiss. Once satisfied, I turn and tangle tongues with my sweet Arran.

I'm completely worked up by the time we are done with our goodbyes, and regret they will be gone the entire day. Geeze. Can I pick a lane? First, I need my space, and now I'm all needy. A classic case of wanting what I can't have.

"Calder is also willing to teach you how to shield your mind," Maxum adds.

"He knows how to do that?" I ask, skeptical since Maxum had made it sound like he was the only one qualified before.

"Yes, he's capable of teaching you the basics, and I can test you when I get back."

I harrumph, because I'd rather not play with the grumpy antagonist.

"I'm sure he just needs to get to know you a bit more, and he will melt in your hands, just like Flint is," Maxum assures me.

"Calder's so damned stubborn," Arran huffs.

"But Calder means a lot to you both," I say. "So he must have some redeeming qualities he has yet to bestow upon me, other than being sexy looking."

"He has a big heart... when he allows himself to care." Maxum kisses my forehead. "I dare say he will fall hard for you once he gets out of his own way."

"Wait, a sec." I ask in surprise, "Do you want me to hook up with him?"

"Do you want to?" Arran asks.

"So you both are okay if I'm with your whole pack?" I ask.

"Only if you are going to be happy with that arrangement," Maxum says.

"Exactly," Arran agrees. "I believe your heart is big enough to love all of us."

"Okay, well, let's just see if he can say hello to me without a snarl. We'll go from there."

19

BUILDING BRIDGES

JADE

*M*axum and Arran leave for their investigations, going the direction we had arrived at the house.

After a sigh and wistfully longing to join them, I climb the stairs to see if Calder indeed intends to teach me a damn thing.

I just hope he doesn't either attack me verbally or physically. Although, I highly doubt even with his crazed anger toward witches that he would actually hurt me.

Just as I'm about to knock on the door, I glance down the hallway and wonder if Flint might help me with shielding my mind. Although, it seems unlikely since I'm sure Maxum would have told me to work with the gargoyle instead if he was an option.

Calder's door flies open before I have a chance to knock. He gives me a quick once over and asks flatly, "Why are you lingering out here?"

Do I tell him I've been working up the nerve to talk with him? Or would that only feed his ego?

"I was debating whether this was a good idea." Yeah. Honesty. That could work. "If you don't want to help me with my shields, then I can buzz off."

"I didn't say I wouldn't help," he grumps and steps aside as an invitation to come into his room.

"You're okay with me in your space?" I ask, a bit taken aback.

"Your spy already invaded my room. I don't see how it's sacred anymore."

I flush pink with the reminder that I had a spy with me for the last few years. "If I would have known... Well, I don't know what to say. Just that a week ago, I didn't even know it was possible for a hamster to be anything more than just a cute ball of floof."

Calder grunts and waves me in. "I know."

"You believe me now?" I ask as I take a tentative step inside his room.

It's nicer than the one at the temporary safe house. But I suppose that makes sense. Maxum intended for this place to be a proper home for them.

Calder's space is filled with burnished wood and beautifully intricate wrought metal—not iron, but another metal I've never seen before. I assume this metal is fae-born friendly since I know iron had hurt Osen.

His room is a mix of deep reds and rust orange—exactly as I might expect a fire being's color choice to be.

I realize I'd like to see Arran's personal room, and Flint's if he'd let me. What would Osen's room reveal that I don't know yet? Perhaps it might draw him forward if there is anything personal he might attune to.

But the most precious thing to Osen that's here might be Calder himself.

Trouble and Sage gaze up at me from a thick shag rug.

I titter over them and squat down to give them a pet. "Hey, are you both doing okay?"

"Birdman gives good ear rubs!" Sage announces.

I peek up at the phoenix, who blushes slightly and turns away quickly, busying himself with something on his desk.

"I bet he does," I agree. "How are you doing, Trouble?"

"I'm mad."

"Oh?" I worry he will say that I've been ignoring him. I haven't meant to, but when I think about it, truly, not much time has passed since my life was turned upside down. Knowing how wild it's been, I relax a bit. Besides, Calder has been keeping an eye on them, and it sounds like he might be a better caretaker than I've ever been.

But Trouble isn't mad at me when I hear him say, "Floofer was lying to us."

"It sounds like that's the case. Did he ever do anything to hurt you?" I ask.

"Uh, no. I don't think so. Not when we were awake."

I sigh with relief, and I hear Calder echo me. He really has a soft spot for the little ones. I just wish he wouldn't be so hard on me because I'm a witch. I never asked to be born this way or have the power to channel spirits.

Well, I suppose it's time to bite the bullet and have him help me. I give each of the fur babies their favorite petting. Sage likes her ears rubbed and Trouble likes a rump scratch.

"You sure you want to help me?" I ask the phoenix. "Maybe I should wait until Maxum gets back."

"Sit down." Calder points to his wooden desk chair. He perches on the side of his bed and stares at me.

I feel pressure at my temples. "What are you doing?"

"You felt that?" He nods and tilts his head. With his movement, I can see the bird part of him clearly.

"Like fingers pressing on the sides of my head," I tell him.

"I'm not a proficient mind reader like Maxum, but I've been known to get into some weaker minds."

"What did you see?" I ask. Because I hope he didn't see how

I admire how he looks in his tight black t-shirt and gray sweatpants.

"Nothing," he says, like it's obvious. "Your mind isn't weak."

"Oh, I thought since Rob could hypnotize me and spirits can invade my mind that I would be considered weak."

Calder leans forward, his elbows propped on his lap. "From what we understand, Rob put a spell on you, likely when you were asleep. That's different from being hypnotized. Essentially, he assaulted you when you trusted him, and he took your choices away. As far as the spirits go, mediumship is a power, not a weakness. You can call on souls and even channel their magic."

"You make it sound like I'm in control of the spirits, but Osen controlled me."

"Only because your magic was weakened by the pendant. Osen is particularly gifted at manipulating things in any dimension—in the shadowscape's astral realm or physically."

"You don't believe I am lying anymore?" I ask.

"I don't know what to think. But yeah, the more I see of you, the more I suspect you don't have a fucking clue."

"Thanks?" I lean back in the chair and frown. "You're right. I don't have a clue. It's like this isn't even my life anymore. Everything I thought I knew about the world and myself was wrong. I believed Rob and I had a typical bad relationship. He was a bit of a narcissistic douche and then straight abusive when I broke up with him."

Calder perks up. "You broke up with him?"

"Yeah. I was tired of him being a jerk. Nothing about the relationship was good. Nothing. So I ended it. All of a sudden, he seemed to care about me. Or rather, that he didn't have free access to me. He even broke into my house a couple of times."

"More than a couple," Trouble adds. "Sometimes, you didn't wake up."

"Shit." I rub my face, and I feel the burn behind my eyes.

But I don't want to cry over Rob—and definitely not in front of Calder.

"What did he do when he broke in?" Calder growls.

I'm surprised by how protective he sounds. "The times I woke up, he demanded I take him back. He would try to... kiss me. I had never been sexually attracted to him and definitely didn't want him touching me after we broke up. When he realized forcing himself on me wasn't going to work, he... hit me. I stumbled into the kitchen and pulled a knife on him, and I was able to call the cops. Then I bought a gun. That stopped him from coming back... or so I thought."

Both Calder and I look at Trouble.

He shakes his head. "Rob came over a few times after that and incanted his spell while you were sleeping, and he asked spirits to talk through you."

I curse and feel hot tears rolling down my cheeks.

Calder's voice is soft as he asks Trouble, "Then what happened?"

"Rob would ask questions about names and places and then he would leave," Trouble says.

"Just using me. That's all I ever was to him—a tool."

Suddenly, Calder is on his knees in front of me and pulls me into a hug.

Startled, I don't know what to make of this new version of the phoenix who is willing to comfort me. For a moment, I'm stiff, but then I give in to the affection and rest my head on his shoulder and wrap my arms around his torso.

"You are not just a tool. Don't allow Rob to make you feel small," he whispers over my hair.

I don't know what to say to that. Calder has hated me since before I was probably born.

"But I'm a witch... and I don't even know the first thing about being one." I suck in my tears and add, "I don't even have my magic."

Calder breathes in deeply and then pulls back to look me in

the eye. "Your magic is coming in now. I suspect you will be at full power soon."

"I will?" I glance down at my hands and wonder how magic works in reality. I need a change of subject. "Does magic get depleted when a magical person uses it? And if it does, does it have to be refilled like recharging batteries?"

"If you use too much at once, you can become drained. Some beings drain faster than others, depending on the magic they have and how much control they have over it. And some take a long time to draw the energy, depending on what their source is."

"Oh, you mean like how Osen draws from sexual energy?"

Sadness flashes over Calder's face. He glances at where his hands still rest on my knees. He appears a bit bewildered by his actions.

"I didn't mean to upset you," I say. "Oh, and I should tell you I thought I felt him. But his energy must be low after Rob's attack. I'd give him what he needs to regain his strength, but I don't know how to do that. Before, he just showed up and you know… did stuff… in the shadowscape."

"You really didn't mind being intimate with him?" Calder removes his touch, sits back on his heels, and studies me.

I pick at my fingers for a moment. I don't know what to say. He was in love with Osen, and it feels like I'm the other woman.

"Hey?" Calder places his hand back on my knee. "We weren't exclusive, even when he was alive. It's okay if you enjoyed being with him. But if you didn't want it, I'd like to know that too. I would be angry if he forced himself on you."

"Even if I'm a witch?" I ask. I can't believe he's being so kind to me. It's like a switch has been flipped. When I think about it, it's often the tough guys who are so damned sensitive that they put up walls upon walls.

Maybe he cares too deeply and can't afford to allow anyone inside.

"I can't keep blaming all witches for what a few have done

to my pack and me. I can see it in your eyes. You could never be that cruel."

I'm stunned by his words, and I feel a weight being lifted that I didn't realize I was carrying. As if I was taking on all the sins of my kind and now I'm able to drop that to only carry my own sins.

"Did he force you to do anything you didn't want to do?" Calder asks again.

"Not sexually. I enjoyed that part. But he coerced me to go to the alleyway. He said he would take my body from me and go anyway if I didn't."

Calder breathes out. "He's a stubborn asshole, isn't he?"

"From what I've experienced, yeah." I bite my lip.

Will he ask about what I've seen in Osen's thoughts?

Just with that worry, my mind flashes back to the scene in the hotel. I remember myself as Osen, with an aching, hard erection. I can actually feel the sensation of sliding into Calder's tight ass. My skin heats, and my clit perks up, wondering if she's going to get some play time.

He cocks a brow, reading me like a neon sign. "You saw me in his memories, didn't you?"

"Uh, yeah. A little." I hurry to explain, "But I didn't mean to see *that*. I just sort of fell into the memories. At the time, I didn't think they were real. I thought they were fantasies."

"And seeing two men together is a fantasy for you?"

"I mean, it's not like an obsession or anything. But two beautiful men, expressing their desire, what's not to like?"

"Do you put yourself in the middle of these men you fantasize about?"

"Well, not always, because it isn't even about that. And sure, sometimes, I imagine being included. I suppose I write romance because I haven't had much love in my life. I haven't had the epic story where someone falls for me so hard that they would do anything for me."

"Except now you have," he says poignantly.

"Maybe," I whisper.

"Maybe?"

I sigh. I might as well tell Calder, as he will confirm my concern. Then I can deal with the painful truth. "I'm going to let you in on something I'm worried about. My theory is that Arran and Maxum are attracted to Osen's energy inside me. Their affection is not really about me, per se."

Calder stares at me for a long minute. Perhaps he's wondering what I've done to encourage their affections. Or he senses that I'm correct. "Sorry. Nope. Maxum and Arran were never gaga over Osen the way they are with you. Flint is definitely into you all on his own. And I haven't sensed Osen's energy radiating out of you in a way that would attract them to you."

"But guys rarely want me... not like how deeply they are hinting at."

"You have a magnetism all your own. It just needed the right people to attract."

"How can you say that? It isn't like you know what's going on with the other guys. It's not like you feel an attraction for me."

Calder drops his gaze, and he tenses. "Even when I was against having you around, I thought you were... attractive."

"Is that why you hated me even more?"

"Hate is a strong word."

"Repulsed? Sickened?" I offer.

Calder chuckles, shakes his head, and makes eye contact again. "Let's go with irritated."

"Okay. I know I can be irritating. It's what my ex-boyfriends call me."

"Witch, you had some terrible taste in males."

"Apparently. Let's see if supernatural guys are any better."

TRAINING

JADE

After Calder instructs me to stand in the middle of his room, he tells me to close my eyes. "Imagine your aura has a bubble around it. Then another one around your body, then another layer around your mind."

I crack open my eyes and look at him, "You sure this is how I shield myself? Imagining bubbles?"

Calder gives me a long-suffering sigh. "Magic is all about intention. I thought you would know this from all your supernatural books you supposedly write."

"I do write those books, but I guess I thought it was all made up bullshit."

"How do you think things get made up? From what is real… or the other way around. You get my point. Form follows thought and thought follows form."

"So the whole 'as above, so below' theory?"

"Exactly." He nods at me. "Now, close your eyes and focus."

I do as he says, because it's hard to focus when I'm barraged by his handsomeness. I hate to say I'm flustered by the intense presence of this hot guy, but yeah… I am.

"Envision those bubbles. Make them as solid and as real in your mind as you can. Imagine that your enemy cannot get beyond your boundaries, no matter how hard they try."

I focus on creating these bubble boundaries, and finally, they feel like they have solidified.

"Good," he praises. "Now hold on to that feeling, no matter what you feel."

I smile at his approval. Then I feel energy moving closer, pushing on my boundaries. I push back with my mind.

"Boo," he whispers.

I jump. My eyes pop open at the sound of Calder so close to me. When I see he's in my space, less than a foot away from my face, I yelp, "What are you doing?"

"Testing you." He smirks.

I sort of want to test him by leaning in a few inches and pressing my lips to his to see what he might do. But I'm being a good girl today. Or trying my fucking best to be. No promises.

I don't pull back or cower. I lean in ever so slightly. His ice-blue eyes widen just a fraction.

"So you testing me includes getting this close?" I glance down at his full, lush lips to make him nervous.

He swallows, fully realizing his mistake. I can almost hear his mind shouting, "Abort mission!"

"I, uh, yes, I have to test you with distractions," he says, regaining a bit of his composure.

"Rub her ears!" Sage suggests. "And she might lick you!"

Calder turns bright pink. Whoops. He's lost the upper hand again.

I have to hold back my laughter. I'm sure Sage doesn't realize how sexual that sounds… right? Oh, my goodness, she *is* a bunny. Maybe she does mean it sexually.

I lock eyes with the phoenix and tuck my hair behind my ear as a not-so-subtle taunt. "Well?" I hint about my petting.

"Well… what?" He pulls back an inch and glances at my ear.

"Did I keep my mind bubble in place, or did your distraction work?" I ask in an innocent voice.

"Oh." He concentrates briefly. He's lost the thread about why he is so close to me. Hmm. Interesting… maybe he's more attracted to me than I originally thought. "Yeah, you were able to keep your shields up. Very good."

"So what do I get as a reward?" I tilt my head, dragging my gaze down his body to egg on his frustration and ire.

"Reward?" he echoes.

I swear he's more of a parrot than a phoenix at the moment.

"My treat. For being a good girl?"

Calder narrows his eyes, finally seeing my suggestive talk for the teasing it is. "Hmm." He steps closer, looking every bit the menacing grump he can be.

I instinctively step back. The back of my legs hit the desk behind me.

He presses closer, his body aligning with mine. He leans over, and I arch backward. His hands land on the desk. His huge arms bracket me in, pinning me in place. "Is this you being good? Because it feels like you are being naughty."

"I suppose it depends on your definition?" My eyes flicker up to meet his flaming blue gaze, noting his teeth are now biting his full lower lip.

"I suppose it depends on the context," he replies. "What do you feel you deserve for a treat?"

Okay. Tables have officially been turned.

I'm flustered, and my pussy is throbbing with his body pressed against mine. I swallow down my nervous sexual energy. I must regain my senses, or he won't let me live this down.

He leans in farther, his lips about to graze mine. "What would you like me to rub?"

Be strong. So many retorts pass through my mind. I want to

tell him I'd like to watch him rub his own cock, but he is just waiting for me to break like this.

I hold my shields strong, or so I hope.

What does he wish to gain from this suggestive scenario?

Does he want to prove I'm a weak-willed slut? Or that he has the power to distract me? Or is he attracted to me too?

Or is he really just trying to test my mental fortitude and figures this is the best way to test me? Because he isn't wrong.

The only other thing he could do that might distract me more is to physically attack me.

I focus on his mind. If I'm coming into my magic, would I be able to read his mind? Is he so focused on my walls that he might fail to reinforce his own?

Without knowing the first thing about what I'm doing, I go with my intuition and reach out with my intention, much like Osen did the night he took over my body in the alleyway.

My energy tickles over his temples. I pick up the vague impression that I intrigue Calder.

As I scramble to probe deeper to understand what he wants, Calder straightens and pulls away.

"Was that you?" he asks, touching his forehead nervously.

"Maybe?" I grimace, a bit concerned he might not have liked that. Will my spur-of-the-moment action fuel his distrust of me?

"How did you do that?" he asks.

"I don't know how I did it. I just wanted to mess with you a bit for trying to antagonize me." Shuffling sideways, I move closer to the door. I might need a quick getaway.

His eyes narrow. "What did you see?"

"Nothing much. It felt like I intrigued you... like you were probably wondering when I was going to break." I offer as a way for him to save face. I'm sure he doesn't want to admit he might be interested. And I want to keep this newfound peace.

"Intrigued?" He saunters back into my space, now pressing me against the door. "Yes, I'm intrigued by you."

"Oh?" Behind my back, I place my hand on the door handle.

"You should know I have a ward over the door. It will zap you if you try to leave."

"Are you trapping me here?" I ask, trying to keep the nervousness out of my voice.

"Your lesson isn't over."

"It isn't?" I gaze up into his intense eyes and wonder what he has planned for me. "What else is there?"

"Protection—what to do if someone gets beyond your shields."

"What do I do?"

"Try reading me again," he dares.

Dammit. I'm not going to let him intimidate me.

My mental intention pushes out again, quicker this time, but I try to keep my own walls up.

In his mind, I see flashes of me—having rough sex with Maxum, Arran, and Osen.

Oh wow. These are all fantasies he's had of me.

A shock like a burning live wire hits me right between the eyes—Calder's defensive measure.

My body slams against the door, and I shout, "Fuck!"

Then I'm thrown forward into Calder. We tumble to the floor. I barely have the wits to pick myself up off Calder's body. The phoenix looks as stunned as I do about our new position.

"Jade!" Flint rushes inside the room and cries out when a magical veil lights up in the doorway as he enters. The big guy looks frantic, as if he might pick me up by the waist. But he quickly changes tactics and holds out a single hand to me.

As I reach out to take Flint's hand for support, I inadvertently straddle Calder. I find he's packing some heat from our recent smoldering exchange.

Can this moment get any more awkward?

"What are you doing?" Calder growls at Flint.

"You hurt Jade!" Impatient with how fast I'm removing myself from Calder, Flint easily lifts me off the phoenix and sets me behind him.

Still surprised by his ability to touch me and how he didn't seem to be affected at all, I stand stunned while the two argue.

"I was training her." Calder scrambles up to his feet and glares up at the taller gargoyle.

"She cried out." Flint takes a menacing step toward Calder.

"Hey, Flint." I step to the side to get both of their attention. "I'm okay. He was training me."

He doesn't look at me. Instead, he glares at the phoenix. "What. Did. You. Do?"

"I zapped her senses when she tried to enter my mind. It's not damaging. She needs to know what's possible so she can protect herself."

"You did it so you could inflict pain," Flint snarls.

Wow. This protective side of Flint is turning me on.

Calder dares to look away from Flint. He asks me, sounding put out, "Are you alright?"

"I think so. It stung, but I suppose I learned my lesson not to go poking around in your mind." I mutter, "I won't do that again."

"See, it's fine," Calder says to Flint, taking a step back. "I get you are protective of… innocents, but Jade needs to learn how to shield herself. She also had an early lesson in someone defending their shields. Not all of us have your innate ability."

"You have an innate ability?" I ask, hoping to steer this confrontation into a more friendly chat.

"My mind is sealed off from others." The big guy turns and his pale gray eyes gaze into mine. "Except for the one who I would have a bond with."

"Like a bonded mate? Or could it be one of your pack?"

"With a mate match." He frowns slightly and heads to the door. "Come, both of you. Time to eat. We need to keep your strength up."

I look at Calder with an *are you okay* expression.

He shrugs it off and gestures for me to go first.

"Don't forget my treats!" Trouble shouts at us as Calder attempts to shut his broken door.

"If you stay in here and behave, I'll bring you something extra good," Calder bargains.

"Fine," Trouble grumbles.

When Calder turns to follow me down the stairs, I'm standing there watching him with adoration. "Thank you," I say softly.

"For what?"

"For taking such good care of them."

He sighs wearily and walks toward me and herds me toward the stairs. "But I messed up too. I shouldn't have been so obsessed with your guilt or innocence and been more attentive to what was right under my nose. It's understandable for you not to know about Floofer, since you didn't know about magic. But there's no excuse for me. I was just blinded by my pain and anger."

"You had just lost Osen, then I showed up. It's totally understandable why you didn't like me. And I was a witch on top of it. I don't even like witches now."

As we join him in the kitchen, Flint watches me as he readies the plates for us to eat. "You don't have to dislike your own kind. Maxum's old acquaintance, Amira, was a testament to a witch doing good. She didn't have to come to help you and Calder."

"I wish I would have been awake to talk to her phoenix mate," Calder says with sorrow in his voice.

"You don't get to meet many of your kind?" I ask.

"No, we are a *dying* species—pun intended." He states it so plainly, I have to take a moment to get beyond my sadness for his kind.

I cover my mouth when I realize the double meaning. "Please don't. Wordplay is foreplay to me."

Calder chuckles and shakes his head. "Be good, witch."

When I look at Flint, his mouth is hanging open slightly, confused by our light flirting.

I get back on track. "So you don't know another phoenix?"

"No." Calder dishes out some fruit and cheese and sits down.

It sounds like that is a loaded subject, so I let it drop. "You didn't get any bad vibes from Amira?" I ask Flint.

"No. She wasn't particularly fond of other witches. However, she was still open to helping you. We may have to take her up on that offer at some point, even if it's just to find another witch to help you with your magic. Maxum's knowledge is limited, and I have a feeling if you are going to remain in our company that you will need to learn to properly control your magic and defend yourself."

With a fork, I poke at the food Flint hands me. "I'm so far behind in my abilities. If I didn't have that pendant draining me, I might have been alerted to my witchiness before now, instead of just thinking I had strange dreams."

"Speaking of the pendant," Calder says. "Trouble says he saw the spirits pulled through it and into you."

"What does that mean? Am I really a medium then?"

"Yes, you couldn't do that if it weren't your affinity," Flint assures me. "But I think it could have been used as a focal, a beacon, if you will."

"Is that why I can't bring Osen back? Do I need to go back and get the necklace to channel him into me?"

"No," both Calder and Flint bark.

"Okay! I'm just brainstorming here."

"I believe you have the natural affinity of mediumship, but just like anyone with an inclination toward a talent, you must practice it," Calder explains. "Like someone might be a natural at music, but that doesn't mean that person can sit down at a piano for the first time and play Beethoven. You have to learn how to use your natural gift. At least the basics."

"Okay. That makes sense. But how do I learn? Do any of you know how to channel spirits?"

"That's a human witch thing." Calder frowns and leans back in his chair. "Fae-born mages don't work with souls or spirits. The closest thing would be someone like Osen."

I grouch, "But he's the one we can't talk to. Is there someone else? Maybe Amira knows of a trustworthy witch with the ability?"

"I don't know. Maybe Amira herself knows enough about the basics to get us started," Calder ponders. "When Maxum returns tonight, we will ask him."

I nod, but when he says this I am hit with a bad feeling. Will Maxum be returning?

21

INFORMANTS

ARRAN

*M*y wolf and berserker do not enjoy leaving our mate behind. Neither do I. They are snarling and growling inside of me. It feels as though their claws are shredding my insides, but I know it's the separation causing it. Perhaps the anguish wouldn't be so overwhelming if we were properly bonded, and she wasn't in danger.

I'm actually surprised that Maxum would leave Jade with only Calder and Flint to protect her.

He must feel that getting this information is more important. I remind myself that this little field trip of his is only meant to last the day. Hopefully, the hamster spy doesn't take this moment to attack. However, I'm soothed by the idea that Floofer hasn't attacked Jade, even with multiple opportunities over the years with her, and at both the safe and lake houses.

The odds Floofer would go after her now are slim to none. Calder and Flint are not to be trifled with and are a deterrent all on their own. And Jade... well, she's a wild card. With her magic coming in, she might be a formidable force. Without training to control her new magic, she could be unpredictable and deadly if threatened.

As we portal to our hometown, we walk down the sidewalk through a quiet part of the industrial area. I've never met his hacker friends, but I know Maxum trusts them more than most. High praise for humans.

"I was thinking—" I begin.

Maxum cuts me off. "That's a dangerous thing."

"*Ha ha*," I grumble. "I'd expect you'd like me to be more thoughtful instead of just reacting."

"Just messing with you." Maxum pats me on the shoulder. "I suppose I'm anxious about leaving Jade behind. I want her by our side at all times."

"I know what you mean." After taking a moment to get my beasts under control, I say, "I was wondering why Floofer would take off now. He could have stayed hidden under our noses, but he didn't."

"Yeah, you're right. We have been so preoccupied with Jade, he could have stayed where he was. Even Calder was mostly oblivious to anything wrong." He comes to a stop and turns to me. "So, what do you think made him run now?"

"Maybe he wanted to get away from Jade *because* she is coming into her power. What if he knows what sort of magic the pendant was blocking? What if he's afraid?"

"Could be that." Maxum nods. "It could also be that someone out there, who Floofer answers to, would want to know Jade's pendant is gone."

We stare at each other for a moment, wondering what power our witch holds in her luscious body. Then Maxum huffs and returns to his long strides toward what looks to be an abandoned building.

He knocks on a large metal door. A minute later, I hear light footsteps down a metal staircase.

The door swings open, and a petite human woman stands

with her hands on her hips, looking fierce and a bit miffed. She has the side of her head shaved and the rest of her straight shoulder-length hair has been dyed a rainbow of colors.

"Mal, still losing fart fights with a unicorn, I see," Maxum jokes, pointing to her unusual hair.

She cocks a pierced brow at him, breaks the stern glare, and snorts out a laugh. "Yep. Maybe if you taught me some of your *Elven* fighting moves, I'd have a chance."

"Wrong again." He chuckles, then explains to me, "She's trying to guess what sort of supe I am. She's not particularly good at this game of hers."

I'm amused that she hasn't figured out he's a demon. I thought his obsidian black eyes and the red tattoos that sometimes peek out of his shirt at his neck and wrists would be a blatant clue.

"Bet I can guess this guy's deal," Mal challenges, eyeing me.

"Are we actually wagering?" Maxum asks. "If so… when you lose, I get to pick your next hairstyle."

"I don't think it's worth it." Mal smirks. "Unless I get to pick out yours."

"Deal." Maxum waves his hand over at me. "Make your guess."

I'm about to bust up that this woman has made a deal with a devil.

Mal steps closer and studies my eyes. Likely, she is wondering what my amber-colored eyes could mean.

My appearance is similar to most wolf shifters—tall, muscular, dark hair, unusually pale blue or golden brown eyes, with warm-toned skin. While I'm not considered particularly beautiful in the supernatural world, I am appealing to humans. However, the only human's attraction that has ever mattered is Jade's.

She might guess just from my standard looks, but who knows how many interactions this woman has with the supernatural world and all their species and halflings.

"A demon," she guesses with a shrug.

Maxum looks downright offended, and I burst out into laughter.

"Dammit," Mal hisses and waves us inside. As she locks the door behind us and asks, "So how bad is my new hairstyle going to be?"

"Mohawk, so shave the other side, but keep the length and color. I want to see it straight up and in stiff spikes."

"Well, I planned on shaving the other side, anyway." Mal chuckles and climbs the stairs ahead of us.

Maxum gives me a wink behind her back. He knew she planned on doing that. "Hmm, maybe I'll change my mind. Shave it all off? But carve 'I lost' into the stubble?"

"Hilarious." Then she stops and spins to look at him, almost eye to eye, even though she is a few steps higher. "You wouldn't make me do that, would you?"

Maxum shrugs. "I get bored."

The door opens up to a stereotypical warehouse apartment. It's spacious and sparsely decorated. There's a living room area and a huge computer station outpost. I don't know that much about computer technology, but I know enough to get by. There are stacks of hard drives and laptops. A wall of screens tower over a massively long desk. Half of the screens are turned off, but I see a few are displaying the security feed from around the building.

The others have Rob's face and what looks like files on him.

After a nod, Maxum greets his other friend, "Dwayne, hope you are well." He then ushers me over to the couches far from the computers. We sit down and make ourselves comfortable.

"Yeah," Dwayne says. "We purchased some mage spells for protection with your donation. Thanks. Seems like it wasn't a terrible investment, considering the community center bombing and the attack at the fae portal."

Both Maxum and I sit straight up and perch on the edge of our seats.

"I knew about the bombing. We helped clean up the mess." Maxum's hands grip his knees, and I'm afraid he's going to crush his own bones. "Do they know who attacked the portal?"

"From what we hear, no witnesses." Mal answers, "The two fae guards stationed there were killed."

"Any leads?" I ask.

"None that we have heard about." Dwayne frowns and pulls up a report. "It happened only a few hours after the bombing. Maybe some random asshole was taking advantage of the distraction."

Maxum and I lock eyes, both wondering if someone was chasing us.

What if the assailants were able to track us somehow? Is Jade in more danger than we realized?

"Or it wasn't connected at all." Maxum stands up and paces in front of me. "We'll circle back to this. Dwayne, I see you have Robert Holden on your screens. Anything become of your search?"

"Yes. But I doubt you'll like any of it." Dwayne clicks and clacks on his keyboards. "Robert Holden is an alias, as we suspected before. From his photo, I was able to determine his real name is Robert, but Robert Blackwell."

"Blackwell. As in the infamous witching family?" Maxum stops pacing and rubs his chin.

"He's not one of the favored lines, but yeah. But he seems to be the family grunt worker. He gets the jobs no one wants from what our sources confirm."

"Did you tell anyone why you were asking after him?" I demand.

"Of course not," Mal snaps. "We are professionals."

"Sorry." Sighing, I pinch the bridge of my nose. "I'm just stressed." I look down and see my claws are out. Running my tongue over my canines, I can feel that I'm on the verge of a shift, but I realize, this time, it didn't hit me the same. Usually, it feels like a wall of painful twisting when my berserker is ready to burst from my skin. Perhaps my slow acceptance of him is helping me ease the shift.

I'm not sure if not noticing a shift is a good thing. I will have to be more aware of myself than before.

"You okay?" Maxum stands in front of me, blocking Dwayne's and Mal's view.

"Yeah. Just the thought of Rob is enough to rile me." I watch as my claws retract and I take a deep breath.

Maxum turns and continues with the reports. "What else did you dig up?"

"He is not all that popular from what we could suss out. He's had a few known acquaintances over the years. Mainly it has been Galiana Collins, an older witch and coven leader and from what we figured out, an activist for witch superiority. I'm sure you already suspect her to be one of ASO's top members. Likely one of their leaders."

Galiana looks much like I remember from when I've spied on her before. She appears to be around forty, but is truly closer to ninety. About the same height as Jade, slimmer build, and only a few streaks of gray to show any signs of her age. She isn't ugly, but she's definitely not my type because of the truly evil glint in her eye. She reminds me too much of Talin, the witch I killed to earn my curse. I heard once they were distantly related, fifth cousins or something. If they were related, I must be more careful around her. Witches are usually protective about 'family' no matter how distant. I didn't see all the faces of the witches who had cursed me, but I wouldn't be surprised if Galiana was one of them.

Maxum grunts a response about Galiana being Rob's associate. "Yeah. One of my people saw her with Rob recently. Who else?"

"A warlock reported having a rare transmogrification affinity, named Sloan Winter." He pulls up a picture of an unassuming guy with mousy brown hair and pale skin. "But he hasn't been seen much the last couple of years. So I don't know much about him or if he's still in contact with Rob."

Maxum gives me a quick, knowing glance. *Floofer.*

"And who is that?" I point to the last image on the screens. It's a woman who looks more than a bit like Jade.

"Jadeana Jones." I don't know much about her. "Rob was seen with her on a few occasions."

"Jadeana Jones?" I repeat softly, still fixated on my mate's face on the computer screen. That isn't her author pseudonym or the name on her driver's license.

"Anything you can tell us about her?" Maxum asks, his tone devoid of emotion.

"You know witches are secretive as fuck. Fortunately, we know a few who aren't particularly happy about the never-ending war between supes and human-born magicals. From what we were told, Rob's been a person of interest for a while. So they knew about his dealings. They had looked into his mistress, but couldn't find much on her. What we do know is Jadeana is sixty years old from a driver's license I finally found when she lived in another state. Records now show she lives in town at 42 Brighton Road. No record of employment. Couldn't find much else on her, actually. It's like someone put a spell on all her records so they would disappear or get mixed up. I've seen results like this before —usually it's a supe or a witch hiding their identities. But other than Rob, I couldn't find any connection to the magical world."

42 Brighton Road? That's Jade's place. It must be her.

"Any more about Jadeana?" I ask.

"Sorry. I didn't know I needed to dig too deep into her. She didn't seem to be of any consequence." Dwayne types on his computer and begins a search. He sits back in his swiveling office chair and spins to look at us. "Patricia is the mother's name on what appears to be her birth certificate. A father wasn't listed. I don't see any other record of the mother, Patricia—not even a death certificate. That's odd by itself." He narrows his eyes at the screen. "The year on Jadeana's birth certificate is also smudged on the form. Like I said, weird."

Maxum and I walk out of the hackers' building in a bit of a daze. Once clear of the building, we both glance around to see if there is anyone in the area.

I say, "What do you—"

Maxum cuts me off. "Not here. Too many eyes and ears in this realm."

We duck into a dark alcove of a building, and he opens a portal to Elfhame. After he shuts out Earth behind us, he does a quick mental scan of the area for active minds and I give the air a sniff.

Once satisfied we are alone in the meadow, Maxum begins in a hushed voice, "We know nothing yet. So we must keep our worries about Jade's truthfulness to a minimum."

"I can't believe she would lie to us like that."

Maxum growls. "I never picked up that level of deceit."

"What if Rob did more to her mind than we realized? What if he tricked her into believing a false persona?" I ask, my voice rising with the fear my mate has been twisted so thoroughly she doesn't even know who she is.

Maxum sighs. "Fuck, I hope not. But there is another, more feasible possibility."

"What's that?"

"The information they found about Jadeana is wrong."

I blow out a huff of air, feeling a bit of relief just from the thought. "You're right. Most of what Dwayne said was rumors, and he noted how records were missing. Her grandmother may have put a spell on them."

"We must wait to freak out until we get Jade's version of the facts," Maxum says, then grinds his teeth. "But if she wasn't honest about her age, then what else did she lie about?"

I don't want to believe she lied to me. Because her being my mate match *isn't* a lie. I feel that in my bones. But if I'm matched to a liar, I don't know what I'll do. I've fallen for her. My wolf and berserker have already bonded to her.

No matter the truth or the reasons—we don't want to lose the one person who has made us feel whole again.

I suspect Maxum feels similarly.

He's right. Until we talk to Jade, we can't dwell on this information. There must be an explanation. Hopefully, a simple one.

TESTED

FLINT

*J*ade has cracked my mantle, and I'm experiencing a tectonic shift.

I don't think I've ever felt this way. My usually cold insides are churning lava. I feel like a volcano about to erupt. Parts of my body I believed to be long defunct are now awakening. My crotch aches from only listening to Jade's voice.

Closely, I watch her eating the meal that I made her. I observe, as she builds a foundation for a relationship with Calder. I'm not jealous. Not that I ever expected to be a jealous male. Her worry lines around her eyes are easing with his acceptance of her being in our lives, and they are beginning to talk to each other.

I overreacted when I heard her cry out when I was in the hallway, listening in on them. I didn't mean to spy, but I worried that Calder's hostility toward witches would cause him to take it out on Jade. And I will not stand for that behavior anymore. His pain allowed him some leeway, but he can't keep spitting his angry fire at others.

"Flint?" Jade looks at me as if she had been calling me more than once and perhaps she did. "You okay?"

"Just thinking." I smile, hoping I'm doing it right. I'm so out of practice with human expressions and nuances.

"Do you feel like sharing?" she asks gently.

"I shouldn't have interrupted your lesson. I just don't enjoy hearing you being hurt."

"Uh, yeah, Jade..." Calder appears shy and unsure of himself. "I could have warned you, and I feel badly that I didn't."

"I appreciate the sentiment, but you both can stop treating me with kid gloves. I need to know all of this, and I'm sure there will be a few bumps and bruises as I learn about my powers. I'm a grown-ass woman, and I'll let you know when I've had too much."

"I wasn't trying to make you feel less than the powerful witch you surely will become," I hurry to apologize. "I just... I feel protective of you. If that makes you uncomfortable, I will stay away."

Jade grabs my hand, and I freeze... At least, my hand is unmovable stone. Apparently, I'm not completely beyond my psychological block.

Her eyes widen, and then an almost imperceptible frown pulls at her beautiful lips. "I don't want you to go anywhere. I like that you are protective of me, but I'm asking for you to realize I might get hurt as I learn."

"I don't like it."

Jade strokes my hand. "I know, my giant sweetie."

She returns to finishing her meal, and Calder and I do the same.

He gives me a helpless grin when Jade isn't looking, and I return it. She has cracked open his chest too. Soon, she will have all our hearts at her mercy.

"What's next in my training?" Jade asks, then smirks. "Or are you just planning to zap my brain over and over?"

"Your magic seems to be coming in," I say. "You may want to meditate and become familiar with how it feels inside you."

"It feels a bit like I'm high on sugar or adrenaline. Or I shocked myself with an electrical outlet. My whole body sort of feels like it's buzzing." Jade holds out her hands and stares at them. "Is that how your magic feels?"

"We don't have a lot of active magic like you will have," Calder explains. "I have some magical ability, but it has mostly to do with mental shields, my rebirth process, sensing impending death, and… nevermind." His cheeks turn pink, and he picks at his food.

Jade glances over at me. She's curious, but doesn't push the obviously flustered phoenix. I believe I know what he avoided mentioning, and I don't blame him for omitting it. However, I find it interesting that he came so close to disclosing his intimate secret.

I divert attention to myself. "As you witnessed the other day, I can camouflage my presence, essentially becoming invisible."

"Hold up. Did you ever do that inside my house? I had felt like someone was watching me. But I suppose that feeling could have been from Floofer…"

"I didn't watch you from inside your house. But I stood guard outside of your home the day Rob came by and almost killed you." I remember the first time she truly caught my interest. "You kept looking in my direction when you would peek out of the window. I thought you might have been able to see me."

"I felt you. Were you over on the side of the blue house with the pink oleander bush?"

"I was." Though my delight quickly falters as I remember the rest of what happened. "I wasn't able to protect you. I believed you had let Rob in on your own volition. I should have known better."

"From what you told me, Osen let Rob into my house without a fight. Besides, you didn't know me then. You barely do now, so I don't blame you."

I don't like the reminder that I barely know Jade. I believe I know the most important part—how she makes me feel. She is also caring, forgiving, smart, funny, and thoughtful. There's no doubt in me she is a good person.

Now that I'm coming to know her, I see how beautiful she is on the outside, but her inner beauty is what's awakened my attraction.

I must finally show her my true gargoyle form so I will know if she can endure to even hold my hand again. I dare not hope for her to ever kiss me or to mate.

If all she wishes to give me is an occasional hug. I will have to be okay with her decision. I don't believe I can live without her in my life in some way—however that may be. Her comfort and happiness comes before all else. Even before my makeshift pack, but I feel in my bones she *is* my pack, so fortunately, there is no conflict.

Perhaps with her human sensibilities, she might never understand the depth at which I will love and adore her. I have perceived that she doesn't quite comprehend how deeply Maxum and Arran feel already. Their feelings and commitment to her will only solidify and grow.

"May I ask what else you can do?" Jade eyes me. "You mentioned sensing the danger of an innocent. And I know you can turn to stone. But can you explain how that is possible?"

My heart dances in my chest that she is interested in what I am. "Our people are said to have first come from huge magical stones. Fae mages found us over a thousand years ago and carved our forms from the blocks. They claimed they could sense there were souls ready to be born from the earth. They just removed the excess material to reveal who we were. The first of us were even larger than I am, and the elves taught the first of us to come alive, to move and then to fight and protect. They taught us to shape our magic, and we were able to mimic the softness of humanoid flesh. Over time, we became more Elven-like in our natures. Or what you might say… we became more humanlike. We began to eat food and have emotions. It was then that our own people began carving the rest of us into existence. I am one of the last born from the living stones, made by my own people."

"Holy shit," Jade says, her mouth hanging open. "You were really made from stone? You are like… walking, talking magic." Her pretty hazel-green eyes twinkle again. I want to understand what that means, but I don't think she knows she is doing it or what it could mean.

I grin at her awe. I really expected her to be turned off by my origins, but she surprises me at every turn.

"My origins aren't that extraordinary. Technically, we all come from the earth." I downplay my uniqueness. I don't want to be so different that she might not see a future with me.

"No. Don't dismiss how cool you are." Jade leans back and smiles widely. "I mean, yeah, humans being born out of a woman's body is the miracle of life. Blah, blah, blah. Or being hatched from an egg is amazing too. All great stuff. But to be brought into consciousness from being carved out of stone and given a form? Whoa. My mind is blown."

I tuck my head down and hide my huge smile. She sees me as special, not odd. But what did I expect from such a loving woman? Why did I fear she would shun me?

My fears have controlled how I live. No more.

"Hey," Jade calls me softly. When I look up and make eye contact, she says, "Please, don't hide your smiles from me. They make my heart glow."

"They do?" I ask, surprised she could see such a thing.

"It's a metaphor, but it makes my heart feel warm and joyful to see you happy."

I nod, then glance over at Calder, but he isn't looking at me. No. His sights are locked on Jade. His face is soft, and he appears to be longing for what this wonderful woman has given me... acceptance. I suppose I should show her my true form soon. I have to know how to proceed with her. Because I am falling hard and fast, and I don't want to hope for something that will never be.

After a long silence while we finish our plates of food, Jade finally breaks the quiet. "A thought occured to me... before the guys left, I was able to sense Arran and Maxum outside my office door. Do you think I could sense others?"

Both Calder and I ask at the same time, "You didn't feel me?"

Jade nervously takes a sip of water before she answers. "I hope I didn't just make a supernaturally sized faux pas." Her gaze snaps to Calder, since he would be the most likely to throw a fit for her spying on us.

"No," Calder says. "Your magic is coming in and you have no control. Although, I'm surprised by your natural ability to wield it. Typically, you would have learned how to manage your magic as it developed over time and fully bloomed at adulthood. Spying on people is definitely frowned upon. However, getting a vague impression of where someone is located is done often and as long as it isn't more invasive, then it's acceptable."

Jade lets out a breath in relief. "Flint, I had a vague impression of you in your room. But Calder, I didn't pick up your energy."

Calder seems oddly tense that Jade didn't sense him. He is so confusing. Maybe he wants the witch after all. I offer an explanation. "If I were to guess, it's because you have deeper connections with Maxum and Arran. You and I had just had an emotional conversation, so we had bonded on some level. But until your training with Calder, you both hadn't talked or been around each other much."

"True." Jade gazes out the window toward the lake. "I was around Floofer for a couple of years. Do you think I could pick up on Floofer's location? Should I even try?"

"He might not sense you reaching for him." Calder scratches his chin and frowns. "I don't want you risking yourself reaching out. However, you seem to have a natural talent for that and maybe if you can track him down, we can capture him."

My protectiveness rises within me. "I don't relish the idea of calling on the unknown with only the two of us to protect Jade."

"He's out there, so he could attack any second. I'd rather be proactive." Calder huffs. "We don't even know if she can do it."

"I think it's worth the risk," Jade says. "Calder's right. He could be lurking right now, ready to strike when we go to sleep."

Goddess, give me strength.

"Then I won't sleep." I stand abruptly and snatch up our empty plates.

Jade flinches ever so slightly, but I notice. What have I done? I'm proving that I'm the monster I fear I am.

I drop to my knees and the plates fall to the floor. "Forgive me. I didn't mean to scare you."

Her soft hand cups my chin, and I completely turn to solid stone. When I freeze, regressing in my progress, tears roll down her cheeks.

"Oh, sweetheart." She keeps her hand on my skin, and her warmth seeps into me. I am greedy about absorbing anything and everything she will bless me with. I would lick up her tears for an eternity until she was finally happy again.

"I wasn't scared of you," she explains. "I have had a lot of unpleasant experiences, and I suppose my body just reacts to certain stimuli. We aren't much different that way. My triggers are someone's frustration combined with movements toward me. It's okay. We're okay." She drops her hand, likely hoping I will return to my 'fluid' state.

It works, and when I can move again, I miss her touch

desperately. In a fit of emotion, I stand, pull her to my chest, and hug her.

Since I'm so tall, her feet are dangling.

"May I hug you with my legs?" she asks. Her cheeks bloom with color.

"Yes," I whisper.

"Flint," Calder says. "I'll clean up here. Why don't you go spend some quiet time with Jade... If you are cool with that, Jade?"

She doesn't break eye contact with me. "Yes. I would like that, if you want to, Flint."

2 3

REVEALED

JADE

*M*y sweet, sweet gargoyle.

I do not know how to help him heal except to show him support and understanding whenever and however I can.

Flint nods. "Yes. Calder, thank you for cleaning up."

"No problem." Calder waves us away. "Now go before I change my mind."

I'm not sure where this new and improved version of Calder came from, but I like him. I just wasn't expecting the phoenix to be a bit of a matchmaker by essentially telling us to go off and fool around.

Flint shows no signs of letting me down, so I wrap my legs around his hips.

Oh hellstone, our private bits press against each other with only our pants separating us. He practically impales me with his grappling hook. Yeah, I'm sure it probably isn't that, but damn if it doesn't feel huge.

I'm so flipping curious that I'm tempted to accidentally pants him if he doesn't show me what he's working with soon. Perhaps I can ask him to show me his equipment for "research purposes." Would that make it better or worse?

Nah, I'll get there the old-fashioned way, through hard work in seduction. Because it is hard work for me. It doesn't matter that I write this stuff. I have zero game in real life. Okay, zero might be hyperbole, but I'm not naturally gifted.

Thankfully, Flint won't know that I have no game since he probably doesn't even realize there is a game to be had.

Flint lets out a groan when I wiggle a bit to adjust myself when he carries me toward the stairs.

"You can hold me by my ass or thighs if it's easier." It also would be easier on my back since he's carrying most of my weight in a bear hug.

"Oh." Flint moves one giant hand down, cupping my full ass, and then the other. "Is that okay?"

"Yes," I whisper, wrapping my arms around his neck. My body is alight with tingles. I don't know how far this will go with my innocent guy, but I'd be happy with snuggles. I'd be even happier with a make-out session. *Fuck*. He's probably never kissed someone before.

Now I'm sweating, I'm so nervous. This is an enormous responsibility.

Sweet grandmother moon… When he climbs the stairs, my pussy rubs back and forth and side to side, and I'm about to come just like this.

Deep, calming breaths, Jade.

Flint carries me into his room, down the hall from Calder's.

I'm not sure what I was expecting his room to look like, but just as with Maxum, Flint surprises me.

The glass balcony doors open up over the unending forest, allowing in enough sunlight for me to see without having to turn on a light.

He's filled the generous sized room with soft velour and

chenille fabric comforter, pillows, and curtains. The colors are all in muted gem tones. A huge fluffy rug is on the floor. In contrast to the softness, there are rocks, crystals, and stones displayed everywhere.

I gasp. "It's beautiful!"

"You really think so?" Flint sounds so vulnerable.

These guys are breaking my little witchy heart. They are all so amazing and such a catch, and none of them really feels like they are.

I suppose they'd say the same about me.

They are so gorgeous, strong, and sensitive. I've only known them a short time, but I could make a list of wonderful attributes that could go on a mile long.

Separate from the rest of his collection, a plain rock sits on his desk. It looks to be the size of the regular gravel from my yard. "What's this one?"

"Uh." He blushes again. "It's from when I kept an eye on your house, watching over you."

Holy hell. My heart melts to heat my core. Has he liked me from the beginning?

I'm unsure what happens from here, but I want Flint to take the lead. I don't want to pressure him into something he's not comfortable with.

He glances at the bed, finally breaking his intense gaze that's lasted from the dining room to here.

I smile. "Whatever you want to do." I nod at the floor. "I'm happy to sit on the floor and just talk. Or we can snuggle on the bed. Or sit on the balcony and stare out into the forest. Or if you have the strength to hold me up like this for hours, which it seems, most impressively, that you do, we can do that."

"I'd like to do the snuggle thing. How does that work?"

I grin, feeling lighter just with the innocence of my guy. "We have a few common options. We could spoon or you could lie on your back and I tuck to your side."

"Spoon?"

"That would be both on our sides. Think of it as one of us sitting on the other's lap but lying down. You can drape an arm around the other person's waist."

"Is there one where I am on my back and you are on my front?"

Geezus, man. My body heats instantly from that visual. That kind of snuggling can escalate quickly.

"Is that how you want to… snuggle?" I worry for a moment that he doesn't know the difference between a snuggle and sex. Is he asking for sex?

Either way, I'm in, so I will adapt to his cues.

"Yes."

Flint walks over to the bed, and I move my legs to let them dangle. He lays back and shifts to the center of his king bed, taking me with him. I swear these huge, powerful guys make me feel so petite and dainty.

For good or bad, my legs fall off the sides of his hips and since he didn't pull me up his chest, I'm pressed to his pronounced bulge.

I rest my cheek on his upper chest and allow my body to relax.

His massive hands are still gripping my ass. I wonder if that's their new future home. But slowly his right hand moves upward, caressing my lower back and up, until his fingers are tangled with my hair.

"So soft," he breathes out, playing with my long wavy locks. "I've been wishing to touch your silver hair since I saw you."

"You like it?" I ask, because I've debated for a while if I should dye it, chop it off, or both.

"It's the most beautiful hair I've ever seen."

Not what I was expecting, but I love the compliment.

"May I touch your hair?" I ask, because I'm not sure if it will be hard as stone or soft. It's a few shades darker than his travertine colored skin, thick, and may well be as hard as a helmet for all I know.

"It isn't as nice as yours." I hear a pout in his voice.

I lift my head, bracing my arms under my chin, and look him in the eye. "I would like to explore you as you explore me, if that's okay."

He nods, and I touch the incredibly and oddly firm but soft short hair. "It's like nothing I've ever felt before."

"I'm sorry."

"Are you kidding me? I love it! You are precious to me. Understand that, please. If I'm mesmerized or excited by your uniqueness, take it as the praise and for the compliment it is meant to be."

"You are such a blessing, Jade." He squeezes me tightly to his chest.

"Flint, you are too." I say, "You are a completely unexpected treasure, and I'm so happy that we are here together right now. Understand, my delicious, spicy muffin?"

He grins at the reminder of his unusual baking choice.

I love being with him like this, just being. But I'm also itching to kiss him. My hands want to explore his flesh and see if it brings him joy.

"What does my skin feel like to you?" I ask.

"Wonderfully soft and warm. Why do you ask?"

"People go through life usually assuming everyone feels like they do. Or sees the same way they do. But that isn't true. Some people can't feel certain emotions or they feel them more intensely. Or someone might not see colors the same, or at all. And with supernatural and witches being real, that likely expands the parameters of what's possible. One thing that I try to do as an author or a reader is to get into the headspace of another person—to know how someone might be made differently than me. And my goal is to love and embrace that uniqueness. You truly are made differently from me, and I want to know more."

"So you can learn to love… my uniqueness?" When I nod,

his huge hand that was cupping my ass moves up and under my shirt, skimming my lower back.

His touch is so light that it tickles.

"You're so gentle with me," I say.

"My strength and size are used to crush our enemies. I've had to learn to be careful with my actions so I don't break things."

"I trust you. And if you hurt me... too much, then I will let you know."

"Too much?" Confusion fills his face. "You need to tell me if I hurt you at all."

"Uh, yeah. About that." I bite my lip, and his eyes dart to my mouth. "Sometimes when people are enjoying each other intimately, a bit of pain can feel good."

He sits up, and I'm fully straddling him now. His arm is around my waist and the other is still tangled in my hair and massaging the nap of my neck. "You'd want that with me?"

"When and if you were ever wanting that with me."

"But..." He glances down at where I'm riding on his bulge. "What if you can't be with me like that?"

I swallow hard. I have no idea what he's working with. I know it feels big, but I shouldn't be making promises I can't keep. He very well could be too big for me to take without perforating my vagina or rearranging my organs.

"There are many ways for people to bring each other pleasure. If there are challenges, we can find a solution."

"I don't know how I am so lucky to have met someone like you," he says with reverence.

I'd like to say he was lucky if he had to wait four hundred years for me. But I feel just as lucky to be in his arms.

His eyes drop to my lips and in my mind I hear a faraway voice say, *I want to kiss you.*

"I hear something... in my head," I say, reaching for the owner of the voice.

"Osen?" he asks.

My first instinct was to think it's Osen, but it sounds like Flint's voice.

"I don't think so," I answer without confidence.

"What did the voice say?"

"I want to kiss you," I repeat the words.

Abruptly, Flint crushes me to his chest in a possessive embrace.

"What's happening?" I wheeze out.

"Sorry…" He pulls back. "It's just I was thinking I wanted to… and… you *heard* me."

"But isn't it only your mate match that can hear your thoughts?"

"Yes. But don't fret. Being someone's match doesn't mean you must mate with me. If you don't wish to have a bond, you can reject—"

I interrupt him. "Slow down. No one is rejecting anything. Let's just see how this all goes, yeah? If anything, I'm worried that I'm not a good fit for you. Perhaps you would be the one to reject me."

"Why would you ever think that?"

"I'm a witch, remember? And we don't know what's going on with me or my magic. We don't know how Rob might have messed with me. What if it's permanent and what if I'm damaged? What if I'm a danger to you? You mean too much to me to hurt in any way."

Flint announces, "I am kissing you now."

That shuts me the fuck up. Flint's taking the lead, and I don't mind one bit. His massive hands cradle my head gently.

He waits a beat for me to protest, and when I don't, he leans in with no further hesitation.

Slightly cooler, his lips are smooth yet firm as they press to mine. Both our eyes open, studying each other's responses.

I explore his mouth with mine, kissing his bottom lip and his top. He's a quick study and does the same with me. When I suspect he's ready, I let my tongue dart out and skim over his seam. He gasps and touches his tongue to mine.

It's all too much for him suddenly. He pulls back, but then presses his forehead to mine, staring into my eyes and breathing heavily as if he's running a marathon.

Something below grows more pronounced.

Holy bell towers. This guy is packing.

"I need to show you who I am. It's only fair, as you are my match. You should know before we proceed further with our courting."

"Courting?" I blush. "You make it sound so formal."

"I want to do what is right by you." He strokes my cheek and then lifts me off his lap like I'm nothing but a tiny thing and sets me down on the bed. "I should inform you I won't be able to give you children."

"I'm sorry if you had wanted them. But if I had wanted kids, I would have had them by now. I only need you, not children."

"And you need Maxum and Arran? Maybe even Calder? Or Osen, if he returns?" he asks. He doesn't sound jealous, but curious.

"Would that bother you if I were to share my affection?" I ask, because we should deal with this now if it will be an issue for him. I don't see breaking things off with Maxum and Arran, not willingly anyway.

"I don't mind. It's not uncommon among supernaturals to have multiple partners."

"Okay, good. I will do my best to be a good girlfriend," I promise.

"I shouldn't delay further." He stands, his face is devoid of everything except sadness. He believes I will reject him because of his appearance.

Slowly, he pulls over his head the tight-fitting, thin sweater he enjoys wearing.

His beautiful flesh is sculpted beyond my expectations. The

unusual tone and coloring only adds to his unique beauty. So far, other than on his head, he hasn't any body hair to speak of.

He pauses as his thick fingers find the waistband of his pants. The fabric at his crotch is stretched from what he's hiding.

He shuts his eyes tightly to block out my reaction. Poor sweetie. My heart aches for him. I don't know what he hides or what his true form is, but I know the fear of rejection.

Rob used to make me feel ugly with his degrading words. It's only with Arran's and Maxum's affection and appreciation for my body that has me starting to feel confident in my skin again.

No matter what's unveiled, I won't hurt Flint like that.

The pants fall down around his ankles.

I sit stock-still, stunned. Between two powerful thighs, not one but two generous hard cocks jut out toward me.

He's a doubleheader.

Whomever carved him had naughty things in mind. And I appreciate their skill. He's definitely large, but not to where I couldn't take him with a bit of stretching involved. The possibilities are fascinating.

"I'm sorry. I know I am not made right."

I snap out of my admiration, realizing that I haven't said a damned thing. I scramble off the bed and grab his hands. He finally opens his eyes and gazes down at me with fear.

"You are perfect."

"But I have two cocks. Males should only have one. They are too big for you, aren't they?"

"With the right preparation, they will fit. And well, if you were open to the idea, you could use both of them at the same time with me, satisfying me in ways other males can't."

"At the same time?" His eyes glaze over. "You mean one in your vagina and one in your anus?"

I nod, because I don't know yet if he's disturbed or intrigued.

Then, in my mind, I see him visualizing pumping into me. His cocks harden further.

"Yes, I like this idea." Flint takes a step backward. "But now, for my original form."

His huge wings unfurl from his back, and I squeak happily.

"You like my wings?"

"Very much," I say.

"Then if you accept me, I will not hide them from you anymore." Flint turns serious again and a sparkling shimmer washes over him, revealing an even taller form. He's thicker in his chest and hips, too. His wings have grown with his size, scraping the ceiling.

The biggest difference is in his larger face, head, and horns. His brows and cheekbones are more prominent. His smaller fangs have now become larger lower tusks, like an orc in my romance novels would have. He definitely would not be mistaken for a human.

"You are gorgeous," I say in awe.

"What? No. You lie." He turns his head, refusing to look at me. "This is the face and body that made Marie terrified and fall down the stairs. This version of me kills people."

I reach up and have to stand on my tiptoes to reach his cheek. "I don't know what was going on in her mind. But likely, she never knew someone as marvelous as you existed. Being surprised isn't the same as repulsion. Besides, I find you sexy."

"Sexy?" He whips his gaze back to me and studies my eyes. "Truly? You would want to still be intimate with me now that you have seen what I am?"

"Yes. Very much so." I want to run my hands over his body and bring him pleasure. "May I touch you?"

"Feel free to explore me… anywhere. Everywhere."

Frisky gargoyle. I like it.

I run my hands over his stone skin on his chest. Delightfully, I discover he feels like smooth marble, but yielding at the same time.

He watches with interest as I drop my hand over his thick, muscular torso. Not wanting to out myself as the perv that I am, I don't immediately grab onto his dual joysticks. I have to approach this tactfully. Warm him up to my touch first.

I run my hand over his bulky arm and step around his huge wings, grazing my hand over his batlike feature. The bones are solid and thicker than I expected, but his wings feel almost like thick leather. I'm surprised he could fly given how big he is.

He shivers when I place my hands on his back where his wings grow from his body. Maxum seemed to appreciate my touch there too, and Flint groans happily with my caress. I trail my fingers down, letting my nails lightly scratch his back until I reach his perky ass. I try to cup his bum, but my hands are too small to take the whole thing.

I walk back around, keeping contact with him the whole time. He stands so still for me he might as well be frozen into stone.

My hands slide over his waist and move toward his groin.

My fingers can barely circle around his first hard cock. Gently, I test his rigidity, and find he has just enough flexibility to make it easy on me.

Flint's huge hand takes hold of mine. I stop moving immediately, worried I've crossed a boundary he wasn't ready to cross. His firm grip doesn't allow me to release his cock, and I don't know what to do now.

24

BONDING

FLINT

*J*ade gazes up at me like I'm actually someone she finds attractive.

I only recognize the look because it's how Arran and Maxum look at her and how she looks at them.

How could she see me as anything other than a hideous monster?

Her soft warm hands on me are so much more than I ever dreamed possible. I collected all these soft pillows and fabrics to approximate the touch of someone who may have affection for me, but they are so far from being like the real thing that I'd laugh at myself right now if it weren't so sad.

Her reverent touch makes me question my belief that this is all for my benefit. Her eyes follow her hands, over my chest, stomach, and my sensitive wings.

When her hands finally circle my first cock, the moment overwhelms me.

I grab her hand. Thankfully, not too hard.

Her beautiful eyes widen, and she appears as frozen as I can become.

"I thought... I'm sorry," she whispers.

"It's just a lot of sensations," I breathe out. "I'm trying to stay calm while a frantic need almost takes over me."

"If it's too much, I can stop."

"No," I blurt. "I like it. But I am having urges."

She smiles, and there is a glimmer of mischief behind it. "What kind of urges?"

"Ones I've never had before. I wish to rip your clothes from your body and dive into you. But I'm afraid I'll be too rough, and I'll hurt you. I don't know how to please you and prepare you, as you mentioned earlier."

I hate that I am so inexperienced. I'm failing her again.

From the look on her face, she hears my thoughts. "I'm going to do that complete honesty thing again. So... sure, I like a guy who knows how to please me. But it's also a fantasy of mine to be with a guy who I can show what I like. That I will be his first experience."

"You actually desire a... virgin?"

"You were a quick study with the kissing. I'm sure you will be with everything else." Jade shrugs. "And you don't have any bad habits to break."

"So, then it's a good thing? It makes you, as you say, *turned on*?" Relief washes over me when she nods.

"Would you like me to show you my body now?" She blushes. "To see if you will be attracted to me, too?"

"I don't see how I couldn't like your body. It's connected to you—to your soul."

Tears well in her eyes. Through our developing bond, I finally sense her. She isn't upset with me, but overwhelmed by my acceptance of her.

Jade pulls off her t-shirt, revealing a silky bra. I'm thankful for the bit of modern knowledge I have and know what to call some things.

Her full breasts are pleasing to my eyes. I can see her nipples are hard. From Maxum's jokes, I know that is often a sign someone is sexually excited or they could be cold. Given the context, I suspect she is becoming excited.

When she drops her pants, she takes her underwear with them. Then she reaches back and unties her bra. The fabric falls to the floor, and I gaze upon her naked flesh.

"You are beautiful. Like a masterpiece painting by the artists of old. Full hips and breasts. Soft and inviting."

Her hand covers her waist. "I'm soft alright."

"And absolutely perfect because of it." I step closer, wishing to touch her—needing to touch her. "May I?" I reach out.

She takes my hand and places it over her left breast. I feel the wild thumping of her heart. "I need your hands on me, please."

I restrain myself from grabbing everywhere and feeling her all at once. I have seen mating dances before between people. There is a time and place for being frantic. Besides, I'm huge and overly strong, and this is my first time exploring a woman. I also want it to last for more than a few moments.

I allow my hand to slide down and cup her breast. She takes my other hand and places it over the exposed one. I feel the lovely weight of them in my hands and bounce them slightly. Then I run my thumb over her tight, pert nipples and she sucks in a breath.

"I like my nipples pinched or sucked as I'm about to climax," she tutors me.

I'm pleased she feels comfortable telling me this, and I log the information with top priority in my brain.

I walk around, admiring her backside. My hand grazes the full ass I had been naughtily cupping earlier. It's just as plump and perfect as I was hoping.

"May I see… between your legs?" I ask, my voice low.

Jade shivers and nods.

I lift her and place her on her back onto the bed. "I know

females often like to be licked, and I want to taste you." My huge hands spread her thighs wide.

Her skin is darker there, has folds, and it's glistening.

"My pussy is wet to prepare it for your cock. You can touch me there."

I use one finger to slide over her silky slit, and I instantly want my cock inside it. "It's so soft!"

"Move your finger up to the top. You will feel a bud of flesh." She bucks when I find it. For a moment, I worry I have pushed too hard. "That's it. I like that. That's my clit, and it likes to be touched, or licked and sucked."

I run my finger down and find her entrance. She tilts her hip and the tip of my finger slides into her. Slowly, I sink my thick digit all the way in and my woman groans, wiggling her hips.

"Yes," she whispers.

I pull out and slide in again, feeling inside her.

"You can add another finger to make me ready for you," she instructs.

"You want my cock this time?"

"If you'd like to give it to me."

I add the second finger, and she winces, whimpers, and then finally moans.

Instead of towering over her, I kneel and drag my cheek down her inner thigh. Removing my fingers, I find I cannot wait any longer before I taste my mate. Because that's who she is.

She is mine now. I will not let her go.

My long tongue snakes out and slithers up her center.

"Oh, Flint," my goddess whispers my name, and I'm an addict.

I need more. "Yes, say my name."

She glances down her body at my face, going in for another taste. My long, thick tongue first teases her hole and then swirls around her clit. "Flint, I'm going to come if you keep doing that."

"Then come on my tongue so I may taste your pleasure and memorize it."

"Damn, just like I thought. You're a fucking natural," she praises me.

I bury my face in her pussy, my tusks rubbing her outer folds, and suck on her bud. As I slip my finger back into her channel, she cries out.

Then she tenses. Her body bucks and trembles. Her vagina clenches around my finger and I'm rewarded with another dose of her slick hitting my tongue.

Jade is panting heavy breaths and reaching for my horns. "I want your cock inside me." When she finally gains purchase of my horns, she pulls me to move over her body.

I grip the bedding on either side of her head and pray to the Goddess that I don't hurt my love. "Maybe I should be on the bottom so you can control things? I'm afraid I will crush you, too."

"I trust you, but we can do that."

I roll over and lay nervously in the middle of my bed that suddenly doesn't look very big anymore, with my full gargoyle size sprawled out on it.

"Hmm, with your size…" She looks at my wings. "Do you think you would feel comfortable propped up slightly by the headboard? Like, almost sitting?"

I scoot up the bed and move pillows under my low back.

My cocks are standing straight up, craving to sink into her.

"Perfect." Her wide, expressive eyes lock onto my oddity, and she licks her lips. "I want to taste you, too."

"You do?" I don't know if I'll be able to handle her soft, warm, and talented mouth on my sex. I was nearly undone by her kisses and her touch drives me to insanity. Her taste is like the nectar of the goddess. I was worried about sinking into her sweet pussy, but now I worry I will lose control with her mouth. "Oh… okay."

I feel her magic brushing up against my heart and mind, making sure I'm actually okay.

Satisfied that I'm only nervous, she crawls over and gently strokes both cocks with her hand. "How does that feel?"

"Good. Incredible. Unbelievable." As I watch her caress my cocks, a bit of liquid leaks out of my tips. "I've never had that before."

"Uh, Flint..." she pauses. "Have you never had an orgasm before?"

"No." My skin heats with embarrassment.

Jade stares at my cocks for a moment. "You've never played with yourself?"

"I haven't had a sexual urge until you," I admit.

"Holy shit. I did this to you?" she whispers, then looks at me. "Okay. I should tell you what to expect. It might be overwhelming. It will probably feel like losing control. You sort of have to surrender to it. I've even blacked out before. Or seen stars. I don't know how it will feel for you, but I'm here for you. And please feel comfortable telling me how it feels. I get turned on with sexual talk. This is a safe space. At any point, if you want to stop, we can do that too."

"*You* are my safe space."

"I believe you're mine." She smiles. "I'm going to lick and suck on you now, and I won't mind hearing how good I make you feel, even if it's only sounds."

Her tiny tongue swipes up between my two cocks and flickers between the two heads.

"Goddess," I gasp.

"Oh, fuck, you taste so damned delicious." She licks and sucks on my head, trying to get more of my fluid. "Like rock candy!"

Then she slides my first cock into her mouth, gripping the base, while stroking the second with her hand. I grab the sheets in a vain attempt to hang onto my control.

She pumps her mouth on me and then swallows me down

until I feel the head hit the back of her throat and down. She swallows, and I cry out.

Is this an orgasm?

No. The impending wave recedes as I resist the urge to buck into her mouth and down her throat again.

She sucks on my second cock and gives it the same treatment.

"I don't know how much longer I can hold off if you want me inside your pussy," I warn her.

Her mouth pops off my cock, and she crawls up my body, giving me sweet kisses over my chest as she goes. When her sex is spread over my groin, she pauses and looks deep into my eyes. "Are you sure you want me as your first?"

"You are it for me. There will be no other," I tell her.

She kisses me without warning, and I taste the sweetness of my cocks' fluids on her tongue. It isn't as satisfying to me as her nectar. She pulls back and asks, "Does one of your cocks have more sensation than the other?"

"I don't think so."

"I can focus on one or the other in my pussy, but I'm willing to take one in my ass if you'd like that."

"At the same time?" I nod vigorously. "Yes, I want that. I want all of you."

"Okay, first I'm going to sink down your second cock to get it wet. And then I will attempt to take them in both holes. But I will have to go slow to stretch."

I nod and brace for the sensation of entering my lover.

She notches my second cock with her hand and squats down onto me, lovingly gazing into my eyes the entire time.

Her slick warmth envelops me. I moan as she slowly works herself down my shaft in waves.

Finally, she is seated as far as she can take me. She's sweating and panting.

I feel guilty that she's working so hard to please me, but her cute whimpers as my first cock rubs against her clit makes me realize she is pleased too.

She grinds her hips into mine, finding pleasure with one cock rubbing the outside and the other inside her.

"That feels so good, my goddess," I groan. My voice sounds nothing like what I am used to. I sound desperate and crazed and entranced.

"I could come again just like this," she says in small gasps.

"Then come on my cock," I say, my voice hoarse with need. The cosmos is pressing into me, and at any moment, I will burst apart in response. But I must wait until I know she is fulfilled.

"Flint, oh, Flint," she says, closing her eyes and thrashing on top of me. She is losing herself in the bliss I've given her.

Her channel grips me like a vise. Finally, I allow myself to hold on to her hips. But it isn't enough. I need to touch more of her. My hands move up, cupping her gorgeous, lush breasts. I give each nipple a squeeze as she mentioned she enjoys, and her orgasm hits another level.

Oh, I could do this for an eternity, keeping her riding this wave over and over.

Blinking her eyes, she looks dazed as if she's lost. She takes a few centering breaths and asks, "Ready?"

My second dick is coated with her slick. She lifts off it and notches herself with my first dick.

"I might need your help here." Her already flushed cheeks turn a brighter pink. "Can you guide your second cock into my ass?"

Instead of answering her, I have a creative thought that I hope she will enjoy. I move my hand over her full ass, then finger her wet pussy around where my cock is aching to dive into. She moans happily.

Satisfied I have enough wetness, I slide my thick finger into her asshole and she gasps and pushes up my body a bit. I curl my head down to sample her breasts with my mouth. With my free hand, I bring her nipple to my lips and suck, all the while preparing her ass for my cock with my thick fingers.

Jade looks down at the sight of her tit in my mouth. "I have to say your tusks dimpling my breast is probably one of the hottest things I've ever seen."

I suck and then graze my teeth over her sensitive flesh, and she is squirming again.

"I'm ready. Please, I need to be filled up by you," she begs.

I guide her hips back down, helping to take the work out of it for her. Her hungry pussy seems to be a magnet for my cock. And I place the head of my second cock in her back hole. Easing down, she gradually takes all of me.

Something in my mind snaps.

I pull back and buck up into her, fucking her from below.

"Yes," she chants over and over as I make her ride my cocks.

No longer satisfied being underneath, I spin both of us, still inside her. She's below me, as I pump into her… She appears so tiny like this. I don't know if her shocked look is good or bad.

I feel like a beast ravaging her as I thrust my weight and huge double cocks into her.

Her hair is spread out like a fan behind her like a halo.

Images of Jade broken in the alleyway, and then of Marie, flicker in my mind.

But I am a beast. A monster. I don't deserve this affection—this pleasure. I failed in the past. I failed to keep Jade safe. She almost died because of me. I wasn't powerful enough to sense the danger or magical enough to heal her wounds.

What if I'm damaging my mate now? My love?

No. I can't go there now.

I completely freeze into stone, mid-thrust.

"Flint?" Jade cries out. "What happened? What should I do?"

She wiggles to get away from me, but I've now trapped her on my cocks. The way I'm holding her shoulders so I could get leverage, brokers no room for her to escape me.

"I'm so sorry," Jade apologizes. "I pushed you too fast."

I want to tell her she isn't to blame. This is all because of me and my hangups.

"I don't know what to do." She reaches up and strokes my frozen face.

I need to move past this, but how? Perhaps if I kept going, I'd break free. I remember it was my fear of failure... of losing her. That I'm too much of a brute.

I remember our fledgling mental connection and try to communicate. *"Keep going."*

"You want me to keep going?" she asks, confused. When she senses my agreement, she says, "You are afraid of hurting me?"

I send her a mental agreement.

"Okay," she says and cants her hips to take me deeper and then tilts away. Fucking herself on me. "Goddess, this is weirdly hot, but I want you to unfreeze at some point. Because you haven't hurt me yet. I believe in you."

After several more thrusts, I feel myself returning to my fluid state. Her words have worked their magic over me.

She believes in me.

I should believe in myself too... after all these years.

"That's it, my love, come back to me," she coos.

My love? Does she feel for me what I feel for her?

My hips regain their motion, matching her rhythm.

A strange tingling at the base of my spine grows and grows, and my thrusts increase in intensity. And then it feels as though the entire universe has broken apart and reassembled just for my pleasure.

My mouth crashes down on Jade's and she greedily licks into my mouth, consuming and transmuting all my doubts and fears.

My body freezes with a tension I've never had before. But I'm not stone, I'm living magic at this moment.

I am free, and I am anchored only to her. My mate.

Pulsing fluid gushes into her, and she cries out with surprise, then pleasure.

"I love you," I yell as I spill into her, and she milks me until I'm dry.

My head collapses on the pillow by her head, and I fight to regain my composure.

Thankfully, I didn't crush her. I had braced myself with my elbows, but the effort is too much now. I am spent.

Rolling over onto my back, I feel my softening cocks slide out of her. She grunts and moans when I plaster her on top of my chest.

We lay there for several minutes, until she says, "That was… amazing sounds too shallow. Life changing?"

"Life changing is an excellent choice," I say as I rub circles over her soft back.

She squirms up my body and gives me a peck on the mouth between my tusks. "I should probably clean up." She worries her lip, as if she has more on her mind, then says, "I… I don't know how it happened so fast, and I'm sort of freaking out about it, but I love you too."

I never expected her to return my feelings so quickly, either. And although it would have saddened me, I would have understood if she never had felt the same.

If someone told me a week ago that I'd be in bed with my mate making love, I would have thought them insane.

However, here we are, blissful in each other's arms.

If I didn't wish to spend every moment with her for the rest of her life, I could finally die happy. As it is, I must wait to die happily years and years from now.

25

RETURNED

JADE

I've fallen, and I can't get up. No, I don't *want* to fall out of love.

I'm in a bit of daze after my experience with Flint. He's still in his full gargoyle form, and I'm teetering on top of his enormous chest with his massive arms keeping me in place.

After my confession of love, he remembers I need to clean up. He shifts to his smaller, more human-like form and pulls his wings into his back. I pout a bit at this, but I understand he's too big to move around easily if he remains in his true form.

Besides, I don't think he's used to showing that side of himself. I'm filled with pride that I was the one he felt he could be vulnerable with and the one he trusted to be himself and connect with.

Of course, the sweet gargoyle doesn't let my feet touch the floor. He carries me to the spacious bathroom off his bedroom. The walk-in shower is thankfully large enough for both of us. Flint steps in, turns on the water, and sets me down, blocking the stream until it warms up. Then he cleans us both. I do my best to wash him and maybe thoroughly hand clean his cocks.

He's quiet the entire time, meticulously touching every inch of my body to the point he's kneeling down and stroking the bottom of my feet.

"Flint! It tickles!" I try to dance away.

Instead of letting me go, he grabs my body, pressing me to him and leisurely licking between my legs with his long tongue to clean up his release.

I *might* be able to come again, but honestly, I'm exhausted. I don't even know if he wants to ramp me up again, but the sensations are wonderful, so I relax and enjoy his attention. He seems content just to be touching... and licking me. I have a brief flash of a fantasy that I wake in the mornings with him between my thighs, licking me as my very own orgasmic alarm clock.

"If I stay in the water any longer, I'll turn into a prune," I joke.

He pauses mid-lick and stares up at me in shock. Then he grins when he gets my meaning.

"That workout has me craving a snack," I say as my stomach grumbles.

"Alright, I suppose I should feed you... actual food." He chuckles and the deep, resonant sound delights me. "Do you get it? Because you tried to eat my cocks."

I giggle with him because he's so sweet and innocent that he doesn't even know that it's an old joke. "You are catching onto my humor quickly," I praise, because he is. None of the sexy stuff came naturally to him before me, apparently. I'm still coming to terms that I'm someone's only flame, especially when it's someone as wonderful and thoughtful as Flint is.

And it appears he's an extreme case of a demisexual—that he's only sexually turned on by someone he truly likes.

I'm honored and humbled that I'm this special person to

him. Out of all the people he's met in four hundred years, I'm the one he wants.

We are still making googly love eyes at each other when Flint carries me downstairs. It seems I might never have to walk again. I glance out the windows and see that it's almost dark out. I begin to worry since Maxum and Arran should have been home by now.

Sitting on the floor of the kitchen, Calder gives us a strange look when we arrive. Trouble and Sage are keeping him company and literally eating out of his hand. Sage is adorably munching on a carrot stem, and Trouble is blissed out of his mind with his banana slice.

"So, you two have officially mated?" Calder asks, his tone lacks any of his usual indignation. If anything, he sounds depressed.

"Officially?" I ask. *Did we? Are we?* I know nothing about real supernatural bonding, but I thought Maxum and Arran needed to bite me.

"Yes," Flint answers confidently.

Shiitake mushrooms. Did I just accidentally mate Flint for eternity? I don't regret being with him, but I hope we haven't rushed this.

"I am courting Jade, and our bond will soon solidify," he continues. "She has heard my thoughts, and I have heard hers."

Nervously, I fidget and hope to shield my nerves from Flint.

Calder glances over at me and reads me clearly with just a look.

Bless his soul, Calder doesn't draw attention to my fretting, but diverts it to another subject. "We should talk about Floofer."

"No." Flint sets me on the countertop and pulls out a variety of cheeses and freshly baked bread from the fridge and pantry.

"You don't even know what I'm about to say," Calder huffs.

"I'd like to hear him out," I announce. Flint needs to understand he can't make my decisions. Not that I'd expect him to. I know he's just trying to protect me.

He captures my hands and kisses my knuckles. "You're correct. I just don't want to put you in harm's way unnecessarily."

"I know, sweetheart. But harm's way is already my road."

"Truer words and all that," an unfamiliar voice says from the back patio door.

"Fuck!" Calder shoots to his feet and places himself between me and the intruder.

When I spin around from my perch on the countertop, I see not one, but three intruders. The first is a mousey looking male who I sense is Floofer in his human form.

Of course, one of them is Rob, and the other one is a woman. I'm guessing she's a witch.

Flint shifts back to his larger gargoyle form in anticipation of an attack.

"I hear you lost your trinket." Rob strolls inside, swinging a locket on a gold chain from his finger, as if he were attempting to hypnotize me. I can see from here that it isn't the same one my grandmother gave me.

"You didn't get me jewelry when we were together, so I don't think it's appropriate for me to accept any now," I sass.

"Oh, yes, I hear you are creating a little coven of supernaturals. But now, you are coming with me."

"Hmm, I don't think we're the right fit for each other," I say, like this isn't a standoff. "Trying to kill me was kind of a red flag that I can't quite ignore. Plus, you're a douche on top of being an abusive jerk, an idiot, and a lousy lay."

"You're the idiot who stayed here when you must have known I would be coming for you," he counters. "And did I really ever try to kill *you*? Or did I only try to rid you of the psychic parasite? You should be thanking me for that."

I think about what I know about his attacks. Rob might have

accidentally gone too far when trying to exorcize Osen both times. Maybe he hadn't meant to kill me. Not that he gets points for that. He still did all the other horrible things, and he's been using me for years to interrogate ghosts.

"So what's the play here? Why do you want me so badly?" I demand.

"You haven't figured it out yet? I suppose you have been too busy fucking monster cock to learn a damn thing."

Out of the corner of my eye, I see Flint opening the drawer that contains random weapons.

To distract from his movement, I shout, "Hey, jerk! No slut shaming. And it's only been a couple of days since I found out about all this shit."

The other man and the woman move into position, likely readying to attack.

The witch looks at me with pure hatred in her eyes. I start to worry if looks can kill, because I'd be dead soon with the way she glowers at me. What the hell did I do to her?

I shore up my mental shields because I sense magic gathering around Rob and his associates.

"Calder." Flint states, "Remember Rome."

What is that? Some secret code?

Keeping his eyes on our unwanted guests, Calder jerks his head in acknowledgment.

Then I recall what Calder said about intention. The magic has been bubbling inside me all day. The bonding I had with Flint actually seems to have settled the turbulence, and I wonder if I am able to defend myself with my magic. But I have no idea how to wield magic or what I can do other than channel spirits. What if I accidentally unleash some deadly power and hurt Flint, Calder, and my fur babies?

Combat magic is not an option then. But I do need to create protective bubbles, since I'm worried Rob will activate his spell on me, and I will lose myself and become his zombie to do his bidding.

I glance at the dark sky, and again I worry about why Maxum and Arran aren't back yet. Did something happen to them? Are they about to walk in unsuspectingly and get hurt?

Focus, Jade. I can't afford to spiral now.

Rob looks at Calder and Flint. "If you stand down, you don't have to get hurt. Just give us Jade and we'll leave."

"Right." Calder sneers, "You're just going to leave peacefully and let us be."

"You hate witches, so what do you care?" Rob looks him up and down with disgust on his face. "All of your group hate our kind. So, give her back."

"Nah. I think I'll keep her just to piss you off," Calder taunts.

"Wrong answer, pigeon," Rob mocks.

Then all hell breaks loose.

The witch shoots an energy ball at Flint, but fortunately, he doesn't seem fazed.

Formerly known as Floofer, throws actual daggers at Calder. They look like they are made from iron. He curses as he bats them away faster than any human could.

Rob murmurs a chant, and I feel a wave of pressure roll over my body. He collapses the first level of protection, my auric bubble.

He chants in some strange language even louder when his first attempt to reach inside my mind fails.

The pressure builds until I fear he will pop my energetic shield around my body.

"Calder, now!" Flint shouts as he leaps into the air and, with his expansive wings, lands in front of the phoenix, blocking our attackers.

Thank goodness for high ceilings in the open great room.

Calder snatches me up and races down the hallway.

I want to protest that we can't leave Flint behind, but I can barely fight for my consciousness.

I'm losing the psychic battle with Rob.

What? You mean a five-minute training session doesn't make me a super-witch with unlimited powers? All the books and movie montages have lied?

However, I'm proud that I am able to fight off Rob at all. I just don't know how long I can hold out.

"It's okay. I got you," Calder whispers.

My mental shields are crumbling as Calder places his hand on a door I hadn't seen before near Maxum's room. He mumbles a chant, and the door opens. It shuts behind us, and we are in total darkness. I can't see a damned thing, I only know we are moving down stairs from the jostling.

He must figure out that I'm scared because his wings catch fire, not huge flames, but a low burn and enough for me to see.

My last shield is crumbling to Rob's will. I grip Calder tighter.

The last thing I register is that we are running down an underground tunnel that's cool and damp. And we keep going deeper.

BUNKER

CALDER

I should have known Floofer was going to return... with fucking Rob.

We don't seem to get any breaks.

With Jade in my arms, I race down to our bunker, nicknamed by Maxum as *Rome* after their ancient catacombs. I sense she is losing her psychic battle. She's fighting the spell Rob tried to activate to make her a puppet for his use, and his spells are eating at her fledgling defenses.

I shiver, thinking about what he has done to her in the past. I know all too well how devastating it is to lose one's power to another.

For Jade, this means he's forced spirits into her body... into her mind. It's a disgusting violation that raises the hackles of my protective nature.

"Hang on," I encourage her, even if she might not hear me. "Keep fighting."

I risk looking down at her while I race down the steps. She

winces with pain. It is no simple thing to fight a spell at all, but one that already has its roots in you. It's near impossible.

I hate leaving Flint behind, but if anyone can fight them off by himself, it's Flint or Maxum. They are both naturally resistant to witch and warlock spells—most of them, anyway. I also know he wouldn't survive emotionally if they took Jade.

Hopefully, Maxum and Arran show up any second to help.

I try to pull on our pack connection, even if it isn't a formal, magically bonded one. Often in a pinch, such as the time in the alleyway, the others can sense when something is wrong with one of us.

The ground rumbles under my feet. Debris shakes loose from above me, raining down over Jade and me.

Picking up my pace, I worry that the battle above ground might bring the tunnel down upon our heads. We'll be safer in the reinforced bunker. We just have to reach it.

Another earth rumbling magical blast makes the tunnel quake. Behind us, I hear a collapse. A plume of dust wraps around us as I reach the bunker door, and I quickly chant our pack's spell to unlock it and rush inside the panic room.

When I see what sits in the center of the room, I jolt to a stop with surprise, bile rising in my throat. I can't process what I see, not yet. I have to keep my shit together. Ignoring the disturbing sight for now, I slam the door shut behind me and seal it with a warding spell.

I set Jade down on one of the large cots we have in here. She doesn't seem to register anything around her. She makes small noises as she fights her internal war.

Maintaining my focus on her, I keep my back to the horrid sight in the center of the room. I kneel beside her and hold her hand, wishing I had more magic to help her repel the spell that's working to take her over.

Suddenly, she goes limp, and I fear she has finally lost her battle.

"Jade?" I call, actually hoping to hear a sassy retort from the witch.

"How may I be of service, master?" she says, her voice is flat and void of emotion.

Fuck! I launch to my feet and pace back and forth beside her cot. I don't enjoy seeing her like this.

Quickly, I realize that this might be a unique opportunity. She believes I am her master. Perhaps she will be in a state to answer questions she doesn't have access to otherwise.

I sit down on the edge of her cot. With one of my rarely used talents, vocal mimicry, I ask, in Rob's voice, "Do you have a spirit with you now?"

"He won't come forward."

"Is it Osen?"

"Yes, he's hurt and hiding."

My chest aches with the thought of Osen still hurting. I thought in death he could rest, but apparently that blessing is not for him.

Time to get answers—for all of us.

"Do you remember the other times you've helped me?"

"Yes," she answers succinctly.

"Were you there when Osen died?"

"No."

Okay... one-word answers aren't getting me very far. I must use open-ended questions from now on. I've never been good at this sort of thing. I'm not the interrogator. This is the sort of job that Maxum or Osen used to do.

There's another rumble from above. I take heart that it likely means Flint is still alive and fighting.

"Do you know how spirits come to you?" I ask the spellbound Jade.

"You send the spirits to me so you can speak to them."

Damn, I hate pretending to be that asshole, Rob. "What happens after I talk to them?"

"After you finish asking questions, you take them from me. You absorb their power... their magic."

This explains why Rob has become powerful in unusual ways. He's stealing magical souls.

"What sort of beings have you hosted?"

As if listing a boring grocery list, Jade says, "Witches, warlocks, fae born, shifters, demons—"

"Okay," I cut her off. It's what I suspected. Osen wasn't a fluke. For some reason, Jade can channel the spirits of supernaturals, which should be impossible. Or maybe it's as Maxum says and we just never knew about someone like her before.

"When you are *not* under this spell, you don't remember doing this?"

"You told me to forget. Do you want me to remember now?" Jade asks with a hint of confusion. I'll give her credit. Her mind and reasoning processes are strong enough to be able to formulate a deduction even while under a spell.

"Yes, I want you to remember everything that's ever happened to you after this conversation," I answer, hoping I can snap her out of this state soon.

Something occurs to me. If Osen is still with her and hiding, maybe I can call him forth. "Osen? It's me, Calder. I need to talk to you."

Jade intakes in a sharp breath. Her eyes, that had been closed this entire time, pop open. They are the swirling shadows of black irises of an incubus... *Osen.*

I doubt our witch can fake something like this.

Our witch? Ugh. I think I'm definitely maybe falling for her charms.

"Osen?"

"Calder? What's going on?"

I'm not sure how much he needs to be reminded of. Does he remember his death? Jade? Anything?

"What is the last thing you remember?" I ask instead.

He frowns as he struggles to collect his thoughts and perhaps his very spiritual essence. "I... I was in a witch's body." He lifts Jade's arm and looks at it. "I suppose I still am linked to her. Jade, is it? And then... we went to the alley where I died. We both saw her there during my murder, but... we realized that person might not be her. Then Rob attacked and drained me. It felt like he was ripping me to pieces, trying to separate my magic from my soul. How am I still here?"

"I pulled you... well, Jade, out of his grasp. Then Rob took off, leaving all three of us in the alley to die."

He struggles to sit up and grasps at me in desperation. "Oh, no. I didn't know you'd died again. How bad was the regeneration? Dammit. I didn't know it would spiral out of control like that," Osen says, actually sounding remorseful for his actions, which is a rare thing.

"Fortunately, I was able to recover without a death."

"Thank Goddess." He breathes in deeply and relaxes his grip on my arm. But then he leans forward as if to kiss me.

"Osen. No." I pull away. I know he forgets what his touch does to me. I can't experience that right now, not when I'm on the verge of losing my mind. We haven't had that since my last rebirth. Besides, I'm afraid he might get carried away. "Your powers... I can't... Also, it doesn't feel right to kiss with her body. She didn't give you permission."

"Fine." He sighs, as if I'm being difficult. But I won't use someone's body against their will—even my enemy's. "Sometimes, I forget how things are."

"That isn't your fault."

"Wait. We snuck out when you all were gone," he reasons. "So, how did you know Jade and I were in the alley?"

"My phoenix power. I sensed her potential death moment."

Osen nods and then realizes the next issue. "But how did Rob find us?"

"Apparently, Jade's pendant had a tracking spell. It was also slowly draining her power to keep her weak and malleable."

The earth shakes again, and Osen glances at the ceiling. "What is that? And why are we in Maxum's lake house in the bunker?"

"Uh, longish story. The guys rescued Jade and me. We all retreated to Maxum's lake house, but we accidentally brought a spy disguised as a magical creature with us. The spy escaped, then returned with Rob and another witch. They attacked. Rob triggered Jade's spell, and I got her out of there before she could be taken."

"You?" Osen shakes their head. "I thought you didn't like the witch. You hate all witches."

"She's not so bad. And the guys are sort of falling in love with her. I won't be blamed for losing her."

He narrows his eyes at me, detecting my deflection of my own feelings about the witch. "I'll let that excuse slide... for now." Osen rubs their temples, likely feeling the residual pain of Jade's fight against the spell. "So the three of them are up there fighting while you hide away down here?"

I grit my teeth. I don't like his implication that I'm hiding. "It's only Flint up there. Unless Maxum and Arran have returned by now."

"The witch seems to be regaining her wits... Her soul is fighting to push me aside and surface," my incubus grunts out as if he is fighting her return.

"Osen?" Weakly, Jade's voice sounds like herself.

"It's me, *witch*," Osen says back to her out loud.

"So, I'm just the witch again, huh?" she asks, sounding hurt.

Their gaze travels back to me. It's Osen, watching for my reaction.

"Is there a reason for you to no longer call Jade by her name?" I ask, wearily.

"I... I don't like being this way. Trapped. Weak," Osen admits.

"I don't think any of us are happy with you being dead," I say. "But I'm done blaming Jade for this situation."

A tiny, shy smile graces her face. "Thank you." She looks around, taking in the room. Luckily, I'm still shielding her from the horror that's right behind me. "Are we in a bunker?"

"Yeah. We're locked in a panic room of sorts," I say.

"Talk about a forced proximity trope," she mutters.

The witch makes no sense to me half of the time. "What?"

Another earthly boom rattles the bunker.

Jade's green eyes shine through the shadow of Osen's presence. "Where's Flint?"

"He's still dealing with our invaders."

"We need to help him! If anything happens..." She can't continue as her voice chokes up with emotion, already grieving for the gargoyle.

"If anyone can survive a witch attack, it's Flint," Osen calms her.

"But we know that there's something more going on with Rob. He seemed to have incubus shadows. What if they use a freezing spell on him, like in your memory?"

"He's tougher than he appears and resilient to most magics," I assure her. "I wouldn't have risked leaving him otherwise. Besides, they all would be upset if I let something happen to you."

Reluctantly, she nods and doesn't argue.

"Uh," I begin, then pause, rubbing the back of my neck nervously. "Osen, I need to take advantage of this opportunity to talk to you. I regret not doing so before."

"Um..." Jade hesitates, then finally seems to make up her mind. "If you guys want to... like touch or kiss, I'd be okay with that. Calder, not that I'd presume that you would want to... because... it's me in here too. But I'll try to give you some space."

"You would do that for Osen?" I ask, shocked by her generosity. It's no small thing she offers.

"For Osen, but for you as well." Jade worries her bottom lip, and my gaze catches on her lush mouth.

Earlier, during our training session, I'd been tempted to kiss her. But now, it's confusing. I don't want to mix up my feelings for Osen with what might happen with Jade on its own.

"Thank you for the offer, Jade," Osen says, using her name once again. "But Calder and I no longer had that sort of dynamic when I was alive."

"Oh, sorry." She pulls away.

I see her spirit retreat, feeling foolish for offering.

"Hey, Jade." I reach out and grasp her hand. "I appreciate it."

All three of us seem to be startled by my gesture. Sure, I've touched her before. But it was in the context of rescuing her from Rob both times. Oh, and I suppose she fell on top of me when Flint knocked her down. Then I hugged her when she was upset, but this is a kind touch that I don't often offer to anyone.

"I'm going to try not to pay attention now, and you can talk freely. And the offer still stands for any affection you need to show each other." Jade closes her eyes, and when they open again, it's clear Osen is back in control.

27

VOYEUR

JADE

*N*ow I feel a bit like a creep for offering my body for their reunion. At least Calder didn't seem to take offense.

Osen, however, seemed strangely opposed to the idea. I'm trying not to dip my consciousness into his. I don't want to go back into any of his memories. Now that I know they are memories and not some crazy dream I came up with, it doesn't feel right to see them anymore. My gut tells me it has to do with his powers, and that perhaps things weren't great between them when Osen died.

Except, even though I'm trying to block out what's happening, I can still hear and see Calder.

"I, uh, I want to say I'm sorry for how I pulled away after my last resurrection," Calder begins. His icy blue eyes seem to melt when he looks at Osen. Part of me craves for him to look at me this way. But I'm being greedy.

"It's understandable," Osen says, my voice coming out deeper and with a hint of an accent to match how he sounds in my mind. "You were paralyzed then. I'm sure my magic reminded you too much of that torture."

"It did. But I should have gotten over it," Calder argues and rubs his eyes with the heel of his hands. "Why didn't I just push past the memory?"

"You might have, if we had more time," Osen's voice holds so much sorrow. "But I messed that all up. I failed you. I failed us. I'm so sorry, my love."

Emotions overcoming him, Calder clasps our face and kisses my lips… kisses Osen. Years of repressed passion and love pour into us.

Calder peppers kisses over my cheeks and forehead. "I missed you so fucking much."

My heart pounds, and my sex tingles. Osen's turned on. To be fair, I am too.

Then I feel Osen's shock. He didn't expect to be turned on and have his lover still able to move. He believed his incubus feeding shadows would paralyze Calder like they had always done when he was alive.

Was that why he was hesitant to touch Calder when I offered?

I mentally nudge Osen to respond instead of him remaining in shock.

He catches Calder's frenzied mouth with his, and they kiss. Their tongues tangle and they hold each other so tightly I can't help but to feel like a third wheel. And damn if these guys don't know how to kiss.

When they gasp for air, Osen speaks to me, *"I never got to kiss him like this. So freely."*

"Never? Because of your powers?"

"Yes." A wave of gratitude hits me square in the chest. *"Thank you, Jade. But I need to pull away before I'm tempted to take over your body and do more than kiss."*

I don't know what to say to that. Part of me wants to be generous and offer myself for them to connect more. The other part doesn't want to be a passenger in my own body. While I'm debating what to do, Calder comes to his senses.

"We should slow down." He presses his forehead to mine, closing his eyes, likely imagining that it's just Osen with him now.

"I love you," Osen says. "I didn't say it all these years, and I should have shouted it every day."

Calder sucks in a breath. "I love you too. It breaks my heart that I've lost you."

"I'm not gone completely yet," Osen reminds him.

"But how long until you move on from this plane?" Calder asks.

"I don't know, but it doesn't feel like I'm going anywhere for a while." Osen looks down at my hands, turning them over and studying our shared body. "I would have thought I would have been exorcized when Rob attacked Jade. I think it might be her who must cut some sort of tether to let me go."

He's probably right, but I don't like knowing I have that kind of power over someone's soul—holding onto it.

I try to remember how I released the spirits in the past, but the returning memories are fuzzy. It's there, just out of reach. Calder's suggestion, when he pretended to be Rob, seems to have opened the door. Perhaps, over time, I'll be able to remember all that happened under Rob's spell.

Osen's emotions are crashing into him again, and he embraces Calder in a tight hug. Calder melts into me and strokes my back lovingly. The love that these two have for each other resonates in my own heart. I just wish I could fix the broken pieces.

But right now, all I can offer is this... this strange moment, deep underground, wondering how many more moments we have left.

Something different tugs on my heart, and it isn't the scene we're playing out here.

"I think it may be Flint. Or even Maxum or Arran," Osen tells me mentally, reading my thoughts.

My concern for my guys puts me in a spin. They should have been here by now. At least Flint should have come for me if he won. I want to reach out using our developing mental link, but I don't want to be a distraction if he's still fighting. But what if he didn't win the battle?

"Jade, don't," Osen says softly.

"I'm sorry. My brain is being too loud for you to enjoy this moment," I convey inside my mind.

"That's not what I meant. And I'm not complaining... I wouldn't have this moment if it weren't for you."

In the shadowscape, Osen appears standing in front of me. He's in his shadowy form as usual, and I'm barely able to see what he might have looked like when he was alive.

"What are you doing here with me? You should spend this time with Calder," I say, with a bit of reprimand.

In our private moment in my mind, he caresses my face and hugs me. *"Until we know what's happened, we can't worry. But our guys are tough."*

"Our guys... You don't mind me being with them anymore?" Previously, he had expressed a hint of envy.

Osen sighs heavily. *"I'm a jealous, possessive prick. Not sure if you picked that up before."*

"There might have been a few crimson flags waving around," I tease.

"Ah well, I see in your mind that you finally broke Flint open like a geode, revealing a sparkling center. I was never able to do that. And Arran? He's accepting his beast, which is healing his pain. Maxum never wanted me for more than my friendship and an occasional fuck." Osen tilts his head and stares into my soul.

His shadowy appearance takes form. He's still not completely whole, but I can see his eyes are dark gray, not just shadows. And of course, he's as handsome as I expected, with a fit, but not overly muscled, build.

I gasp. *"I can see you."*

"With your bonding with Flint, and the moment with Calder, I have enough power briefly to show you myself, before I will need to rest and restore my magic again."

"Why show me yourself now?" I ask.

"You gave me a moment with Calder that I hadn't had before. Ironically, it took you to be my open heart so I could be present with my love. Thank you for helping to heal his wounds, too."

"I'm not really doing anything." I shake my head.

"You are being you. Genuine, and that's enough." Osen corrects himself, *"No, that's exactly what my pack needs. What I need. So... thank you."* He leans down and presses a sweet kiss to my lips.

"I have to go for now," Osen says and fades away from the shadowscape.

I open my eyes and find I'm still embracing Calder. "Uh, Osen had to rest. It's just me. Sorry." I pull away from the embrace.

However, Calder doesn't let me go. He tightens his grip.

"Thank you, Jade," he whispers over the side of my neck.

Goosebumps rush down my flesh.

When he releases me and leans back, he traces a thumb over my cheekbone. "I'm sorry I was so unpleasant before."

"It's not a big—" I begin, but he cuts me off by placing his thumb over my mouth.

His eyes stare at my lips, and his hand on me. "No. Don't be dismissive of your amazing patience with my behavior."

His thumb traces my bottom lip lightly. I feel he's debating if he should kiss me. If it were only up to me, I'd lean forward and take the lead, but it isn't.

It sounds as if his choices were taken from him during his last death, and I won't pressure or force him into anything. Especially not with me, a witch.

Calder blinks a few times, shaking himself out of whatever

lustful thoughts he might have been having. He stands up and walks over to the center of the bunker.

He had been blocking something from my view this entire time. I stand, unsteady on my feet and walk over to the glass and metal casket-sized box.

"What the fuck is this?" I hiss. "Is that… *him*?"

28

STUCK

MAXUM

*M*y other contacts don't give me much more information than Mal and Dwayne did.

Arran is restless, and I don't blame him. His bond with Jade is incomplete, and he won't be settled until they formalize the mating process. *If* they formalize it.

First, we need her to explain her name, and why she lied about her age.

Once again, I remind myself that information might not be accurate.

"It's getting late. We should go back." Arran glares at the evening sky like it's his enemy.

"I have one more person I'd like to visit and then we can return." A string is plucked at the back of my mind as soon as I say this. Someone has crossed my wards. "Fuck."

"What?" Arran grabs my shirt collar and growls in my face. "Is it Jade?"

"My ward alarm was triggered." My eyes lock on the place I had planned to portal out, and I race toward it.

Arran is on my heels and in his full werewolf berserker mode by the time we get across the street and into an alley. Thank fuck no human is around to see him. We don't need to be reported for revealing our supe natures to the mortal realm. He's been caught too many times already, and the authorities will punish him if it happens again.

We rush through the portal and stare at the lake house. It was reckless to portal directly to my home, but time is of the essence when my sanctuary is potentially threatened. Besides, my home has already been compromised by the enemy.

There's an actual magical skirmish happening on my front lawn. The area is about an acre of mostly open space, dotted with large ponderosa pines. If I'm correct, by the look of the damage, this battle began at the back of the house, or perhaps inside.

Flint is limping but throwing a boulder at someone who looks very much like the bastard Rob. Blasts of magic hit Flint's back, and he staggers from the impact. When I look at where the blast originated, it's just as Mal and Dwayne said. Sloan and Galiana are indeed Rob's companions.

"Where's Jade?" I mutter. "Or Calder?"

Arran's berserker shakes his head, telling me he doesn't see them either.

I don't appreciate trespassers... especially witches and warlocks threatening my pack and my mate.

"Let's take these assholes down," I snarl.

Arran's berserker charges right at Rob.

Bummer, I was going to call dibs. Oh well, if he has issues, I'll tag in.

Sloan. This is the dickhead who snuck into my fucking sanctuary—who tricked Jade into staying in her home. Spied on her. On us.

Yeah. I could definitely satisfy my bloodlust with his death.

I reach out with my gift to read him, then I plan to scramble his brains. Ah, Mr. Fucking Floofer has great mental shields. It will take time for my magic to smash them down, but I will make it happen. Then I'll see what's inside and scramble his memories and personality so damned much that he believes he actually is a hamster, after all.

I storm over to Sloan's hiding spot behind a tree trunk.

Righteous anger rises in me—mostly at myself for believing I could leave Jade today with Floof-Sloan escaped and still missing. He likely had been watching and knew this would be a suitable moment to attack.

Perhaps to snatch up Jade?

Sloan spins, finally realizing that I'm almost on top of him. His eyes widen and the magical blast he intended to lob at Arran hits me square in the chest, burning my shirt.

It stings a bit. He's either weakening due to all the magic he's thrown around or he's not that powerful to begin with. Probably both. And sure, most spells bounce off of me, but that doesn't mean it can't be painful when they do.

I swat the flames out on my shirt, then grasp his head. He squeals like a rodent. That's a little too on the nose.

Tightening my hold on his head, my magic works double time to crack his shield. The witch, Galiana, hits me from behind with a blasting spell. Wow! I would have thought she'd have more punch, but maybe she has been exhausted already.

It makes me believe the witches' claim that supernaturals aren't the only ones suffering horribly from the disappearing magic in the realms. Perhaps witches are being hit even harder than we are and won't admit how bad it is.

Perhaps the excuse that they believe that supes are depleting magic by just our existence does have a more desperate origin. Weaker witches are likely to be hit harder than those with more innate power.

It makes me wonder if they expect Jade to have more power

than they do, and if they wish to harness and manipulate her magic for themselves.

Not on my watch.

My vengeance for them having dared to invade my home gets the better of my control, and I hear the telltale sound of cracking a skull. I refocus and realize that I haven't killed Sloan… yet. However, he goes into shock and drops his shields.

Well, that worked out nicely.

Fortunately, Galiana is busy assisting Rob against Arran and Flint, so I now have a moment to probe into Sloan's mind and rummage through it for information before he dies.

Unfortunately, it's a freaking mess in his pathetic mind. He's pretty upset about dying and all the pain. *Boohoo.*

Maybe he shouldn't have messed with a demon or his witch.

When I search for his memories of Jade, I see flashes of her. He watched on as Rob interrogated the ghosts they had placed inside her.

Sloan would shift and sneak out of the room when the guinea pig and rabbit were asleep and go through Jade's computer. He'd send emails of information that she had accidentally channeled from Rob's victims and written into her books, notes, or journals. I also see he would watch Jade sleep and ask the spirits questions when Rob wasn't around.

She truly had no clue what was happening to her or who was spying on her right under her nose.

I dig for Sloan's connection to Rob. From there, they met during a secret Anti-Supernaturals Organization meeting. They had conspired to become major players in the movement. Galiana was already one of their leaders, but Rob has been slithering his way up to the top by being her lackey. Then several faces of the ASO members flicker through my mind, and I make a point of memorizing them.

I see the trio plotting to target Jade. I also get a vague impression Galiana believed there's something unusual about our witch. Something… *other*. Galiana first wanted to destroy

Jade because of whatever she is, but then realized they could use Jade for her abilities before they finally eliminated her.

Why is Galiana so intent on destroying Jade? What is different about Jade from any other witch?

I try to press for more, but Sloan's heartbeat falters and I feel his soul slip away. I wish I had gotten more out of him, but he was a minor player even among the three of them. He was expendable enough to live at Jade's home during the last couple of years. Honestly, he was only a grunt. The real power player is Galiana.

When I turn back to the ongoing fight, Flint and Arran are cornering the witch and warlock against the side of the house.

Galiana sees that I'm free to turn my ire on her, and that they are officially outnumbered. She chants and throws out her hands. A portal opens up, and they both race through, escaping our wrath.

Flint collapses onto the ground and grunts in pain. The warlocks and witch did more damage than I would expect to the magically resistant gargoyle.

Arran is in terrible shape too. Half his berserker's fur is burnt off. Hopefully, a shift into his human form will heal most of the major damage.

I'm fucking losing my mind with worry, since I don't sense them in the house or the nearby forest. "Where's Jade and Calder?" I ask, trying to not lose my wits.

"Rome," Flint says.

"The bunker?" My eyes widen. "Fuck!"

"Rob activated his spell on Jade," Flint explains. "It wasn't safe for her to be around the warlock."

He couldn't have known not to send Calder down there, so I remind myself not to be upset with him. It makes sense on a strategic level to have the phoenix take her there. But Calder might freak out with the sight of Osen's body and take it out on Jade.

"Arran, can you shift?" I ask, because I assume he's going to want to go down there with me. I need him to heal up and be in his more logical human form to help Jade and Calder.

He howls in agony as he shifts. Painful burns have healed a bit, but his usually gorgeous naked body looks fucking rough, and I wish I could do something to help him. But I can't even offer him a salve before we find Jade. He wouldn't accept it even if I did.

"Flint, can you walk?"

"For Jade? Yes." He struggles to find his feet, and I give him a hand. Not that I can mind-read the gargoyle, but I sense something has changed about him.

"I can't reach her mind," he says.

"What? Why would you be able to—" He must have realized she is his mate match, and they have bonded on some level.

The same realization must have occurred to Arran as he asks, "Did you... were you... with Jade?"

"Um, yeah," Flint blushes his bright peach.

"Goddess." Arran is shocked, but not upset. "I'm happy for you."

"I'm happy for all of us," Flint says. "But first we need to ensure our mate is alright."

"True." I pull Flint's massive arm over my shoulder and help him walk through the front door and to the bunker's access door. After chanting to disable the first warded spell, I continue to help Flint down the wide stairwell. "I should tell you... Osen's body is down there."

"What?" Flint is downright frantic. He now knows what he's accidentally done to Calder. "Why did you keep his body instead of securing him in the ice caves until we could arrange a funeral?"

"I... I don't know. Well, you'll see. Something odd is going on."

"We aren't supposed to keep secrets. Look what it did for Osen," Arran reprimands.

"I know." Then I stop moving with the sight just ahead. "Dammit."

The tunnel has collapsed. My heart beats wildly, imagining Calder and Jade never even making it down to the room. What if this crushed them? What if they are underneath all this rubble?

Flint urges me forward, and I panic because I had added extra wards to the bunker to not allow portaling in and out of it. I remind myself that might also be why we can't sense Calder and Jade.

Calder would have a nightmare of a time if he died under the weight of the rocks. If we couldn't dig him out, he would keep dying over and over until his magic was exhausted. Then he would finally experience his last death.

Part of him wants to go. I know this. He hasn't been the same since he came back from his past rebirth. But I will not let him leave us so easily. And I will not allow him to suffer an ongoing death like that.

If they are under this mountainous weight of debris, I also need to get Jade's broken body out.

I won't be the same if she is lost.

Arran appears strangely unaffected. Has he finally shut down emotionally?

"I don't think she's under all that. My wolf says he still feels she's alive."

The pessimist in me, who has seen centuries more devastation than the wolf shifter, doesn't argue that maybe she isn't dead *yet*, but she may still be dying.

At the blockage, Flint falls to his knees since his injured leg barely works and tosses huge pieces of rock behind us.

"Wait, we don't know if they are under this." I grab the current small boulder from his hands and set it down. "We should check the bunker first. I should be able to portal just outside of the room, if it's clear on the other side."

We move back. I open a portal and sigh with relief when I

see the bunker door. First challenge down. Now, to see if they made it safely inside. Then to see what condition they both are in.

I leave the portal open, since we may have to retrace our steps if our people aren't in here.

Chanting my unlocking spell, I crack open the door and hear Calder cursing.

Not good.

The door slams back shut, and I try to push it open again.

"Maxum?" Calder asks and then releases his hold after peeking around the door and seeing my face.

Flint and Arran storm inside after me. We all stand in shock at the sight.

Jade is lit up like a candle, her aura so bright she looks to be on fire. Her eyes appear unseeing, although they are cast toward Osen's glass casket. As if seeing him this way has triggered her, but she is no longer herself.

"Jade?" Arran calls, stepping closer.

"Don't," Calder warns.

"Why not?" Arran snaps.

"Because you'll get zapped," Calder says, rubbing his hand. "Her magic finally manifested when she saw Osen. Not sure what the fuck sort of magic this is."

I can't make horns or tails of the kind she has either.

Flint limps closer to Jade. I'm not sure what the hell he's doing. He's in no condition to take any more damage.

"She needs an anchor to draw her out of this. I feel her mind swirling," Flint says.

When I let myself skim her mind, I sense it, too. "Do you have a suggestion?"

"Don't come near the witch," Jade says.

"Osen?" I ask.

He whips her head to stare at me. His shadows are in her eyes. The shadowtendrils undulate, reaching for the glass. His spirit wants to return home.

"How did you return?" I ask.

"Her magic can feed my soul… my magic. With her, I can take my revenge… for this." He points to his body on display. Then he steps toward the door.

At first we allow him to maneuver by us, because he might lash out. It could hurt Jade. But then I realize he might hurt Jade more if he gets away.

"No." I step in his way.

Osen narrows their eyes.

It surprises me when Calder jumps in front of him. For a moment, I wonder what he plans on doing? Will he aid in Osen's revenge or stop him?

"You aren't going anywhere with Jade," Calder growls.

"But with her power and my ability, we could kill them all," Osen argues.

"No. Give control back to Jade right now." Calder fires up his wings, displaying how serious he is.

"But she doesn't know what to do with it." Osen takes a step closer, challenging.

"You got yourself killed. You can't risk her like this. She is too important to her mates."

"To you?" Osen asks Calder, sounding concerned for the first time.

"Yes, even to me," Calder admits. "I don't know if I want to pursue something or not, but I want her alive. *Your pack* wants her alive and healthy. And with you in charge, that doesn't seem likely."

The power emanating off Jade lessens. Osen reaches out and kisses Calder. I don't like him using Jade this way, but maybe if he does this, he'll leave her be.

The magic sputters out, and Jade passes out in Calder's arms. The gentle way he looks at her and holds her, I realize Jade not only captured Flint's heart today, but something has shifted between the phoenix and our witch.

"We can't stay here," Arran says as he collects Jade from

Calder. He winces as her body presses against him, agitating his burns.

"You're right. This place is compromised now," I say and hold out my arms for Arran to hand over Jade. "Let's collect our things and get out of here before Rob returns."

"But where will we go?" Flint asks. "This was the last place we had left."

"There's one place... it might solve all our problems... if they let us stay. Finding out what sort of witch Jade is, how to use her power, and a place to hide off the map."

29

ALL WRONG

ARRAN

*a*fter we get back up the tunnel to the house, I shift back and forth again to help the healing process along and do a quick sweep of the house to make sure no one is lurking.

I throw on a t-shirt and sweatpants and pack up Jade's things from the office, knowing she wouldn't want to leave them behind.

I really love our home here, and I wish we could have stayed longer. But with our lifestyle, I've never been able to set down roots for long. With the ASO and the witch attacks escalating and the missing supes, we haven't felt settled for a long while.

My wolf and berserker whine within my chest as we all wish to hold Jade, but Maxum has her resting unconscious on the bed in his room as he packs up Jade's clothes and his own.

When I enter the bedroom, he's finished up, zipping up his duffle and staring at our witch. I observe him, wondering what's going on in his mind.

Tossing my clothes and toiletries in my bag, I ask, "You picking something up?"

"She's in there. Strong. Stronger than before." He finally looks at me. "Her magic makes no sense. It doesn't feel like anything I've felt before."

"Is it bad for her?" I ask. "Maybe we shouldn't have been so quick to have Jade ditch her pendant."

"I don't think the magic is hurting her. But it feels all wrong."

"Could it be because her magic had been blocked for so long?" I ask, wandering over and caressing her cheek with my fingers.

"Arran?" she murmurs.

"Yes, my sweet love?" I say, hoping to coax something from her. Maybe my words will wake her. Sitting down on the bed beside her, I wait and hope for a response.

"I feel weird," she says, opening her eyes and blinking at the light.

She sighs in relief when she sees both me and Maxum. "You're alive. I was so worried when you didn't show up when you said you would." She holds my hand and reaches out for Maxum to do the same.

Instead of coming closer, he apologizes, "It took longer than I had expected, but we returned as soon as I sensed a problem here."

"Are you hurt?" I ask, because I haven't had the chance to do a thorough inspection of her body. Although, I assumed Calder would have told us of any injury she sustained during the attack and their retreat.

"I'm okay… I think." Jade sits up and sees the bags. "Are we leaving?" Her bottom lip poofs out in a pout.

"Yeah, as soon as Calder finishes packing upstairs."

"Where's Flint?" It hits her that she hasn't seen or heard mention of the gargoyle. She moves to launch off the bed to track him down. "Is he okay?"

Maxum catches her as she runs for the door. "He's banged up, but he will recover."

She hugs Maxum now that he's in her grasp, but he seems resistant. Sensing something is off, she pulls on Maxum's hold around her waist. "What's wrong? Let me see him."

"In a minute, we need to clear something up first," he says with all the seriousness he can muster.

"Why does it sound like I'm in trouble?" Her energy recoils.

She withdraws her hands from Maxum and holds them protectively over her chest. He releases her and gestures to the desk seat.

I want to snarl at Maxum for even questioning her, but I also know why he must.

"We heard some rumors, and we need the truth."

"Okay." Jade glances over at me, wondering what fresh hell is coming now.

"What is your name?" Maxum asks.

"Which one?"

Maxum blinks. "How many do you have?"

"I have my author name, my birth certificate name, and my new name."

"Then who is Jadeana Jones? Who is Patricia? And how old are you?"

"Jadeana Jones is my mother. Patricia is my grandmother. And I'm forty... Well, next month I will be. Why? How old do you think I am?"

I look at Maxum, then back at Jade. "You took your mother's name?"

"She named me after her for some bizarre reason. Obviously, she didn't know at my birth that she would later disown me. Anyway, she often goes by her middle name, Ruth. I still liked Jade and legally changed my name to the shortened version. Then for my author name, you've seen my book covers so you know it's Juniper Jade."

"I'm confused. Why would my informants think you were

your mother and she was dating Rob?" Maxum's voice still holds a shred of suspicion.

"Well, years ago, when I first leased my house, I hadn't changed my name yet. Maybe that's where they got my name and got us mixed up?"

"And you aren't sixty?"

"I would say that's ridiculous, but now that I know witches age better than humans… No. My mom is sixty. However, I'm sort of used to having mixups all the time. I suppose people rarely expect women to pass down their names. We'd often have problems with paperwork and such because we had the same name and look a lot alike. Apparently, my grandmother's genes are dominant, because we could all be mistaken for each other. Although, from a picture I found on the internet, my mom mostly looks her age."

"My guess is that your grandmother put an obscuring spell on your records to hide you." Maxum sweeps Jade up in an unexpected hug, and she squeals as he picks her up and crushes her to his chest. He says with complete relief, "I figured it had to be something stupid like this. Thank Goddess."

"Yeah, stupid seems to follow me around."

Calder peeks his head into the room. "We're ready when you are."

"Need Flint, now!" she orders Maxum, pointing to the door.

He obeys and carries her out to the living room where Flint is sprawled out on the couch. Already, because of his supernatural nature, he's healing, but he looks beat up. His skin is more marbled with discoloration than normal.

Jade scrambles out of Maxum's arms and rushes to Flint, hugging him fiercely when she reaches him. His massive arm circles around her waist and gingerly pulls her closer.

"I'm so sorry! I wish I could have helped fight so you wouldn't have gotten hurt."

"Your magic is still coming in, my love." Flint strokes his

large hand up and down her back as she holds him. "We don't even know what you can do with it once it does."

Jade lifts her head off his broad chest and stares lovingly into his eyes. "The magic feels so strange. Maxum thinks there might be something wrong with me."

Maxum corrects, "I didn't say anything is wrong with *you*, but there is something different about your magic."

"Hey?" Flint cups her cheek gently. "You are perfect. Being different isn't wrong."

Jade kisses Flint, and he returns it, claiming her mouth like a pro.

My brain still takes a minute to process this new version of the gargoyle who can touch... and who can touch *our mate*. Fortunately, my alpha nature, my wolf, and my berserker all accept Flint into our mating pack.

Electricity arcs off Jade's body and into Flint's chest.

Well, that's fucking new.

I have a feeling our witch will continue to be full of surprises.

Flint gasps, but quickly looks as though his injuries are mending.

"Did I...?" Jade strokes down his body where his flesh had been damaged and is now healed.

"See," Flints says with a wide grin. "I told you. Perfect."

"Perfect or not," Calder says with a bit of irritation. "We need to get the fuck out of here before someone returns. None of us are ready to handle another fight right now."

"Birdman is right," Maxum teases, using Trouble's name for him.

"Shit!" Jade glances around. "Did anyone check on the little ones?"

It's then we hear scratching coming from the kitchen.

"Oh, yeah." Calder mumbles. "I put them in the cupboard for their safety." He points to the kitchen island. "I was waiting to get them out until we were ready to leave, just in case we were attacked again."

Jade rushes to the kitchen and Calder guides her to the correct cupboard. He stands closer than I'd expect him to. He's warming to her.

"Is it safe *now*?" Trouble grumps.

Opening the cupboard, Jade picks up Trouble and Calder gets the bunny, Sage. Our witch and phoenix face each other, smiling, and take turns petting the fur balls. Several times, I notice their hands touching. Hmm.

Something dramatic has shifted in Calder.

Both our affection-phobic pack members don't seem to mind Jade's touch anymore. Perhaps they even crave it. Speaking of which, I crave her touch, too. But that will have to wait until we are safe.

"Let's go!" I bark.

Everyone snaps their gaze at me. I suppose that came out more aggressive than necessary, but I'm suddenly feeling a sense of urgency to get us somewhere safe.

"Yes, Mr. Bossy Sweatpants," Jade teases, but quickly puts Trouble and Sage in their travel carrier.

Maxum picks up his bag and tosses it onto his shoulder as he heads out to the front. The doors begin to seal and lock around the house... not that we will be able to return any time soon. Well, not until we kill Rob, Galiana, and anyone else who knows its location.

Jade can walk without issue, but I still want to hold her in my arms. I need to confirm she is okay—that she's alive.

If I wasn't carrying all Jade's stuff and my own, I'd be holding her, but I'll bide my time and make use of it later—wherever Maxum is taking us.

I just hope for our sake, it's somewhere we can rest for a damned second, breathe, and figure out what sort of witch our beautiful mate is.

30

HELL

JADE

$\mathcal{I}$ understand why Maxum needed to ask me about the rumors. I'd probably have one of my characters do the exact same thing. To be fair, my situation is a bit wonky, growing wonkier all the time.

Is wonkier a word? Well, it is now. Even with everything that's happened, I still have the Shakespearean flare.

"Ready?" Maxum says as he pauses, surveying what is left of his huge front yard.

The damage around the lake house makes me stagger a bit, imagining Flint fighting on his own for so long. He's lucky Maxum and Arran returned when they did.

"Jade?" Osen calls me in my head.

"What?" I'm not feeling overly warm toward him since he almost ran off with my body. Again.

"I fucked up."

"No shit," I snip.

"I don't mean to be so insane. I mean... I was always a bit of a

hothead. It's one reason I understood Arran so well. But since I died... I'm not okay. I'm broken. I don't mean that metaphorically. Something is missing in me. It makes me do dumb shit without thinking it through."

I sigh as I watch Maxum create his portal. I know this is hard for Osen to admit his weakness. From what I hear, he didn't do that in his life—ever. To admit it now, when he is so vulnerable and reliant on me, must be killing him. Well, not exactly, since he's already dead. But it's dang hard, I'm sure. He's struggling to deal with what's happened to him.

"I get it," I say, softening to the incubus' plight. *"Are you okay after seeing your body?"*

"Not really. Why the fuck did it look like it's preserved?"

"I don't know. Can Maxum perform magic like that?"

"Not that I know about. But why would he do that?" Osen asks, completely confused. *"Our traditions would have him burn or bury my body, not keep it frozen in time."*

"I can ask him," I offer.

"Not now. Let's all get settled first. Otherwise, they might fight if they don't like his answer."

"Okay. That's smart, to be patient." Then I say what I need to get off my chest, *"Speaking of patience... All of us want revenge for your death and will help you find it. So how about you stop stealing my body and trying to run off?"*

"I'll try. I promise."

"Do. Or do not. There is no try," I sass.

"You are seriously quoting science-fiction to me?" he asks. *"I thought you were strictly into fantasy-paranormal romance."*

"My horizons are broader than that, thank you very much."

"Jade?" Maxum calls.

"Huh?" I snap out of my mental conversation with Osen to see all four guys are staring at me. "I'm coming!"

"Not yet, you aren't." Maxum winks and holds out his hand for me, pulling me through to our next destination.

· · ·

Okay, not quite our final destination.

Maxum uses the same tactic to lose any potential tracker as we did when we traveled to the lake house. We crisscross through the realms and countries. Flint, Arran, and Maxum take turns giving me piggy back rides when my short, human legs have a hard time with the terrain.

Maxum asks me to come to him just before he opens a new portal. I'm losing count. Maybe our fifth? "Stick close to me."

I don't like the urgency or concern in his normally even-keeled demeanor. When I peek through the magical doorway, I see darkness, barren land, and orange flames in the distance. The vibes aren't exactly welcoming.

"What the fuck?" I whisper.

We step through, and Maxum informs me, "It's the second ring of hell."

"You take me to all the best places." I joke. But then I feel bad. It's his origins, after all. "Sorry."

"Don't be. I hate it." He strokes his hand down my back and for a moment I wonder if he's making the gesture to soothe himself too. He watches the rest of the guys join us and simultaneously keeps an eye out for danger. "Sure, it isn't what humans believe it is, but it's usually an unregulated, lawless place. And its inhabitants are often out for themselves. It's dangerous for anyone, but especially so for anyone not from here."

There's a smoky aroma in the air, but it's not the inviting scent that Maxum naturally has.

"Let's go," Maxum says as he rushes toward what looks like a cavern.

Not to be a 'fraidy cat, but I'm nervous.

Then I realize. I'm literally in hell. I don't think many paranormal authors can claim that and mean it. Although, we often feel like we are when we run up against deadlines.

The atmosphere feels heavier, thicker. My breathing is labored as we tromp across the rough and barren landscape.

"Where are we exactly? Are we under the Earth like some humans believe?"

"No. It's in another dimension layered over Earth's plane, just as the fae realm is. And just like the fae realm, there is energetic overlap, where the mortal realm and hell bleed into each other. That overlap is destroying a lot of hell, just as it has with Elfhame."

"Humans are destroying the other realms?"

"Not to mention their own," Calder adds.

"So it's not wrong when some fairytales say the fairies are dying off?"

"Where do you think those stories come from?" Maxum frowns. "The truth."

"And there are a lot of supernatural beings who have contributed to the mortal literary world," Calder explains. "Books even stolen from other realms and distorted to fit human sensibilities."

"I've known some famous supernaturally inspired authors in my day," Maxum grins at my excited face. "Also, I helped invent rock n' roll… at least the human version."

"Fuuuck," I say, but I sort of always wondered about the arts being otherworldly inspired. I can't wait to learn about all the things he's done in his life.

And this guy… this demon… this fine ass male, who has experienced more things than I can imagine (which is saying a lot), wants *me*?

As I hurry to keep up with his long strides, Maxum pulls me closer to his warm body and gives me a kiss on the top of my head. "You don't give yourself enough credit."

I snap my gaze up to him. "You read my mind too easily. I didn't even feel it."

"This is my power source. My magic is stronger here."

I think about his compliment. I suppose I'm more interesting now that I'm a witch.

"You aren't special to me because of your magical side. That's a dime a dozen in my life."

"Okay, so why?"

"Even when faced with adversity and abuse you have suffered, you are yourself. To still be genuine and kind after a hard life is a rare thing."

"Many people are nice. I'm not unusual in that."

"No. Kind and nice are two different things. Being *nice* is doing things because they are expected in your society's norms. It isn't necessarily genuine or good-hearted. Being kind sometimes doesn't even mean being nice. Kindness comes from the heart. It's thinking of someone's needs and suffering, then doing what is best for them to grow."

"I get what you are saying. Like someone might not be sickly sweet about it, but they will save someone's life or help them in an important way."

Maxum tilts his head toward the other guys and says in a low voice, "Your kindness, understanding, and compassion have healed them."

He gives me a grumpy look when he hears my brain, wanting to argue that I haven't done *that* much.

"Okay, fine. I'll play along. But I haven't helped you."

"Jade, you have. In my long life, I have never had love, with the exception of my affection for these guys. Honestly, I've never cared if I died. Then you showed up, and for the first time in six hundred years, I have something to live for. Someone to love."

I feel my face heating with emotion.

Or perhaps it's more than that, because Maxum snatches me up and breaks out in a full run for our destination. Bouncing in his arms, I glance over his shoulder and see a huge dog-like creature racing toward us. I swear the thing is as big as a mule.

Its eyes are flaming with orange fire. The cracks in his dark gray skin reveal lava circulating underneath.

A hellhound?

The rest of our group races to keep up with us. The demon dog is hot on their heels. Genuine fear reflects in my guys' eyes.

Maxum chants, opening a portal ahead of us.

Mid-stride, Arran shifts to his berserker form.

Calder is the slowest of us. He's carrying the fur babies, slowing him down further.

The hellhound snaps his massive jaws at him.

Calder unfurls his wings, but beating them only slows him further.

I know this won't end well. My power swirls inside my body and, with an instinctive gesture, I throw my hand out to stop the hellhound from harming my phoenix. A bolt of lightning shoots from my fingertips and crashes into the hellhound's snout.

Its head hits the ground with the force of my assault, and it flips over, letting out a painful howl.

A portal opens up in front of us to what appears to be a dark forest, and we race through.

Maxum snaps it shut and grips me to his chest. "You okay?"

"Yeah?"

"What the hell was that?" he asks.

"She threw a damned lightning bolt like a mage!" Calder's eyes are round, and I'm not sure if he's scared or excited.

"Is that bad?" I ask.

"Having a huge aura and getting zapped in the bunker was one thing. That could easily have been a regular yet powerful witch's magic, reacting instinctively," Calder explains.

Maxum continues, "But the way the magic came out of you now was more like a mage. You didn't need to use a spoken spell to create it."

"I need a spell?"

"Witches usually need a verbal incantation to focus their intent," Flint elaborates. "You are too new to magic and untrained to throw a spell like that."

Calder rushes up and hugs me, surprising the *hell* out of me.

Wow, any phrase with the word hell in it will have a lot more weight after my last field trip.

"Thank you for saving me," he whispers.

"Who dares to trespass?" a deep, growly voice echoes from the surrounding forest. Then the fiery eyes of a hellhound appear.

"Oh, fuck, it followed us," I say and feel my energy swirling and waiting to be unleashed again.

With a quick squeeze of my shoulder, Maxum silently pleads for me to bring my anxiety down a notch. Then my demon holds his arms up in a show of surrender. "It's Maxum, a friend of Amira. I seek asylum and a witch's protection."

"Dammit," the hellhound grumbles. "I thought I was going to get to eat you."

The huge demon dog glowers at all of us. I get the impression he's psychically reading us. He flicks his head at me. "What the fuck is she?"

"She's the reason we are here," Maxum says.

The hellhound sniffs the air. "Mostly a witch, but why do I pick up an incubus and something else?"

"Long story, but she won't harm you."

"This is the same witch Amira and Raithe aided?" the hound asks, with a curled lip.

"She is," Maxum confirms.

"Very well, come with me," the hound gives me a suspicious glare.

Nothing like a warm welcome.

SANCTUARY

JADE

*V*ery much like Maxum's lake house, Amira's place seems to be in the middle of nowhere. As we follow the giant hellhound, I get a strong urge to turn away, avoid this place, and forget it exists. I wonder why. Is it not safe?

Osen perks up in my mind. *"That's a witch ward. Well, it's their first line of defense. If they can make you go around and ignore their existence, then they don't have to bother with people wandering onto their property. I'm impressed you identified the intent, since the point is for you not to notice."*

I hate to admit I preen a bit with Osen's praise, but I quickly dismiss what I did. *"Could it be that I only noticed because I'm following someone and going against the spell?"*

"Hey, sweet witch. Don't downplay your accomplishments. I bet the guys only feel anxiety. They might have put it together by now since they know what to expect, but you don't have their years of experience."

I let the subject drop. *"Why did Maxum phrase it like that—we seek asylum and a witch's protection?"*

"Because it's an ancient custom, before the witch-supe wars. We used to be able to come to each other and seek refuge."

"That sucks that we can't get along anymore."

"I suspect Amira is getting along quite nicely with her supes."

I chuckle at that, but I admit I'm curious how the trio are able to overcome their differences. *"After we were attacked, I met Raithe, and he seemed nice enough. A bit more amenable than this hellhound,"* I say.

"Hellhounds are nothing to be trifled with. You saw the one in hell. This one is much older, and has become more human-like with his sheer will to evolve, probably to be a suitable mate for his witch."

"Evolve—?" I'm too busy concentrating on my conversation with Osen, and I trip on a root.

Flint catches me so I don't tumble onto my face.

"Great. She doesn't even know how to walk," the hellhound grumbles.

"Leave her be," Flint growls. "She has a spirit distracting her."

My gaze swings to take in my gargoyle. I'm shocked that he figured out what was distracting me, because to be honest, it could have easily been Maxum's tight ass swaying in front of me. "How did you know?"

"I hear your mind, remember?" He blushes. "I wasn't meaning to eavesdrop."

"Why don't I hear you anymore?" I ask, frowning at my inability to use our mate connection.

"Well, my mind isn't as busy as yours. It's quieter. And I've been shielding, so you wouldn't be overwhelmed by your magic coming in, as well as Osen's return."

My heart melts a bit with his thoughtfulness.

"Thank you, but please don't hide completely. It felt like something was missing," I tell him.

He grins shyly. "You missed me?"

The hellhound looks over his shoulder and eyes Flint. "Looks like this witch is collecting herself a coven."

"I'm Jade, by the way. You don't have to keep speaking about me as if I'm not here."

"Until you prove you aren't an issue, I'll behave how I see fit, witch." He stops abruptly at a clearing and glowers at us. "If I discover any of you are a danger to my family, I won't hesitate to eliminate the threat. Understood?"

We all agree. He isn't fucking around. But I don't really blame him. I'd probably say the same thing in his shoes to protect my guys.

"I think they've been fairly warned, you can stand down," Amira says as she steps out from nothing. "So, demon, your witch seeks asylum?"

"I know you usually only protect supernaturals or humans anymore, but we are being attacked by witches and warlocks," Maxum explains. "And Jade's power is coming in, and we could use your help to guide her in how to use it."

Amira looks me up and down. "Her power has come in, but it's erratic and unusual." After a thoughtful pause, she sighs. "Fine. You may stay here under my protection while we sort out her magic and figure out a new place for you to go."

It's always fun to be talked about like I'm not even a person. But I keep my mouth shut. My instinct says she's testing me.

Osen chimes in, *"Witches and warlocks are known for their quick tempers—especially those with a tendency to turn dark. Amira is trying to push your buttons to see what you'll do. If you are prone to snapping. If you'll turn evil."*

"Thank you for taking us in," I say with as much genuine gratitude as I can squeeze into the sentiment. Because even if they're attempting to taunt me, they are also doing us a huge favor. They are risking their safe place to take in a known risk.

I can handle some bullying, if I would even call it that. This is nothing compared to what I've experienced in my life. I was brutally bullied in school. Even my mother abused me after her mother died. This is barely on my radar. Hell, even Calder was a bigger pain in the ass than they are being, and I'm already over his attitude.

Amira turns and vanishes in front of us. Then the hellhound does too.

Maxum turns and winks at me. "Let's disappear." He holds out his hand, and I take it, but keep hold of my gargoyle's, too.

We step forward and a large cabin, a barn, and small cottage now sit in the middle of the clearing.

"Wow, was that illusion made with Amira's power?" I glance up at my demon. "Do you think I will be able to do that? I mean, I'd love to pull a disappearing act when I don't want to chat someone up."

"Someday. *Maybe*." Maxum squeezes my hand when I frown with disappointment. So much for insta-magic.

When we reach the large log cabin, Amira points to a smaller outbuilding—a bungalow about fifty long strides away. "You will all have to stay in the guest house." She glances at all the guys and takes in their size. "It will be a tight fit, but it's all I have to offer you for accommodations. It has the basics, and it was where we stayed while building our home. Let one of us know if you need anything, since I suspect you left your former safe house in a bit of a hurry. We'll have dinner in a few hours."

"Thank you. As long as my pack is safe. That's all that matters." Maxum bows to Amira.

We follow him over to set our stuff down and get a look at our new hideout.

"Witch?" Amira calls, as we walk away. "Tomorrow, come see me."

"Will do." I salute casually. *Oof.* What was that? I don't salute, but perhaps it's because I expect she will be part drill sergeant and part witch.

Maxum looks as though he's holding back a chuckle.

Arran looks like he might consume me right on the lawn.

With a determined stride, Calder rushes ahead to check out our small cabin.

Flint scans the surroundings, likely assessing the threat level. With my attention on him, he says, "I have to ensure your safety, my mate."

Will I ever get used to the guys calling me their *mate*? The thrill of finally being desired to that level may never wear off. It makes my heart pound harder and my skin heats up.

Calder comes back out of the cabin and actually blushes. "All clear. But uh, Amira wasn't joking about tight quarters."

We all walk in and notice the space is mostly open, with an enclosed bathroom. The bedroom, if you could call it a room, has a partition wall to separate it from a living area and kitchenette. There's only one large bed. We might all be able to fit on it, but it will be a dog pile. Thankfully, there's a long couch, so Calder has that as an option. I doubt he wants to share a bed with me even if he was overwhelmed with emotion and wanted to kiss me, we are still getting over our differences.

It could have been a friendship kiss... okay, maybe it wasn't *that* innocent. But it doesn't mean he wants me for more than a sweet moment of thanks for allowing him to speak to his dead lover.

"I think he might have wanted to kiss you for more than just a thank you," Osen whispers in my mind.

"Perhaps, but I'm not going to dwell on it. I have bigger issues to deal with, like survival. Learning about my magic. Smiting our enemies," I tell him.

"I'm all for that, especially the last one," he says happily.

"I figured. And remember, I want to get revenge for you. For all of us. So don't get a wild hair and stick it up my bum."

"I'd love to put something else up your bum."

I bark out a laugh, and everyone turns to look at me. "Sorry, Osen's being a brat."

"The more things change, the more they stay the same," Calder jokes with a playful grin.

Damn, I wish he'd smile more. He's always devastatingly handsome, but even more so now. My panties have caught on fire.

We quickly tidy up the place and put our limited items away.

We are all covered in dust and sweat. However, being the gentle-monsters they are, they tell me to go first. I pout a bit since I've gotten used to them washing with me.

As soon as I close the bathroom door and strip down, I hear the muffled debate between Maxum, Arran, and Flint about who will get to join me.

I grin like a fool that they all want to be in here with me. No matter who it is, I'll be happy.

I turn the faucet knob to warm up the water before stepping in. My back to the door, I hear someone enter. Immediately and without question, I know it's my demon.

"Maxum, how did you win the fight?" I ask.

"Sneaky witch, how did you know it was me?" He wraps his hulking arms around my waist and lifts me into the shower tub stall.

I squeal as the cold water shocks me, but my devil just laughs.

Osen seems to fade into the background, allowing me some alone time with my demon.

Maxum gently wipes the wet hair from my face and gives me a passionate kiss. "You can't scare me like that again."

"What did I do now?" I ask with sincere confusion.

"I was so worried when Rob attacked," Maxum growls. "Again." He squirts some of my liquid soap into his hand, and uses his hands to wash my chest.

Of course, he starts with the boobs. But fuck, I love it. However, it's very distracting.

"You know I don't blame you for the attacks," I try to

console him, figuring out he blames himself. "And unfortunately, I doubt that's the last we will see of that jerk."

"I'm not really blaming you either, but…" He leans down to give me a good scrub between my legs.

"You aren't used to not having control," I finish for him.

"Yeah. I'm not used to it. But recently, my life has been chaotic. With Osen's death, falling for you, and then the attacks, I'm about to lose my mind," he says.

"I know how I could make you lose your mind in a good way." I use some of the soap to make his cock and balls slippery and stroke him, making him moan.

Wanting to take this further, I rinse off the soap on his cock. Kneeling down in the tub, I take a moment to look back up at my demon's face, staring into his obsidian eyes that reflect the flames of my desire.

He grips my hair and holds me in place, not allowing me to move forward and take him into my mouth. "You want to suck my cock, sweet witch?"

"Please," I beg. I can tell how much that pleases him as his cock jerks, trying to reach my lips all on its own.

I stick my tongue out and open wide.

He moves my head forward, shoving his huge, ridged cock into my eager mouth.

Using my tongue, I play with the soft spikes along the base, as he pumps into me, reaching my throat.

"Good little monster fucker." He pulls out and asks, "You want to swallow me down?"

"Yes, I want to taste you."

He squeezes the base of his dick and pre-cum leaks out. "Here, taste me."

I swipe the tip of my tongue, and his warm, spicy taste explodes in my mouth. Overcome with need, I grab the backs of his thighs and plunge down onto his cock, slurping and sucking like a madwoman.

"Rub your clit," he orders.

I do as he says and moan with the arousal that rushes through me. I'm on the edge.

"Goddess, Jade." His grip on my hair tightens, and he grabs the shower curtain as if that could support him. "I'm coming," he warns.

His hot and spicy cum fills my mouth and throat. It's too much. But I do my best to take all of him. With a strum of my fingers, I bring myself off. It's not a brain-numbing orgasm, but I doubt this is the end of our fun. He lifts me immediately and plunges his cock into me without warning.

"Fuck!" I shout, more out of surprise. It barely twinges with pain, and I'm quickly given over to pleasure.

"I will claim you, my sweet witch," he says, and my heart races twice as fast. "But when it's the right time." He pins me against the tile and slowly pumps into me.

"What if I'm ready now?" I ask.

"It's not the right time. Besides, not in a bathroom. I want it to be… as perfect as it can be."

"I love you," I say, then kiss the ever-loving hell out of him while he brings me closer to my bliss.

"I love you." He whispers over my lips, "You've ruined me… in the best way."

3 2

HUNT

ARRAN

I know hiding out at Amira's is for the best, but I wish we were back at our lake house. There's no space to move in this tiny cabin. We aren't little creatures. Well, the magical creatures are, but they are running around without a care.

I envy them.

My skin itches to claim my mate. Instead, I've had to listen to Maxum giving her pleasure just mere feet away.

Flint stares at the door, longingly. And Calder surprises me by doing the same. He even casually grinds the heel of his hand against the erection contained in his tight pants.

I can't stand it anymore when I hear her shout out with her orgasm. I crash through the door. She's dripping wet and bent over the vanity with Maxum taking her from behind. His hand is wrapped around her hair, pulling her head up and making her arch her back. In the reflection of the mirror, her eyes lock with mine.

Maxum has dropped his glamour. His horns are out and his skin is deep red. With a loud smack to her ass, he orders her, "Look at me when I come inside you."

"Oh, fuck," she hisses, turned on by his demands.

He finishes inside her, crying out her name.

When he's done, he glances over his shoulder, grins wickedly, and pulls out. His hand knotted in her silver hair, holds her in place with her ass in the air and on display.

"Clean her up," Maxum orders me.

I fall to my knees and lap at her swollen and abused pussy, cleaning out Maxum's spicy cum.

"Arran!" Jade shouts and squirms. "Holy hell." Her body is on the verge of another orgasm. I can feel it.

I also now sense Flint standing in the open doorway, watching.

"Do you wish to join us, gargoyle?" Maxum asks with a bit of mirth. He loves this new side of our reserved pack member. "Maybe have Jade suck your cock?"

"I do, but this is Arran's moment. So I will refrain and just enjoy our mate's sounds of pleasure."

I'm thankful for Flint's judgment, because I don't know if my berserker could hold back if he touched Jade. He's barely holding out from coming forward and taking control. He's putting up with Maxum's hand on Jade's lower back only because he's allowing us to clean her out.

I'm pretty sure my berserker is going to insist on licking out their cum whenever he can, to remove their scents. His small protest that we have to share our mate.

My nails turn to claws as I get excited by this thought, the tips dimpling her plump ass.

But my naughty witch loves that feeling of danger, and she immediately comes on my tongue.

I want to dive into her pussy and knot her, but I must wait. It will be a sweet torture. But I have a surprise brewing in my mind—one that I believe she will enjoy and will scratch one of her fantasies off her list.

So instead of satisfying my urges, I pant and lean back against the open door, still on my knees.

"Did you like the wolf tasting you?" Flint asks. "And the demon fucking you?"

Stars and stones. Even I'm turned on by his gravelly voice, dirty talking after all these years.

His two thick fingers slide down her ass and dip into her honeypot, stretching her. "Are you sated, my witch?"

"Flint," she whines. I can hear in her voice she is spent. "Why do you have to be so fucking sexy? But..."

"I know, sweet mate," he soothes. "You are tired. But just know, I'm going to take you again, and soon. I will claim you completely. I will lay claim to your body, your mind, and your soul."

"Bloody hell," Calder whispers from the main room. His cock is out, and he's stroking himself. As soon as we lock eyes, daring me to call him out, he comes.

Witnessing this break in his armor makes me happy.

We *will* have a pack with Jade as our nexus. We will all finally be whole.

Jade doesn't see Calder's release or when he races out of the cabin to clean himself up in private. But by the knowing look Maxum gives me, I'm sure he sensed our phoenix's pleasure.

Damn, I can't wait until Jade experiences Calder in the bedroom... or wherever they decide to fuck. I'm excited to see how it will blow her mind with what he can do. Goddess, I hope for his sake he finally overcomes his intimacy hang-up.

After a quick rinse, Maxum dries off Jade and carries her into the bedroom area to get her ready for our dinner with Amira and her mates.

Flint rinses off, then I do.

With a downward cast of his eyes, Calder returns and also takes a quick shower.

We hear a dinner bell ringing from the main house and head over.

Our entire pack is nervous. Though, I suppose we are also curious to see how a witch gets along with her supernatural mates.

The phoenix, Raithe, is standing outside his front door and gives us a friendly wave as we approach.

"I hope Darius didn't scare you too much," he says with a smirk, indicating he knows he did. "I'd say he's a big softy, but that'd be a lie... Well, to anyone else but Amira and me. So if you need anything, I recommend asking me for it."

"Thank you." Jade smiles. "We really appreciate you helping us out. I apologize that we have to impose at all."

"Don't worry your pretty little heart over it." Raithe waves her off, then his eyes settle on Calder. "Hello, brother-cousin."

"Are you related?" Jade asks with a gasp.

Raithe is the first to correct her. "Not in the way you think, but all phoenixes are related in some way. It's tradition for us to acknowledge we are family, since there are so few of us in existence."

"Hello, brother-cousin." Calder dips his head in respect. "I look forward to getting to know you during our stay."

"As do I." Raithe grins welcomingly at Calder and a lot of the tension I had about being here fades. Perhaps between Jade's compassion and now a connection to his people, Calder might heal.

When we sit down at a large dining table, it's clear there aren't usually more than three seats. Someone has brought in huge wood stumps and brought over another table to extend the existing one, making room for us all.

Flint bows as Amira comes in. "Thank you for accommodating us."

I guide Jade to the seat next to where I intend to sit. I would like for her to use my lap as a chair, but I don't want to make her uncomfortable in another witch's home.

We make formal introductions after all the food is put out to share. It isn't a huge feast, but it will do. We did come by unannounced. None of us would ever think to complain. Besides, if we are still hungry later, we actually brought some of our non-perishable provisions from the lake house.

Maxum and Calder offer to help hunt for wild game in the area. And that perks up my wolf and beast.

"How safe are these woods?" I ask. "And how far does your magical influence extend?"

"We have one hundred acres. The line goes up to the ridge and to the top of it. Then along the creek, to beyond the meadow, the way you entered," Darius explains. "Why? Do you need to let your wolf free?"

"I do," I admit as I dish some offerings onto my plate. "And I was concerned for Jade's safety if she were to wander the property."

"You both will be safe within our boundaries. If someone were to trespass, I will know immediately," Amira assures us.

Good. I smile, thinking of what I have planned.

For the night, we barely fit on the large bed. Calder opts to use the couch as I had thought he might. He's not ready yet, and I understand.

Flint sleeps on Jade's one side, Maxum on her other. My need to be near her has me between Maxum's and Jade's lower halves. I'm holding her legs, burying my face in the seam of her thighs, and breathing in her fragrance.

After they are all asleep I decide I need to find the perfect spot for what I have in mind.

I make it just outside the front door when I hear rustling behind me. Jade.

I spin and pin her to the outside of the building and capture her mouth with mine.

She sucks in a breath of surprise, but quickly melts into my arms. When I break away, she asks, "Are you okay?"

"I'm fine, my sweet witch." I grab her ass with both hands and pull her hips into mine. She can feel my growing member wishing to claim her. Only a thin, long t-shirt she borrowed from Maxum and tiny panties separate me from my dream woman.

"Then what are you doing out here so late?" She glances down at my nakedness. "Are you going to shift?"

"Yes, I was going to hunt for something. But now, I think I'll hunt you." Nipping at her bottom lip, I scent her perfume blooming with the arousing thought.

"Me?" Her hazel-green eyes widen and glow with excitement.

Her magic is coming in, and it doesn't quite feel like any witch's magic I've felt before. But perhaps she is something different. She's able to channel supernatural beings after all.

I grin wickedly when I see she's wearing her slip-on shoes. "How does that sound? Would you like me to chase you, catch you, and fuck you into the ground like the naughty, delicious witch you are?"

"I don't approve of running as a rule, but I'm willing to make an exception in this case. Sign me the fuck up."

I chuckle and inhale her natural perfume along her neck. Then I rub my cheek against hers, marking her with my scent. I step back, letting her see my bare form.

She licks her lips in anticipation.

"You better run, because I'm going to devour you once my berserker catches you."

"Holy hell," she curses and runs for the trees, her plump ass jiggling perfectly.

My wolf and berserker want to launch forth from my body and give chase now, but I force them to be patient. We need to give her something of a lead or it will be over too soon.

I sniff the air and pick up the harmless creatures of the

surrounding forest. I approximate where the river is, which Jade is heading toward now. We hate letting her out of our sight, so I shift into my wolf form to heighten my senses, and trot after her.

It saddens me knowing that my sexual time with Jade will always be with my berserker. He's the one in control when I'm feeling too much. And I'm so deep in my emotions when I'm with Jade that I don't see how I, in my human form, will ever be the one to make love to her. Thankfully, I'm present and conscious when he's in control… even more so in the last few days, since Jade helped me accept that cursed side of myself. I no longer believe he will hurt her.

My wolf scents Jade's excitement, and my berserker bursts forward, no longer content to wait. He was patient when we licked her sweet pussy in the bathroom earlier, but he's done waiting.

Honestly, we're all done. We want her. We want to claim her as ours.

I howl at the moon, knowing it will happen tonight.

She. Is. Ours.

33

CAUGHT

JADE

One of my most reckless fantasies is coming true. I just hope it turns out okay. Arran had warned me that his berserker is exactly that: he's out of control. And I've agreed to be hunted by the most dangerous hunter out there.

I don't think the berserker wants to hurt me, but he's huge, much bigger than Arran's usual form. Standing over six foot six, he's pure muscle, claws, and teeth. They created the berserker as a curse to represent how beastly and out-of-control Arran can be. He was created to keep him separate from his humanity and lash out at the ones he loves.

Except the berserker has shown me kindness and care. Perhaps it's because I'm a witch? Am I breaking the curse? Or is Arran's acceptance helping him integrate this wild side?

As I race through the forest half naked, the adage to be careful what you wish for buzzes in my mind. The berserker might forget his affection for me in the middle of a hunt—an act that will only feed his primal nature.

Fuck, what have I done? Have I put too much trust in them?

I push harder to run, but I'm already winded. Okay. Seriously, I need to do more cardio. I make a resolution that I will start tomorrow if I survive tonight. Sitting at a desk for hours on end has done little for my endurance. Besides, I'm pretty sure I'm going to need a lot of endurance to keep up with my guys in bed or running with them in a forest.

A bone chilling howl cuts through the night air. *Crap.* If I didn't know that was Arran, I would have pissed myself.

I'm reminded that even though my guys are sweet to me, they are apex predators guided by their primal natures.

Fear courses through me now. My adrenaline answers the call and races through my bloodstream, making my legs move faster than they have ever moved before.

A presence brushes against my mind—a spirit. It's probably Osen, but I don't have the time or energy to deal with him now. This is Arran's experience. I shut down the intruder with a magical shield, partitioning my mind.

I'll deal with it later.

I don't even hear his footfalls, it's his breathing that gives him away.

Daring a glance over my shoulder, I see it is, in fact, Arran's massive and dangerous berserker form chasing after me.

His hard, swollen cock bounces menacingly with each stride. His knot is engorged and ready to lock inside me. I shiver at the sight.

What will it be like to experience it for real? Will it hurt? Will it make my body spasm over and over in bliss like the romance books suggest?

His claws swipe out and shred the back of my oversized sleep shirt. With another swipe, he tears the rest of the ruined shirt from my body. All I am left with now are my shoes and panties.

Like the klutz I am, I trip over a rock and fall on my side, knocking the air out of my lungs. The frantic excitement takes over my rational brain, and I scramble to get up.

My effort only makes me present my ass to my werewolf like a dang omega in heat. I might as well have served my pussy up on a platter.

Arran's beast slices off my underwear and grabs my hips with his huge hands. He lifts my ass up and licks my throbbing pussy. His licks quickly turn to frenzied nipping and laving at my sex.

It has me moaning and whimpering into the damp leaves on the ground.

After he gets his fill of my taste, he drops me back to my knees and plunges his thick cock inside me all the way up to the hilt of his knot.

This is taking doggie style to a whole other level.

Thank goodness I've been stretched out recently. Otherwise, his sudden intrusion would have hurt a lot more than just the sting that quickly turns to pleasure.

His claws dig into my tender flesh without breaking it. My werewolf pulls back and slams home again, mindlessly seeking his bliss.

This will be an untamed fucking.

Part of me is more than a bit nervous. He might forget I'm a fragile, human woman, so I move to get away again.

His massive, furry body leans over and presses against my back. He growls a warning in my ear.

I glance over my shoulder and see his golden eyes, wild and glowing with unbridled lust.

One paw-like hand takes hold of my entire full breast, which is an accomplishment in itself.

The beast ruts into me again, hard and fierce.

He pinches my nipple with his sharp claws, sending a fire to my clit. Somehow I know that it is Arran. He's breaking through and adding a bit of his own intention.

Knowing my Arran is here with me alongside his beast makes this whole experience more fulfilling and powerful. My arousal slicks my passage for his intense thrusts.

"Fuck," I shout, while the knot hits against my outer pussy, sending me straight toward a climax cliff.

His large balls bounce off my clit, and I'm launched into a gripping orgasm. Stars flash behind my eyes, and the world falls away. All the struggles and worries vanish. Nothing exists except us.

My pussy clenches around his dick.

The werewolf roars, spilling into me and filling me up.

But it doesn't end there. While I'm still coming, he shoves his knot into my channel.

I cry out with the stretch. He ruts into me with shallow and yet vigorous thrusts.

My orgasm is prolonged, and I shout and curl my toes from my uncontrolled release.

Arran's voice comes through in his full beast form, which I thought was impossible. "You are mine. My mate."

I crave for him to claim me with his bite, just as his essence is with my insides. "Yes, yours. Make me yours."

His razor-sharp teeth pierce the juncture of my neck and shoulder, claiming me.

Our bond immediately snaps into place.

Wholly.

Completely.

We are one.

My body glows with sigils and strange writing, just as Maxum described before. The unidentifiable magical symbols over my body dissolve like they are evaporating into the ether.

Have they vanished for good? Or is this how they always appear and disappear? I wish Maxum was here to see this.

"Oh, Jade..." a woman says in my mind. She sounds completely mortified and distraught. *"What have you done?"*

I shake my head to clear my confusion. "Abuela?"

"You made the same mistake I made."
Mistake? What mistake did my grandmother make?

TO BE CONTINUED…

Find out now what happens next in
ENCHANTING HER MONSTERS!

THANK YOU FOR READING!

If you enjoyed this book, consider leaving a review on Amazon. Check out some of my other books and completed series below:

If you love Maxum, he has an appearance in
Shadowcraft Academy (Completed) Series
I didn't want magic. I was supposed to escape.
I'm forced to attend a magic academy with five males
who won't leave me alone—my fated mate dragon,
a dangerous vampire, a protective druid, a seductive incubus,
and a hot professor wolf shifter.
https://books2read.com/ShadowcraftAcademy1

Fae Hearted (Completed) Series
A human servant with a secret.
A tempting deal with an Elven prince.
Three elves willing to break all the rules for her…
https://books2read.com/faehearted1

Chained Fates: Shadow Myths Book 1:
Four Demon Warriors. The last Serafim. One dark cell.

I find myself imprisoned with four gorgeous males
from a violent warrior species.
With their massive size, horns, and tails, I worry they will seek
revenge for my reluctant part in their torment.
When my healing hands wander, their growls turn to purrs.
Will they take me with them if we can escape?
Will they give me what I crave—their touch?
https://books2read.com/chained-fates

Rebel Fates: Shadow Myths Book 2
The Egyptian gods were aliens, and their people still exist...

I'm done with Earth. The moon base has to be better.
Famous last words…
However, my plan didn't go as I had hoped.
I end up on a ship with three intense warrior aliens who look
like gorgeous Egyptian gods—all who I begin to crave. They
have heads of animals and bodies of men. They look like
Anubis, lion man, and a minotaur.
And they're furious I'm a stowaway.
I'm not out of trouble yet...
https://books2read.com/rebel-fates

Need bonus content? News on new releases?
https://yvevale.com/newsletter

ALSO BY YVE VALE

SHADOWCRAFT ACADEMY:

(Dark Paranormal Academy Trilogy + Bonus Novella)

Hexed ~ Jinxed ~ Cursed ~ Blessed

BEWITCHING MONSTERS:

(Grown-Ass Woman & Monsters Trilogy)

Bewitching Her Monsters

Charming Her Monsters

Enchanting Her Monsters

Possessing Her Monsters

SHADOW MYTHS:

(Science Fantasy Standalones)

Chained Fates ~ Rebel Fates

FAE HEARTED:

(Fantasy / Shadowcraft Universe Origins Prequel)

Between Realms

Tangled Secrets

Chaos Tempted

Bonds Eternal

GODS ARE HIRING:

My Karmic Destiny

A Why Choose / RH continuation of

My Instant Karma by Raven Vale

ALSO WRITING AS

WRITING AS RAVEN VALE

GODS ARE HIRING:

M/F PNR Standalones

My Instant Karma

Cupid's Last Arrow

WRITING AS JADE VALE

CAGE BROTHERS:

M/F Dark Billionaire Contemporary Interconnected Standalones

For more book details, visit:

ValeRomances.com

ACKNOWLEDGEMENTS

A special thank you goes out to my husband, Mr. Vale, for supporting me. Thank you for being my editor and catching any rogue plot points.

Thanks to all my author and reader friends for their great advice, support, and friendship.

Also, I appreciate all of my wonderful fans! I love reading the beautiful reviews you leave or when you reach out to talk about my books. They are gifts to my heart and soul.

And my deepest gratitude goes out to all of you who have encouraged me in my life.

ABOUT THE AUTHOR

Yve Vale loves spicy romance, fated mates, and redeemable supernatural bad boys who end up as cinnamon roll alphas for their woman.

She writes about strong females and their magical males, all set in paranormal worlds.

She is a lover and a fighter. This is why her books feature a fair amount of action, both in romantic endeavors and in battle.

For more information, visit: ValeRomances.com